Gloria Buenrostro is NOT My Girlfriend

PRAISE FOR
Gloria Buenrostro is NOT My Girlfriend

"The friendship between Gary and Gloria is one for the ages. I'll be holding these two characters in my heart forever."
—MARGOT WOOD, author of *Fresh*

"Sweet, funny, and bighearted, *Gloria Buenrostro Is Not My Girlfriend* is a treat."
—ELANA K. ARNOLD, author of *What Girls Are Made Of*

"[Gloria and Gary's] easygoing relationship adds levity to thought-provoking themes of wealth privilege, stereotyping, and insecurity."
—PUBLISHERS WEEKLY

"This is a sincere story of unexpected bonds and self-discovery."
—KIRKUS REVIEWS

Gloria Buenrostro is NOT My Girlfriend

BRANDON HOÀNG

SQUARE FISH

FARRAR STRAUS GIROUX
NEW YORK

An imprint of Macmillan Publishing Group, LLC
120 Broadway, New York, NY 10271 • fiercereads.com

Copyright © 2024 by Brandon Hoàng.
All rights reserved.

Square Fish and the Square Fish logo are trademarks of Macmillan and are used by Farrar Straus Giroux under license from Macmillan.

Our books may be purchased in bulk for promotional, educational, or business use. Please contact your local bookseller or the Macmillan Corporate and Premium Sales Department at (800) 221-7945 ext. 5442 or by email at MacmillanSpecialMarkets@macmillan.com.

Library of Congress Cataloging in Publication data is available.

Originally published in the United States by Farrar Straus Giroux
First Square Fish edition, 2024
Book designed by Mallory Grigg
Square Fish logo designed by Filomena Tuosto
Printed in the United States of America

ISBN 978-1-250-79607-3
10 9 8 7 6 5 4 3 2 1

LEXILE: HL650L

To my wife, Beth.
You believed in me before I believed in myself.

Gloria Buenrostro is NOT My Girlfriend

ONE

MY STOMACH LETS OUT A HUNGRY GROWL. Or maybe it's my nerves. We've only been on the road for thirty minutes, and already I'm breaking Audrey's only rule—don't make a sound. And here I am making the most monstrous noise a stomach can make.

Audrey shoots me a look. "You didn't eat before we left?"

"I'm fine." She knows I didn't have any time to eat.

My stomach betrays me with another moan.

"I'm hungry, too," she says. "I'll stop somewhere."

"Let's keep going."

"If I don't eat, I'm going to pass out. Besides, we have like three more hours until we get there, and the last thing I want to hear is your digestive system." Audrey cracks a smile, but she knows this trip isn't a joke to me. Her face softens. "It'll be fast. Drive-through only."

I nod. Sisters can be all right.

Audrey makes good on her word. We're in, out, and back on the interstate in less than ten minutes.

"Hello? You awake in there? I said ranch me." Audrey waves a chicken nugget under my nose.

"Sorry." I peel back the wrapper, allowing her to dunk her chicken nuggets one-handed. I owe her big-time for this. I'll probably be holding her ranch until I'm eighty. She finishes, tosses the empty nugget carton, and uses my shirt to wipe the crumbs off her fingers.

Let me amend my last thought. Sisters can be all right *sometimes*.

"Relax, Gary. She'll be okay."

I rub my nose.

Audrey cranks up her awful pop-punk music. My cue that she's done chatting. I force down a bite of my burger, watch the billboards whip by, and think about what I'm going to say to Gloria Buenrostro when I see her.

If she'll even speak to me.

TWO

THEN

THIS SUMMER WAS A BIT OF A WEIRD ONE—one where time seemed to speed up to a frenzy or slow to a trickle whenever it felt like it. So in that regard, it's hard for me to pinpoint exactly when this whole thing with Gloria actually began. If I have to name the moment it started, I'd have to go back to the very first Thursday of summer break.

When people say they were doing nothing, they usually don't mean that. They're usually doing *something*, like checking their phone, watching something on their laptop, napping on the couch, whatever. When I say I was doing nothing that day, I literally mean I was doing nothing. I was lying on my bed, trying to imagine drawings in the cracks of my ceiling. A pretty standard start to my summers. But I remember thinking that a very specific water stain looked like a horse galloping when my best friend, Preston, called me.

"I'm coming by to get you in five," he said.

"What's going on?"

"I drove by Circus Burger. Everyone's there. I saw Jordan's car. Wear something decent."

Before I hung up, I had already zipped up my least wrinkled hoodie and had one leg in a pair of jeans. It would have to be enough.

Preston ended up being late, but outside my house he blasted his horn like I was the one keeping him.

"Easy," I said, hopping into his Protege. "What happened to five minutes?"

"Had to go through the gas station drive-through. You want us rolling up there in a dust cloud?"

"You just washed your car earlier this week!"

"I'm not taking any chances."

Preston Trương and I went way back. Our moms had met working at the restaurant and became fast friends. His mom was a single mom too, so whenever one of them got stuck working overtime or got called into work at the last minute or any other emergency popped up, they would cover childcare for each other. Our moms worked their magic and somehow managed to snag us boundary exceptions for both middle school and high school on the rich side of town—never get between a Viet mom and her kid's education. Growing up together, Preston and I pretty much didn't have a choice in the matter—we were going to be friends.

We were a lot alike in some ways. We were both Viet kids, we didn't know our dads, we both coasted on decent grades, but it wasn't like either of us were geniuses, and we were practically invisible to everyone in school. If I didn't have Preston, I would have been alone in the vast emptiness that was middle school and high school. We needed each other.

We were barely a week into summer break, and Preston and I were already making a habit of cruising by Circus Burger, seeking out these spontaneous meetups. It was a little pathetic, but what choice did we have? It was either that or Preston and I would end up in his room, playing the same video games we've beaten a thousand times. Rinse and repeat for the entirety of summer vacation.

Circus Burger was a popular hangout spot for the cool kids, despite the fact that it wasn't exactly near our school. The rich kids had to come east, over to our side of town—a testament to just how good Circus Burger's double-fried fries were. It was open late at night, the parking lot was big enough, the lines designating the parking spots had long faded with time, and none of the managers seemed to care that a bunch of high schoolers blasted their music from their cars.

The beautiful thing about these spontaneous hangs in the parking lot was that anyone could go. It wasn't like a house party where you could only get in if you were invited. It was the parking lot of an old burger joint, for crying out loud. Anyone could show up at any time. You just had to know when these gatherings were happening. Luckily for me, Preston had a car.

It was packed for a Thursday night. But it was summer, so I guess every night counted as a weekend. The popular kids (or "the perfects" as we called them) had their expensive cars lined up at the very back of the lot. Of course the one that stood out was Jordan Tellender's baby-blue BMW—windows rolled down, doors open, base thumping like a jukebox on wheels. We got lucky—there was only one spot left, and it was right next to Zac Simmons's pickup truck. A major score.

Preston and I sat cross-legged on his hood as we sipped on bottles of pineapple Jarritos. The perfects were only a car space away from us, but it felt like miles. It was like we were shooting a nature documentary, keeping our distance as if not to startle the very animals we were studying. These were people we'd known since elementary school, but they felt like strangers. Or rather, we were strangers to them. Our whole lives, we'd been watching. *We* were the invisible ones.

I swirled the pineapple soda in my mouth, savoring its sweetness. Jessica Krebs sat in the back of the truck, tearing a piece of a steaming chicken strip before handing the fry basket over to Nicole Warren and Eliza Kennedy. Another car over, a bunch of other people were huddled around a phone, cracking up over some video. Jordan popped his trunk and lifted a soccer ball high above his head to a smattering of cheers and applause.

The perfects were part of something. They were always in sync, moving together like a shoal—those massive schools of fish. There was a glow about them. An unspoken otherness. I knew, logically, they weren't that much different from Preston and me. We grew up going to the same schools. I sat next to them in class. I was even part of their group projects. But they were a complete mystery to us. And they were always smiling, always laughing. What were they laughing about? I'd been asking myself that question for years.

"What do you think is so funny?" It was more like a rhetorical question. It wasn't like Preston had any more insight on the situation than I did.

"Who knows?" He shrugged. "Maybe they're laughing at us."

"You think?"

Preston leaned back on his elbows. "No, of course not. They aren't even thinking about us."

Jordan stole the ball from Blake Haggart and changed course; I thought he might be walking straight toward us. I nudged Preston and we sat up a little straighter. But he went to the girls in the truck bed.

Jordan juggled the soccer ball, keeping it in the air with precise, gentle taps of his shoes. "Gloria coming around tonight?"

Eliza shook her head. "Don't think so."

"What's her deal? She's missed the last few hangouts."

"I texted her. We all did." Eliza checked her phone. The other girls nodded. "She didn't say anything back."

"Maybe she's on a date!" yelled Tyler Myers. That got a real laugh from everyone.

Charlie Dryer jumped on the hood of his Escalade. "Yo, if Gloria Buenrostro is on a date, then everyone here owes me ten bucks."

Jordan kept juggling. He was up to thirty-two. "You only got until school starts until that bet is invalid, brotha."

"Maybe you wish it were you." Charlie smirked.

Jordan grinned, but kept his juggling streak up. "Right. Like anyone here wouldn't give their left nut to be the first person to go on a date with Gloria Buenrostro."

"Ew. You're so gross," said Eliza. "She's not on a date. She probably volunteered for the night shift at the animal shelter."

"Or she's off organizing a coat drive or baking a cobbler or she's signed herself up for another half-marathon," said Jessica Krebs. "You know how she is."

Jordan's eyes stayed focused on the ball. "Too good for us?"

"Too good for you, maybe." Eliza's joke got a good laugh from the others. I noticed that Jordan didn't join in.

The music changed to some catchy bop. Jordan bounced the ball up before giving it a good kick, sending it back to his friends. "How about a dance for hurting my feelings?" He reached out his hand, which Eliza took even though she rolled her eyes. And wouldn't you believe it—they danced.

If I tried to do that, I'd look like a complete clown. I'd be laughed out of the parking lot. How did Jordan make it look so easy? What was the secret to the perfects? How could he allow his mouth to form and say those words with so much confidence?

Maybe that was the key. Maybe it was about not caring about the outcome. Taking a giant leap of faith and hoping for the best.

"What are we doing here? We're going to be juniors next year, Preston." I rubbed the smooth bottom side of the bottle cap with my thumb.

"Tell me about it."

I whipped the bottle cap into a dumpster. "Do you know how many dances our school hosts a year? I'll tell you. Four. And we've missed every single one. And that's not even counting all the ones from middle school."

Preston laid his head on my shoulder. "Okay, I'll be your date."

I shoved him off, fighting back a smile. "I'm serious. Aren't you even a little curious what it's like? We should be doing stuff like that." I nodded to where Jordan was lip-syncing, bumping his hip into Eliza's, causing her to laugh even harder. "We should be doing ... I don't know. Something. Anything! Whatever they're doing."

I knew Preston wanted to be one of them. We both did. It wasn't like Preston could afford his Protege or the meager upgrades he put into it. And he spent a year growing out his hair so he could transform it into a new undercut/heavy swoop. Preston was a peacock trying desperately to get attention.

He snorted. "If you want to go over there and make an ass out of yourself, I won't stop you."

It was a challenge. The annoyance in his tone wasn't lost on me, either—it was something that was becoming more frequent these days. I'd been getting this creeping feeling that Preston was getting sick of me ... that I was bringing him down, holding him back. He was taking his frustration out on me. Not that I blamed him. Maybe two people weren't meant to be each other's only friends. We were two prisoners in a chain gang, locked together forever by a pair of ankle shackles. He was right. I needed to stop whining and do something about it.

"They say fortune favors the bold," I said, gulping the last dregs of my soda before sliding off the hood.

It was Preston's turn to laugh. He stopped when he realized I was actually heading over. "I was kidding. You can't just walk up there."

"Why not?" I tried to play it off like I didn't know what he was talking about, but we both knew that walking up to that crew was a big deal. It wasn't like I was afraid that they were going to hurl insults at me or beat me up or pants me or try to humiliate me—at least not intentionally. They weren't the bullying type. But it wasn't like they ever asked Preston and me to hang out after basketball games. We'd never been invited to the house parties they threw. It was like we didn't even exist to them. Which somehow made it worse.

"Because we're us and they're them," said Preston.

"Maybe I'm tired of being us," I said. If high school was a big game, Preston and I weren't even on the bench—we were in the bleachers. In the nosebleed section. "We only have two years left. We have to do something. Let's be part of something."

"Drop the cool guy act, Gary. I know you're peeing yourself!"

It was true. But I wasn't going to admit that to Preston.

Jordan's dance was interrupted when the soccer ball arced in his direction. He trapped it with his chest and shot it through the makeshift goal made of empty to-go cups. Then Jordan made a victory lap, high-fiving all the outstretched hands. They loved him. Everyone, the guys and the girls, all clung to his every word. If I was going to make a move, I had to wait until Jordan was isolated, away from the pack. When I saw him make his way over to the soda fountain station, I knew that was my chance.

I gave Preston my best two-finger salute and made my way to Jordan. I didn't have a plan. I was hoping that the adrenaline would kick in and miraculously come up with a string of coherent words for me.

Jordan stood at the fountain, his finger hovering over the

Orange Bang! tab. I had to act now before he returned to the pack.

"That's a good choice," I said, the words gushing from my mouth like a broken fire hydrant.

"What is it?" Jordan didn't even look up as he pressed the button.

"It's kind of like a melted orange Creamsicle," I said. "It's pretty good on its own, but my trick is to add a splash of soda water."

Jordan handed me his cup. I couldn't believe I was doing this. I kept telling my brain not to mess this up by spilling it everywhere. I gave the soda water a solid two-second pull before handing it back. "That should be perfect right there."

Jordan took a sip. My fist balled in anticipation. Then he nodded, smiling. "Whoa. This is amazing. Why doesn't every place have Orange Bang?"

"I've been saying that for years." I didn't know how I was doing this, but the words kept going. I only hoped he couldn't detect that I was completely freaking out.

"You're Gary, right? Didn't we have Algebra II together?" he said, taking another sip.

He knew my name? He. Knew. My. Name.

"Yeah, that's right." I knew I needed to throw Preston a bone, too. "I'm here with Preston Trương. You know him?"

Jordan squinted over at the Protege. Preston returned a sheepish wave. "I don't think so . . ." I beamed. He knew me. Me! But I'd have to lie to Preston and tell him that Jordan recognized him, too. "What are you guys doing here?" I had to keep Jordan talking. I had him by the hook. I just had to tire him out.

"Hanging out. Got hungry," said Jordan. "Actually, we were trying to check out that abandoned house over on Poppy Street. Couldn't find a way in, though."

My eyes lit up. Poppy House was only a few miles from me. Preston and I used to sneak in whenever we got really bored.

"Oh yeah," I said, trying to temper my voice. I couldn't believe he was still engaging in conversation with me. "Did you guys check out the cellar door? There's an old lock there. I know the combination."

"How?" Jordan asked. I had his attention now.

I couldn't exactly tell him that Preston and I had way too much time on our hands and had spent weeks killing time trying to crack out the combo. Figured it would be a lot cooler to remain mysterious. "I have my ways. Fourteen, four, thirty-six."

Jordan gave a satisfied nod. "Thanks, man."

Maybe this would be it. Maybe this would be the moment Jordan would invite us to go with them. This was my way in!

Instead he said, "Maybe I'll catch you around this summer. Later, Gary."

And with that, he went back to the others.

Okay, so I wasn't getting an exclusive invite to hang out with Jordan and his buddies. But I wasn't going to let that minor setback ruin my victory. I'd had a conversation, a real conversation, with Jordan Tellender. This was huge. This was major. I couldn't wait to tell Preston. Maybe we were closer to knowing what they were always laughing at.

Thinking back on that night now, I was so caught up in the Jordan Tellender of it all that I missed an important detail that would eventually change everything. If Gloria Buenrostro wasn't with the other kids in the parking lot, where was she? I was about to find out.

THREE

PRESTON TRIED TO DOWNPLAY MY CONVERsation with Jordan, but I knew it was his way of trying not to get his hopes up. It didn't stop him from asking me a million questions on the ride back home.

"Wait, wait, hold up," said Preston, pinching the bridge of his nose. "You're telling me Jordan needed a way into Poppy House and instead of offering to go with him... you just straight up gave him the lock combination? Dude. What's wrong with you? That's called leverage!"

I groaned. Preston wanted this just as much as me. I joked that I'd try to get him an introduction the next time we ran into Jordan at Circus Burger.

My chat with Jordan, which had lasted less than five minutes, had taken everything out of me—I was ready to pass out and call it a night. But when I opened the garage door, Audrey came out to meet me. She was wearing the same faded hoodie and baggy pajama pants from the past three days. For a second I thought she was going to ask me to join her for a spontaneous movie night. It was our little summer tradition to show up to the theater and watch whatever happened to be playing.

"You want to try to catch something?" I asked, waiting to hear her answer before taking off my shoes.

"What? No." Audrey's face scrunched in annoyance. Like what I proposed was the most ridiculous option she'd ever heard. "I've been trying to call you. Check your phone. Mom wants you to run to the Jig and clear out their fish sauce."

The county fair was only a few weeks away, and Mom needed to stock up on as much fish sauce as she could get her hands on. I'd tried to convince her to buy in bulk, but she insisted on going to the corner store, as she'd done for years. Good luck trying to convince a Viet mom to break her habits.

"Wanna give me a ride?"

"It's like two miles away." Audrey typed away on her phone, half listening.

"It's almost eleven. Come on." I tried masking the disappointment in my voice. For months I'd been looking forward to Audrey coming back from her first year at college. Audrey and I always goofed off together during summer break. But ever since she went away for school, she'd been acting totally strange. Like I was the last person she wanted to see. It had been a week, and she was still refusing to leave her room. The only time I'd see her was when we'd wait for each other to finish with the bathroom. She hardly even said more than a few sentences to me.

"Take the bike, then," she said, eyes glued to her phone.

Audrey was gone before she could hear me laugh. The only bike we owned was my mom's, and it was a relic from the eighties. I wouldn't be caught dead riding it around the neighborhood. Walking was worth the risk.

It was about a forty-minute stroll to the Jiggity Jig (we only ever called it the Jig for short), thirty minutes if you picked up the pace. One of those places that wasn't really that far on paper, but slightly annoying when you were forced to actually make the walk. Our family had been going to the Jig for years. It was our corner store, easy to miss if you weren't looking for it. It was the only place within walking distance that carried a decent selection of Asian ingredients, medicines, and vegetables. I jumped and slapped the dusty green awning, as I always did, before I stepped inside.

The only employee in the store was a stone-faced cashier who Audrey and I called Frogger, on account of his wide mouth and his eyes, which always looked slightly farther apart than they should have been. We never bothered to ask his real name, but it wasn't like he ever talked to us anyway. It was the same guy every time. Been that way for years. Frogger was completely bald on top with a ring of frazzled black hair that wrapped around the back of his round head. In all the time I'd been going to the Jig, Frogger had never lost any additional hair. It was always the same amount, which I chalked up as one of the great mysteries of the world—right up there with the ancient pyramids and dark matter. I waved and he barely acknowledged my existence. If he smiled, it was hard to tell, thanks to his bushy mustache. It was our little routine.

The Jig was your typical neighborhood corner store. There was a section for produce where a leaky sprinkler system kept the cilantro and banana leaves hydrated, a wall of cheap liquor displayed behind the counter, and tight, dusty rows packed with standard groceries. I maneuvered my way past the same tower of boxes that I was convinced would someday fall and crush me to death and nabbed the last two bottles of Three Crabs fish sauce—the only brand my mom would use.

I spotted Tulipán, the store's cat, perched on a crate of plantains, and gave her a good scratch behind her mangy ears. It had taken me years (and a lot of cat treats) before she'd even let me get within a foot of her. I was daydreaming, enjoying listening to Tulipán's car-motor-esque purrs, when she leapt from the crate and dashed to the entrance.

"I guess we're done with pets today, huh?" Tulipán reminded me of Audrey with how quick she was to get away from me. I looked to see who had suddenly grabbed her attention. To say I was shocked was an understatement. It was Gloria Buenrostro.

I froze. Like a startled possum caught in headlights. If this was any other kid from my school, I wouldn't have given it a second thought. Even if it was Jordan standing there, I might find it strange, but seeing Gloria standing in my neighborhood corner store caused my body to lock up, my brain to short-circuit. The thing about Gloria was that she transcended popularity. She was somehow bigger than all that. Gloria Buenrostro was known to all, but it was hard to believe that anyone actually *knew* her. She was so talked about that she was somehow more than human.

I'd known Gloria from way back when we were in first grade together. Ask anyone about her, and the first thing they would tell you was how beautiful she was. She'd inherited her mother's sad dark green eyes. Her father's deep-set dimple. The faint spattering of freckles across her nose looked like it was created by a delicate swipe of an artist's brush. Catch her on the right day, and her smile could send you straight to the nurse's office.

Like everyone else, I admired her from afar. In addition to her beauty, Gloria was a busy bee—her grades were immaculate, she did layout for the yearbook, she had her own baking column in the school newsletter, the community fridge down on Townsend was her idea (and was always stocked), she was a favorite volunteer at the animal shelter, and she was the only freshman to ever be cast in the senior play, earning a standing ovation for playing Cecily in *The Importance of Being Earnest*. But off the stage, she was pretty quiet. Most people mistook her shyness for being stuck-up, but I never saw her that way. She always seemed too focused, too busy flitting from one extracurricular activity to the next to ever worry about anything else. Maybe that was why no one ever had the chance to get close to her—there was never any opportunity to.

And here she was. The most popular, most beautiful, most discussed and dissected girl in school standing in *my* corner store and petting *my* corner store's cat. How Gloria managed to get cheek to cheek with Tulipán without getting a face full of claws was a miracle. A pair of sunglasses was perched on the top of her head. Her hair was pulled back in a thick ponytail. Some frayed jean shorts hugged her thighs. She lugged a bulging load of laundry in a worn canvas bag.

I was too far away to hear anything, but whatever she was saying was making Frogger laugh so hard that he was actually slapping his knees. I couldn't believe it. You have to understand that I'd been shopping in the man's store since I was old enough to walk and I'd never seen him so much as crack a smile. And this girl had him giggling like a ticklish toddler.

It went on like this for a few minutes before Gloria grabbed a basket and picked exactly three plums, two limes, a bag of persimmons, and a bundle of lemongrass. I ducked down the cereal aisle to get out of her line of vision. When she went back to the counter, Gloria and Frogger engaged in a couple minutes of haggling. She kept trying to shove a ten in his hand and he shook his head. She finally gave up, or so I thought. When Frogger turned his back for a second, Gloria slipped the bill into Tulipán's collar.

She was good.

Gloria must have heard me chuckle, because she looked right at me. I snapped up a box of Fruity Pebbles, making it look like I was very interested in the nutrition section. "Riboflavin . . . yes, good, good," I muttered. I could have died right where I stood.

When I felt enough time had passed to be safe, I looked up and she was gone. Which was impossible. The front door is fastened with a motion detector that emits an annoying beep anytime someone comes or goes. I would have heard it. I made a quick check of the store. Nothing. She'd just vanished.

I was about to break my eleven-year tradition of never exchanging a word with Frogger.

"Hey, uh," I said, prepping my best middle-school Spanish. "¿Dónde está la chica?"

Frogger raised a bushy brow. Maybe my accent was just that bad. I needed to try again.

"¿Dónde está—?"

"I heard you the first time," said Frogger. "Why do you want to know?"

"I'm a friend of hers from school."

Frogger eyed me again. I suddenly felt very self-conscious.

"Home," he said. "She's at home."

Home? It wasn't possible. First off, she lived on the complete other side of town with all the other rich kids. Second, there was the whole motion-detector mystery that was still unsolved. I repeated the words over and over again as I stepped out into the parking lot. *Home?*

Maybe this was all some hallucination. I was about to chalk it up to the potent cleaning product fumes that permeated the Jig when I spotted her for the second time that night. There was a row of barred-up windows connected to the Jig that I'd never taken a close look at before. But now I could see Gloria through one of them. She was unloading the plums into a fruit bowl. Then I made out a faded house number scrawled on a mangled mailbox so old, it was hanging on its last hinge. The rain gutters barely clung to the roof. Paint peeled off the siding. It must have been in violation of a hundred safety violations. Frogger wasn't lying—Gloria was home. In an apartment bolted onto the back of the corner store, as if it were an afterthought. She *lived* at the Jig.

I took a shortcut home, walking over the freeway overpass. As I felt the rumble of traffic zipping by under my feet, I tried to make sense of it all. Gloria Buenrostro had no business being in my neighborhood, let alone living in my corner store. Gloria lived in a mansion. One with a pristine manicured lawn. An automated sprinkler system. Wind chimes dangling above a freshly painted porch swing. Suddenly I saw my neighborhood in a different light. Our lawns had more dandelions than they did rosebushes. Chain-link fences protected empty, overgrown lots with weeds that went up to your chest, sprinkled with one-shot liquor bottles. Frayed, droopy nets clung to the rims of rusted basketball hoops shoddily nailed above garages. I was meowed at by more than one stray walking home. None of it made sense. What was she doing here? Why wasn't she with all of her friends at the abandoned house on Poppy? Why was she in *this* neighborhood?

Was she in some kind of trouble?

That night, I kept thinking about Gloria. It was as if a Greek goddess had decided to come down from Mount Olympus to live among the mortals.

Audrey knocked on my door before poking her head in. "Did you get that fish sauce?"

I slapped my forehead. I'd left the bottles in the aisle when Gloria spotted me. "Whoops. I forgot."

She shook her head. "You better go back to the Jig tomorrow before Mom wakes up."

I was already planning on it.

FOUR

I SLEPT THROUGH MY ALARM THE NEXT DAY, so walking to the Jig was out of the question. My mom had already taken her car to work, and I wasn't about to risk Audrey's wrath by waking her to ask her to drive me in her precious Geo Metro. There was only one option. And I wasn't looking forward to it. I didn't think it was a stretch to say that my mom had a hoarding problem, a habit left over from the days we'd been really struggling to pay the bills. She kept everything: stacks of magazines, broken fair equipment that we'd replaced years ago, dusty stuffed animals that Audrey and I had long forgotten, camping gear from the seventies she got for free from a garage sale (despite the fact she hates the outdoors). I had to squeeze, push, and crawl my way over a maze of boxes before I finally reached what I was looking for, but there it was hanging on the wall: my mom's old tandem bike.

I didn't recall my mom ever riding the bike, or couldn't imagine who she'd ever have ridden it with, but there it was as if it were waiting for me. It didn't take long to fill the tires with air and grease up the gears. I could only pray to the high school gods for mercy that no one from school would notice me. It was humiliating enough to be riding a tandem bicycle, but to be riding one by myself was a completely new level of loserdom that I wasn't ready for.

Thanks to the tandem, I made it to the Jig in half the time it would have taken me to walk. I bought mom's fish sauce, raced home to drop it off, then circled back. The fish sauce was an excuse—I had to know what Gloria was up to. I waited across the street for an hour, hoping I didn't miss her in the minutes that I was gone. Just when I was about to give up, she emerged from the rusty screen door. The same pair of giant bug-eyed sunglasses she'd worn the night before covered half her face, but today she wore a white dress covered with an orange and lemon print and a ratty baseball cap pulled down low. I almost wouldn't have recognized her if it weren't for her silver bracelet with the whale charm dangling from her wrist. She walked out dragging an old beach cruiser behind her. Stuffing poked out of the banana seat. Frayed tassels spewed from the handlebars. The squeaky chain creaked. It looked worse than my mom's tandem—and that was saying something. Maybe we could be bike losers together.

In one arm she carried a neatly folded stack of clothes wrapped in tissue paper and a crisp dress shirt on a hanger. In her other hand, she swung a dinged-up blue-and-white travel cooler onto her bike rack.

There she was. Right across the parking lot. I gobbled up the last of my breakfast—half of a stale baguette soaked with a little bit of Maggi sauce—then bent down, pretending to tie my shoelaces. For the first time, it dawned on me that I had no goddamn clue what I was doing here. I had just woken up with nothing else on my mind but to figure out why. Or maybe it was bigger than that. Maybe I was riding the high of talking to Jordan last night. Could it be that simple? I came over without a plan. Now was my chance. But to do what? That was the question. I needed to do something. Anything.

Before I could land on an option, Gloria leaned her bike against the wall and walked around into the Jig's front entrance. Maybe I could have gone back inside under the pretense that I had forgotten to pick up something else, but my legs refused to cooperate. She nearly caught me spying on her once. I wasn't about to risk it again. So I waited for her for a solid ten minutes. Watching the heat waves sizzle from the dumpster while I baked in the morning sun. What was she doing in there for so long? If Frogger was running a convenience store, it didn't seem very convenient.

Finally she emerged, mounted her bike, and she was off. I had to do something. Anything. I don't know what came over me. Panic, maybe. But I didn't exactly have time to consider all of my options. All I knew was that if I didn't go after her, I'd miss my chance to see what she was up to. So I shoved off in Gloria's direction. Keeping a safe distance, of course.

All I could do was follow the flap of her dress until my brain decided to cooperate and figure out my next move. What I was doing was so completely outside of okay. I had no plan. Even if I caught up to her, I wouldn't know what to do. I could only hope some inspiration would hit me the longer I rode. With each push of the pedal, I had to convince myself to see this thing through—whatever it was. Maybe if I followed her long enough, I might learn something about her. At the very least, why she was spending so much time in my neighborhood.

The morning consisted of a series of stops at houses and apartment complexes. Every stop was the same: Gloria would fish through the clothes on her handlebars, pick an assortment after checking the tag, and deliver them. Each time bringing her cooler along with her.

By the time noon arrived, I still didn't have a clue what I was supposed to be doing. All I knew was that I was working up a serious sweat following this girl around town while she ran errands.

Then she spotted me. We had taken a right on Pinewood when she whipped her head around and stared right at me. No, it was more than a stare ... It was a glare. Then she took off. I panicked, pedaling faster to keep up with her. She miraculously turned a beach cruiser into a speed bike. And my mom's tandem wasn't exactly the best at maneuvering tight turns. I thought I actually might lose her, until Gloria hit a nasty pothole. She shuddered and pulled to the side of the road. I yelped, slamming on my brakes. I tossed the tandem onto the sidewalk, sprinting toward her.

She couldn't have been more than a block away, but it felt like I was running the length of a football field. I looked down at my clothes and instantly regretted my outfit choice. I'd dressed like a little boy—cargo shorts and a striped shirt. I should have worn jeans. Jeans would have been a much safer pick, even if it *was* eighty-five degrees out.

"This is not happening. This can't be happening." Gloria stared at the sky, her hands balled into fists. She was trembling.

"Are you okay?" I asked, catching my breath.

She turned, looked straight at me. Her green eyes shimmered like tears would overflow at any second. Her face was flushed with embarrassment and accusation. Before she could say anything, I knew that whatever had happened to her was my fault. "Why are you following me?"

My heart stopped. A chill ran through my body. This was all wrong. This wasn't the way I wanted it to go.

"No . . . I . . . wasn't exactly . . . I mean, I was, but . . ."

"No, you know what? Never mind. I don't need this. I don't have *time* for this." Gloria knelt down and held the broken frame in her hands. There was a clean break, right where the rust buildup was the worst.

"Let me help you, at least," I said quickly. The words just tumbled out. I didn't know how to fix a broken bike frame, but I figured the longer I kept talking, the greater the chances were that I'd spout something to save me. Or, manage to squeak out a proper apology. "There's gotta be a bike shop around here somewhere."

Gloria shook her head. "Unless you have a welding torch hidden on you, this bike is done. I have to get all of these deliveries out before he comes over." She inhaled, willing herself not to cry. "And now I have to pay for a new bike. Why is this happening? Why today?"

"Wait here." I backtracked, picking up the tandem. "Just tell me where you need to go." The words kept gushing out like some busted fire hydrant. Chauffeuring Gloria around this neighborhood on my mom's crappy bike all afternoon . . . What was I thinking?

"I wouldn't have gone over that pothole if I hadn't been so focused on trying to lose you."

I blanched. I didn't know why I thought she'd share a bike with me. She was within her right to laugh in my face and walk away. I couldn't even muster up the courage for a proper apology.

To my surprise, she hopped on the back of my bike.

"This thing isn't going to crumple under us, is it?" Gloria bounced in her seat, testing the bike's structure. "I don't know if I can handle two bikes failing me today."

"I doubt it. This thing is built like a tank." I took my place at the front. My hands, slick with sweat, tried to find their grip on the handlebars. Gloria Buenrostro. Right here. Sitting behind me. I hadn't been this close to her since she helped me with that long division quiz in seventh grade.

"You cool?" she asked, eyebrow raised.

"Yeah." At least, I thought I was. I probably should have called a cardiologist to check my heart rate.

"Then why aren't we moving?"

"Oh." I shook my head, trying to recover. "Where are, um, we going?" I asked.

Gloria shoved some purple gum into her mouth.

"Hfcnshon."

"Uh. What?"

Gloria chewed before shoving the gum to one side of her cheek. "Bubbaloo. Got a gooey center. I can't get enough of the stuff. You want some?"

"No. I'm good, thanks." It was kinda funny watching Gloria chew a massive wad of gum. Not exactly prim, proper, or refined. Not at all what I expected from her.

"Blowing massive bubbles helps pass the time, trust me. Well, what are you waiting for? Let's go. Hockinson Ave."

And with that, we were off. Me and Gloria Buenrostro. Pedaling together on my mom's creaky old tandem bicycle. I wouldn't have believed it if it didn't happen to me.

FIVE

"HERE!"

I slammed on the brakes, sending loose gravel flying. Gloria leapt off before I came to a full stop in front of an old apartment building. A crooked, busted-up intercom directory box stood at the gate not serving any purpose. The sidewalks were gnarled and uneven—I read somewhere that developers preferred to plant cheap trees, not caring that the roots would demolish the concrete. The trees were eventually removed, never to be replaced, and the sidewalks were left unrepaired.

Gloria started up the stairwell and when she reached the second floor, she cupped her hands around her mouth.

"You coming?" she hollered down at me. By her tone, it sounded like it was a given that I'd be following her up the stairs. "Grab that cooler, will ya?"

I did as she told me. I found her three doors down, standing in front of a door with chipped orange paint. Gloria knocked, and the door cracked open a bit, stopped short by a chain.

"¿Quién es?"

"It's Gloria, Mrs. Espinosa. I have your cardigan."

The door slammed shut, followed by the sound of the chain

being unlocked. Out poked a wrinkled brown face. The lady's fishbowl-sized glasses magnified her pupils to a cartoonish degree. Her frown full of mistrust.

Gloria thumbed through her stack of clothes, landing on a caramel-colored wool sweater. "Good as new!"

Mrs. Espinosa's eyes darted back and forth as if she were expecting some government agents to pop out from behind the nylon bushes. "Thank you, sweetheart. Although I'll be honest, I thought you were coming with news about Sir Ivan. I printed out some more flyers. Would you mind posting them when you're out and about?"

"I always do."

"Who is this? Who are you?" Mrs. Espinosa pushed the rim of her huge glasses up her nose, giving me a once-over.

I was positive that Gloria wouldn't remember my name, but before I could get it out, she said, "Gary Võ. He's a friend from class."

She knew my name? I was her friend?

"Võ, huh? Laotian?"

"Vietnamese, actually."

Mrs. Espinosa got right up to my face; I could make out my reflection in her glasses. "Full? You don't look full."

"Half."

"Gringo, eh? Do Vietnamese have a word for that?"

"Not that I know of, but I think I know what you mean."

Mrs. Espinosa gave a satisfied sniff before turning back to Gloria. I guess I'd passed her test. Whatever it was. "Good. You finally got some help." She shoved a stack of flyers into my arms—it was one of those "Have You Seen Me?" posters. Except this one featured a green parakeet with a flaming red beak. Mrs. Espinosa clicked open her purse. "It's a tragedy. You're too young to be spending your summer working like this. You *both* should be out there chasing down ice cream trucks, playing in sprinklers, getting into trouble..."

Gloria smiled at me. "I think we're a little too old for sprinklers."

"No one is too old for sprinklers, honey." Mrs. Espinosa gave me a swift jab with her elbow.

"We should get going." Gloria took the cooler from me. "Have you had lunch today?"

A smile crept across Mrs. Espinosa's face, and she pulled out a wrinkled five-dollar bill. "I'll take two."

Gloria plucked out two small wrapped bundles from the cooler, paused for a slight second, then grabbed a third.

"My eyesight might not be what it used to be, but I can still count." Mrs. Espinosa handed a tamale back to Gloria.

"It's fine, Mrs. Espinosa. I... uh, have a special today. Buy two, get one free."

"You're talented at so many things, but you're an awful liar," Mrs. Espinosa said, patting her cheek. "Don't be giving away your product for free."

Gloria smirked, knowing full well that she'd been bested by the old lady. "Okay, okay. Call my mom if you need any more alterations."

"I will." Mrs. Espinosa started to close the door but then hollered, "Can I put in two requests for tomorrow?"

"Always."

"That sweet puerco with ancho is perfect for these hot nights."

"And your other request?"

"Leave your hat and glasses at home. Show the world your pretty face."

Gloria was already walking away when she called out over her shoulder, "I'll save you some puerco!"

"If you run into Sir Ivan, be sure you address him properly!" Those were Mrs. Espinosa's parting words of wisdom before locking the door behind her.

I quickened my pace to catch up to Gloria. "She was... something."

"Just wait until you meet the others." Gloria raised a fist to another door. She gave me a look when she noticed I was starting back down the stairs.

"Oh," I said, trying to hide my embarrassment. "There's more?"

"Yeah." Gloria gestured to the clothes slung over her arm. "You up for it?"

"Totally." I prayed she couldn't hear my hesitation.

Gloria and I spent the rest of the afternoon finishing her deliveries, posting Mrs. Espinosa's flyers, and dropping off various articles of clothing that her mother had either altered or repaired. I got to meet all of Gloria's regulars. There was a stressed-out mom holding wailing twin toddlers who ordered a patched-up pair of overalls. A towering, twitchy man who needed his slacks hemmed for a job interview. A young baseball coach who let out an earsplitting whoop when Gloria handed him a bundle of uniforms, each with a "Championship League" patch sewn on the shoulder.

Every delivery was always followed up with an order of tamales. Gloria even had to tell some customers that they couldn't take as many as they wanted for fear that she'd run out before we finished her route.

I was in awe watching Gloria interact with her loyal customers. Her deliveries weren't just about dropping off product in exchange for money. She'd sit and gab, catching up on the latest neighborhood gossip or asking them about intimate details of their lives—which they were more than happy to dish. When they joked, she'd sling jokes right back. I got the sense that for some of these people, a visit from Gloria was the highlight of their day. Or maybe even their only social interaction. Gloria didn't take notes or check her phone—I don't know how she was able to keep all those different addresses and which clothes went to which person and who ordered what tamale in her head, but she did. They loved her for it. This wasn't the solemn, quiet academic who aced spelling bees and spent hours fretting in front of a mirror. She charmed everyone we came across. I wondered what else we all had wrong about Gloria.

The sun was starting to dip by the time we returned to the Jig.

"Thanks for all the help today," she said, dismounting. "I thought for sure you were going to bail on me after Mrs. Espinosa's interrogation. She can be pretty intense."

"Dare I ask how Mrs. Espinosa lost a pet parakeet?"

"She was taking him out for a walk when he broke out of his leash," said Gloria, as if it was the most normal explanation in the world. "I've been trying to find him."

"She takes her bird out for walks?"

"I try not to ask too many questions," said Gloria, shrugging. "But I figure if I'm running around town anyway, I might as well put up some flyers to help her."

"Do you ever take a break?" My calves were throbbing from riding a bike and climbing stairs all afternoon. I was going to sleep well tonight. I couldn't imagine getting up and doing that all over again tomorrow or even the day after that.

"Some days are lighter than others."

A trail of sweat dripped down my forehead, stinging my eye. "Are you going to be okay now?"

Our eyes met. I caught a hint of sadness in her face. I wondered if I'd said something wrong. "What do you mean?" she asked.

I shifted in my seat. "When your bike broke, you said, 'Why today?'"

"My dad's coming over tonight." Gloria took off her hat, allowing her thick black hair to cascade around her shoulders like some majestic waterfall. "If I didn't finish those deliveries, I would have set us behind, which would put my mom on edge, which would put my dad on edge . . ." She trailed off as she stared at her front door. A sigh of relief. "It would have been a nasty domino effect." She started to her apartment but then turned back. "You really should get a light for that bike. Those potholes come out of nowhere. You almost killed us."

"Oh yeah, sorry," I stammered. "I don't usually—"

"Monday you need to be back here. I start early. Eight o'clock."

My jaw actually dropped. "What?"

"My bike is done for. You got a phone?"

I fumbled to pull it from my pocket before handing it to her. Gloria held my phone up. "You need to unlock it."

"Oh right, yeah." I didn't even question why she needed it unlocked, but I plugged in my pin and handed the phone back. She could have asked me to spill government secrets and I would have given up everything I knew.

Gloria typed something in and then tossed the phone back to me. Someone must have been watching over me that night, because I actually managed to catch it.

"There. You have my number now. The way I see it, unless a new bike miraculously shows up on my doorstep—I own you." She twiddled her fingers at me. "See you on Monday."

Before I could process what I had been signed up for, Gloria disappeared inside.

SIX

I NEEDED TO TELL SOMEONE ABOUT WHAT had happened. I was a bubbling teakettle about to burst with steam. If I didn't let it out, I would implode. I'd spent a whole day with Gloria Buenrostro and I couldn't keep something like that to myself. Preston was going to flip out.

"Oh my God, what the hell is that?" Preston got up from under his car, took one look at my monstrosity of a bike, and dropped to his knees. He was shaking, literally *shaking* with laughter. "Will you ditch that thing before someone sees you?" He stretched his neck out to look down both sides of the street. "Wait. No one saw you, did they? Please tell me no one saw you."

"Shut up, man." I rolled it into his garage. "It's my mom's old bike."

"Well, your mom should keep it." Preston lay back on his creeper and rolled under his car. I should mention that the only reason I know the actual name of that little rolly cart that mechanics use is because cars are the only thing Preston talks about and I once tried to learn all of the terminology before giving up. "Since when do you bike here anyway?"

There it was. My opening.

"Since I started taking bike rides"—I waited, to give it a little dramatic flair—"with Gloria Buenrostro."

Preston peeked out again. "Maybe I need to put my muffler back on, because I didn't hear that right. Did you say *Gloria Buenrostro*?"

Hook. Line. And sinker. "Yeah, that's right." I launched into detail about how I saw Gloria hanging out at the Jig, that I discovered she'd moved into our neighborhood (I left out the part that her new home *was* a convenience store), and that I found out she delivers tamales and altered clothing as her summer job.

Preston was on his feet, rubbing his temples. "I'm sorry, slow down a minute. You're telling me that Gloria Buenrostro moved into our neighborhood and all of a sudden *you're* palling around with her like you're besties?"

"I wouldn't say we're besties, but yeah, that's pretty much it."

Preston laid both hands on my shoulders. "Don't joke about this. I'm serious, man. If this is all some big joke, I'll never forgive you."

"I'm seeing her again on Monday." I couldn't help cracking a smile.

He leaned in so close, I could make out my reflection in his eyes. "Are you falling for—do you think you *like* her?"

"I like her just fine."

"Shut up, dude. You know what I mean."

"She's cool, Preston. Way cooler than we thought. What do you want me to say?"

Before I could finish, Preston smushed my cheeks. "Are you even listening to the words coming out of your mouth? I want you to own this. You're hanging out with Gloria Buenrostro! Do I need to repeat myself? I feel like I need to repeat myself." Then he stepped back, cupped his hands around his mouth, and belted, "Gary Vō is hanging out with Gloria Buenrostro!" Some far-off neighborhood dogs barked in response.

I could feel my cheeks reddening. Hearing those words, for a fraction of a second, I got a taste of what it was like to be cool. I'll admit it felt good to have something over on Preston. A look of what . . . admiration? Certainly better than pity.

Preston put his hands behind his head. "When you said you wanted to do something bold, I didn't think that meant squirreling your way in with Gloria Buenrostro."

"Maybe she could help us?" I said, keeping the momentum going. "She could introduce us to the rest of the perfects."

"You're onto something. She could be the key. The key to getting us in." Preston mumbled to himself. "If you're friends with Gloria . . ." Preston trailed off as he whipped out his phone, fingers flying.

"You think there's a chance she'll put in a good word with Jordan and his buddies?" I asked.

"Anything's possible at this point. Put the bike in my trunk. I'll give you a ride home and save us both the embarrassment." Preston raised his phone to me. "Listen to me though. Keep your phone close."

I could practically see the gears churning in his head, but I was too afraid to ask what he was cooking up. As I tried to angle the tandem in the back of the Protege, an inkling of dread crept over me. I'd known Preston long enough to know that when he had an idea, he was determined to see it through—and his plans always came with headaches. Looking back, I had no idea that telling Preston about Gloria was only the beginning of my troubles.

SEVEN

I DIDN'T HAVE TO WAIT LONG TO FIND OUT what Preston was up to. The next evening, after I washed the dishes, I found about a thousand text messages waiting for me on my phone. My first reaction was to panic—no one had ever flooded my phone with that many texts. I thought something was seriously wrong.

> Gary. Call me back. ASAP.
> Where are u?
> Seriously. This is important.
> GARY.
> GARRRRYYYY?
> Poppy House. Meet me there.
> Jordan Tellender asked for us.

That last text made my eyes bulge. Like a shot of espresso right to the heart. I tried calling Preston back, but it went straight to voicemail. I guess I was going after him. I hollered inside that I was going out for a bit—not sure why, seeing as my mom was already at the restaurant and Audrey couldn't care less where I was going.

With summer vacation only beginning, it meant there was still a bit of sunlight, even when the mosquitoes were starting to buzz. I wasn't about to bike there, but it wasn't far anyway. Poppy House was an old abandoned two-story tucked back in its own cul-de-sac. It had two signs up: a "For Sale" sign that had been there since before I can even remember and another that said "No Trespassing" that we ignored. I didn't think it looked too bad on the outside, and I may have, once or twice, dreamed about buying it and fixing it up someday. But when you stepped inside, it was clear why no one had scooped it up. It was rotting. Copper stripped from the walls, leaving nothing but frayed bare wires. We definitely shouldn't have been hanging out there. It was a miracle the roof had never caved in on us.

When I arrived at the end of the cul-de-sac, I recognized Preston's souped-up Protege parked next to a row of much nicer cars.

"I told you he'd show up," said Preston. He was flanked by Blake Haggart and Charlie Dreyer—the two guys who had been kicking around the soccer ball at Circus Burger. They were both indistinguishable for the most part, but were always seen by Jordan's side. I had trouble remembering which one was which. Blake and Charlie didn't exactly stand out—they would have been forgettable if they weren't best friends with Jordan Tellender. And that was enough to earn Preston's and my envy.

On the other hand, Jordan had accomplished quite a bit. I don't know too many high school sophomores who have established their own brand. Jordan ran his own Twitch channel—kind of a mishmash look into his life. He started off recording himself playing video games (I'll admit that I looked up his videos for tips on how to cheese some tricky boss battles), but then the channel transformed into a way for him to show off his new shoes or hats or gaming headphones or pretty much whatever free stuff companies would send to him. Once he started making prank videos with Blake and Charlie, I stopped watching. Not that he would have noticed he lost a viewer. Jordan's videos get tons of hits. He's a big deal.

"So you're the one who helped us get into this place?" said Blake. I felt a swell of pride. "I'm Blake and this is Charlie," said Blake. Charlie stared at me with the same glossy look in his eyes that he always had.

"I'm Gary," I said.

I wasn't exactly shocked that Blake didn't recognize me. For a long time, I didn't want to be recognized. There's a saying that a single nail that stands out gets hammered back down in the wood. I wasn't the nail—I was the grain in the wood. If you don't stick out, no one pays attention to you, and if no one pays attention to you, no one notices that you wore the same outfit twice in a week or that your sneakers are the same pair from last year or that you eat the same three-dollar Vietnamese sandwich every day for lunch.

"So what's going on?" I asked, trying my best to act casual.

"They need your phone," said Preston.

I kept my eyes on Preston, and he gave me a nod for extra reassurance. I plunged my hand into my pocket, feeling for my phone in panic.

"Relax." Blake raised his hands. "We have to confiscate all

phones. This is kind of an old-school operation. You'll get it back," he said. "I promise."

Preston clocked me rubbing my nose. A nervous tic I've never been able to shake. "I already gave them mine." He rolled his eyes. I hated that I was embarrassing him.

Blake stepped forward, holding out a purple Crown Royal bag. I dumped my phone in with the others. "Follow me."

Preston and I kept pace as Blake and Charlie went around the back. The cellar door was wide open, the lock unlocked with the combination keys set to the numbers I'd given to Jordan. With each step, I felt queasy, a mix of excitement and uncertainty, even though I had no idea why I was being summoned. Preston was practically skipping. He tried to keep his face cool and disinterested, but his goofy grin kept creeping through. To him, an invite-only hangout with the cool kids was like Christmas morning.

We climbed the stairs and entered the living room. It had been a while since Preston and I had last hung out at Poppy House. The lawn chairs we'd brought with us were still there. An incomplete deck of playing cards sat on a broken coffee table. 7-Eleven hot dog containers and some empty chip bags littered the floor, right where we'd left them. Corner store prayer candles were scattered all about, lighting up the room with an eerie glow. Someone had taken a marker and drawn a thick black streak across the eyes of the saints. Apparently, whoever did that didn't want the saints to witness what was about to transpire.

And there was Jordan Tellender, standing in front of the fireplace with his arms stretched wide, welcoming us.

"There they are! The guests of honor!"

I probably should have run a comb through my hair. It wasn't the day to be wearing my old faded tank top with the chocolate stain on the bottom. I straightened up.

"Thanks again for getting us into this place," said Jordan, giving my shoulder a shake. I'd be lying if I said I didn't feel a wave of goose bumps. "We needed a new spot for our little operation. It's perfect." Jordan looked at Blake. "You got their phones?"

Blake tossed the bag to Jordan.

"Cool." Satisfied, Jordan turned back to us. "Sorry about that, gentlemen. Preston, you've heard this all before, but it's worth repeating. Let me remind you that the only reason you know about us is because your cousin is a good friend of mine who apparently can't keep a secret."

"I won't say anything," said Preston, nodding to me. "*We* won't say anything, I promise."

"We can't take any risks. No pictures. No texts." Jordan pointed a finger at me. "And don't even think about posting anything you're about to hear. No one talks about this place or what we do. We don't exist."

That little preamble certainly didn't calm my nerves. Meanwhile, Preston was practically shaking with joy.

"Not a word of this to anyone." Jordan stared at Preston and me. Right in the eyes. "Do you agree to our terms?"

We nodded. I still wasn't sure what I was agreeing to, but it wasn't like I was going to tell Jordan otherwise.

His dead-serious scowl transformed into a wide grin.

"Beautiful. I'll get right to it," he said with a clap. "Gary, you're the man of the hour. You know Gloria Buenrostro, right?"

Jordan mispronounced her last name as "Ben-roost-oh." I started to correct him but kept my mouth shut.

"Well, yeah, I know—"

Jordan cut me off with a wave of his hand. "Of course you know her. Everyone does. Unless you're some antisocial cave troll like Blake's sister."

He chuckled at his own joke. Preston and Charlie followed suit, except for Blake, who looked like he wanted to punch Jordan straight in the teeth. Jordan circled the sagging stump. "I'm not asking if you know *of* her. I'm asking if you *know* her. Preston tells me you and Gloria have been getting chummy."

"I don't know if I'd use the word *chummy*," I started to stay, but a sharp elbow-jab to my rib cage shut me up.

"He's kidding, guys," said Preston. "Gary spent a whole day biking around our neighborhood with her. Making tamale deliveries."

I shot a look at Preston, who gave me a sheepish shrug in return. It wasn't like Gloria had told me to keep any of that a secret, but I didn't expect Preston to blab it to Jordan right away.

"Tamales, huh? On the east side? Interesting." Jordan chewed on this. He wasn't the only one who thought it was weird that Gloria was hanging out on the east side. "I knew something was going on when my mom heard that the Buenrostros registered for tent space at the fair this year. Does your family still do the fair, Voo?"

My cheeks flushed. And not because he butchered my last name just like he did Gloria's. The county fair was a big deal for my family. It was the same weekend every year—smack-dab in the middle of summer. Every year, we had a booth cooking and selling Viet food. I usually didn't talk about it—it's not exactly the height of coolness to be a carney. "No—well, I mean, yeah. We're thinking about it. Probably. Yeah, we are." I was struggling to piece together what any of this had to do with meeting Jordan Tellender at Poppy House.

"That's great news. Those noodles you guys hock every year are top-notch," said Jordan. "I digress. You're probably asking, 'What's all this have to do with us?'"

"What you two are about to see is something that hasn't been witnessed outside of this circle." Jordan cuffed the sleeve of his plaid button-down and reached up into the fireplace chimney. He pulled out an old cigar box and placed it on the coffee table.

"Go ahead." He nodded. "Take a look at our bounty."

Preston and I stepped up to the table, not sure which one of us should open the box. It felt like we were part of some sacred ritual. Preston elbowed me in the side again.

I took a breath and popped open the latch. A series of photographs were taped under the lid. Pictures of girls from school. The first four looked like printouts of screen grabs from social media sites, but the last one, Gloria's picture, looked different. Her picture looked like it had been clipped from a yearbook. In the box itself was a purple ceramic dish with a polka-dot pattern, a single softball sock, a retainer case, a little toy figure of a bells bag from *Animal Crossing* fashioned with a string—one of those charms that dangled from a phone, and a clipped black-and-white picture of Gloria. I still wasn't quite piecing Jordan's puzzle together, but I could feel the hairs on the back of my neck rise. There was something undeniably creepy about these "treasures."

"It started off as a goofy game," said Jordan. "I was talking about how sick I am of social media. It's gotten boring. Everything we do is digital, on the screen. There's nothing you can hold, that you can feel. Do you know what I mean?"

I didn't, but nodded anyway.

"Like, if I wanted to dig up something on Marissa Taylor, all I'd have to do is type her name into a search bar. Everything you would want to know about her is right there at your fingertips. Her birthday, her hobbies, and more photos than I'd know what to do with—"

"We all know what I'd do with them!" Charlie cackled.

"You're an idiot, Charlie." Jordan rolled his eyes. "Anyway, what was I saying? Oh right. The internet. It's too simple. Too easy. Where's the fun? The *challenge*? I want to *earn* it. So one day in art class, I swiped Marissa's project when it was cooling from the kiln. That little dish over there."

"Ah. I'm picking up what you're putting down." Preston was bluffing. I knew he was in the same position I was—he didn't have a clue what any of this meant.

Jordan plucked the pottery dish from the box, turning it over. "Holding this in my hand, I got this rush, man. A thrill. This crazy jolt of energy. Holding something of significance belonging to one of the hottest girls in school. It was like a drug. That's when the club was born."

He cracked a slow smile and waited. The kid certainly knew how to build anticipation.

"We're curators. Curators of rarities. Becoming a member isn't easy . . . You have to make a contribution to do it. We all have to pony up something to what we've been calling a 'token'—one personal item from each of the five hottest girls in school. Charlie over here paid someone fifty bucks to nab Shelby Harrington's old retainer. It almost got him disqualified, since he didn't really get it himself."

Charlie looked hurt. "Hey, come on. I dug into some of my birthday money for that."

Jordan continued. "And for number two on our list: Blake got one of Allison Austin's softball socks." He shrugged. "If she didn't want us to get it, she shouldn't have posted a status about how annoyed she was that her locker's lock was broken."

And this was a game? These guys really needed to take up a hobby.

"Which left two more slots to round out our top five," Jordan continued. "Bristol Katz was easy. All I had to do was wait for her to post when she had an upcoming track meet. Her bag was right there on the bleachers, completely unattended." Jordan held up the charm between his thumb and pointer finger. The strings snaked down his forearm. "Her phone charm is one of my favorites."

My stomach dropped. I went all clammy. By my count, there was only one more girl left. I didn't have to guess who the number one girl would be.

"Which brings me to the name of our little club," said Jordan. "The only club of its kind in existence. Named it after number one on the list. Our white whale. A tribute to the girl who needs no introduction. We're the Rooster Society."

Ah. Rooster. *Buenrooster*, like Jordan's mangled pronunciation of Gloria's last name.

"We got nothing from Gloria. As you're well aware, she's always been a bit of a mystery. She doesn't even really have an internet presence. Believe me, I've searched."

"What about Eliza Kennedy and those girls?" I asked.

Jordan sat in a lawn chair and picked up the deck of cards, giving them a good shuffle. "I'm not convinced that they've really cracked Gloria. Sometimes she hangs out with our little circle, but she's not *really* there. I haven't been able to get close. No one has.

"So that's the trick, boys. In order to be initiated as a Rooster, you need to get an item worthy enough to be deemed a token. It has to be something personal." He shuffled the cards into a bridge. "You're looking at the only members of the prestigious Rooster Society. But we're feeling generous this summer. Thinking of expanding our operation with some fresh recruits."

Fresh recruits? Preston looked at me, his eyes as big as a praying mantis's. He was thinking the same thing I was—this was our chance! The opportunity we'd been waiting for. But then I thought about what I was being asked to do. Was he asking us to steal something? The only time I'd ever stolen anything was a bottle of fancy root beer . . . and that was from our own supplies at the fair tent. And I'd chickened out and put it back.

Preston nodded with a look of determination I'd never seen from him before. He was practically drooling all over Jordan's new kicks. "What do we do?"

"That's the Rooster attitude," said Jordan, snapping his fingers. He slammed the cards on the table. "First things first.

Ground rules. And there's really only three of them you have to remember. You already know the first—never speak a word of this club to anyone else." Jordan paused. "Right? We're still square on that?"

We nodded.

"Second, the target can't know you've swiped her token. If Gloria finds out about the heist or the club itself, you're done. And the final, and most important rule, is: The token has to be deemed worthy by the rest of the group."

"What's considered worthy?" Preston asked. "Because if you need another slobbery retainer, I'm sure I can get you one, no problem."

I caught Charlie's dirty look from the corner of my eye, and Preston's cheeks reddened. Sarcasm was his default. Even I knew that he needed to check himself with these guys.

"Great question. The token has to be something directly tied to the target. Take Allison Austin. Softball is her life. Or Shelby Harrington's retainer. She didn't actually get hot until she got her braces off, so that was a no-brainer." Jordan settled in one of the lawn chairs. "I'll make it easy on you guys. I want Gloria's bracelet."

I knew exactly what he was talking about. In all the years I'd known Gloria, she'd never worn the same outfit twice. The only exception being a thin silver bracelet fastened with a single, tiny whale charm. She could be seen wearing it in every elementary school group picture. She never took it off, not even for gym class. During tests, I'd catch her fiddling with it whenever she was stuck on a problem. No wonder Jordan wanted it. It was practically a part of her. And that was going to be a problem.

"That's impossible," I said. "For all we know, it's grafted to her wrist."

Jordan smirked. "That's the point, isn't it? No one's been able to get close to Gloria Buenrostro, Gary, and you're the most promising lead we've had. If it's true that you and her are buddies, this should be a cakewalk. Not to mention that you'll both be carnies together—manipulate the carney code, if there is one. Whatever you have to do! If anyone can get that bracelet, it's you."

I wasn't exactly comfortable with the idea of stealing something, but this kind of opportunity didn't come around often. Not only was Jordan offering us a way in—he said that *I* was the only one who could do it. If I pulled this off, it would singlehandedly change the course of high school for both Preston and me. This was what we'd been dreaming about. We'd be in.

The creeping dread of guilt and the logistics of how I was going to get that bracelet would be a later-problem. I felt like crowing.

"We're in."

"That's what I like to hear." Jordan started to make a jab at Preston's crotch but switched at the last second to a playful punch to the shoulder. "That's the other part about being a Rooster—you gotta have guts."

Jordan's toothy grin gleamed in the candlelight. "Meeting adjourned."

EIGHT

ONCE THE HIGH FIVES WERE HANDED OUT, the roar of the expensive car engines faded away, and the adrenaline burned off, the gravity of the situation I had gotten us into bubbled to the surface. Did I really agree to steal from Gloria?

"Will you knock it off with the nose-rubbing thing?" Preston pushed my arm down.

"I can't help it," I said, shoving my hand into my pocket. Through the dusty window panes, we watched the taillights of Jordan's BMW disappear around the corner. "There's no backing out of this, is there?" I was hoping that maybe Preston had the tiniest bit of regret that I was starting to feel.

Preston plopped down in the chair Jordan had sat in, picked up the playing cards. His shuffling wasn't as slick as Jordan's. "Why would we want to?"

I paced in front of the fireplace, hoping to walk the nerves off. "Let me throw this out there, just for the sake of argument." I paused, picking my words. I had to tread carefully. Preston didn't like pumping the brakes—when he had an idea, it was full speed ahead. I was always the one poking holes in his plans. "Jordan wants us to *steal* something for him. Put aside the whole problem of how we're actually supposed to pull this off. I want to make sure we're on the same page here. Think about what he's asking us to do. Are you really okay with stealing to get into this club?"

Preston threw a frustrated hand through his hair. "It's a stupid charm bracelet, Gary. Besides, it's *Gloria Buenrostro*. She can afford to replace it—she probably has a whole treasure trove of whale bracelets. Trust me, man, rich kids like Gloria won't even notice. These people wake up every Christmas morning with the latest iPhones stuffed in their stockings. You think she's going to notice a cheap bracelet missing?"

"You got me there." I wasn't entirely convinced, but I knew better than to tangle with Preston when he'd got his mind set on something. Best to keep my mouth shut.

"You can't chicken out now. Besides, this whole thing was your idea!"

I swiped a bit of dust off the fireplace mantel. "How do you figure?"

"'Only the bold get glory' or whatever it was you said back at Circus Burger."

"Close enough," I said. "But when I said something bold, I meant starting a conversation . . . not engaging in theft!"

"Look, you want this, too. We've been waiting our whole lives for an opportunity like this. You want to spend every single lunch with me, at the same table, eating the same chả lụa sandwiches—"

"I like eating chả lụa sandwiches with you."

"Gary, that's not what I—" Preston jerked his head up to the sagging ceiling beams. I blushed, feeling his frustration with me mounting. "I don't know if you've noticed, but we're not topping the guest lists of the cool kids' parties these days."

"Yeah, Preston. I got it." It wasn't like I hadn't noticed him sneaking longing glances at Jordan and his buddies hanging in the hallways for the past two years. But when you were a couple of poor brown kids at a school where most of the kids were white, it wasn't exactly easy to break through. That wasn't to say that Preston and I had those truly awful racist experiences you saw in the news. I'd never had anyone call me a racial slur, or found "Go back to 'Nam" spray-painted on my locker. It was just that no one had gone out of their way to invite me to anything. But it wasn't like I'd gone out of my way to ask, either.

Sometimes I forgot how badly Preston wanted to get in with the perfects. Even more than me. He'd never been satisfied with being stuck on the low rung. He was all about the show—he'd spend hours scouring the internet for the most ridiculous deals on the biggest name-brand gear. Game consoles, laptops, audio equipment. I'd watched him blow all of his New Year's money on a single pair of sneakers, only to bury them in his closet when he overheard some girls snickering about them. Me, on the other hand, I could make a single pair of Chuck Taylors last for years as long as I had enough shoe glue. I didn't even want to know how he was able to afford the upgrades to his car.

For as long as we'd known each other, Preston had always been trying to get me to step out of my shell. To put down my book and pick up a beer like everyone else. Sometimes I wondered if he'd actually be in with the cool kids if he didn't feel an obligation to hang out with me. Sometimes I wondered if Preston thought I was a clunky anchor holding him back.

"You said it yourself. High school is almost over, and I—*we* have nothing to show for it," said Preston. "If you do this, that's your ticket to dances. You'll be neck-deep in corsages—"

"Boutonnieres. I think corsages are for girls."

Preston snapped his finger. "See what I mean? You want this so bad, you know the difference between formal flower arrangements. Once we're in, it opens up the doors for everything else. Dances. Parties. Dates. Girls."

I couldn't help but laugh at that last part. Girls? Plural? Me? Yeah, right. My chuckle was enough of an endorsement to keep Preston going. He leapt to his feet, throwing an arm around me.

"Admit it. You felt something tonight coming here. Something we've never felt before. Let's finish what you started!" I couldn't help but smile—he had me there. He knew he'd hooked me. "You swipe a cheap little trinket. So what? This is the kind of harmless mischief normal high schoolers are *supposed* to be getting into. Let's stop being the sad sack Viet kids and do something about it for once. Two more years left. We can make them count."

I reached to rub my nose, but caught myself. My eyes were trained on the open cigar box—Jordan had left it behind, trusting us to put it back in its hiding spot in the chimney. Each of the tokens staring right back at me. Without context, they looked like the contents of somebody's junk drawer. A mishmash of nothingness. But these seemingly random objects meant something. And they were a ticket to improve our lives.

"You can't get cold feet now. Come on, man. Please. For me."

Preston had never asked me for anything. While he'd tried to cattle-prod me out of my comfort zone, he was usually pretty good about leaving me alone to my own isolated routine. If I didn't do this for him, he'd never forgive me. And if Preston ditched me, who would I have? It wasn't like I could wait around for Audrey to come out of whatever funk she was in.

"Yeah, of course I'm in." I reached my hand out and Preston grabbed it. I pulled him up out of the chair. "I just needed to be sure you were, too."

"Gary. This is going to be life-changing. For you and me both. I promise you." He followed me as I headed outside.

"I don't know how we're going to pull this off." I locked the cellar door and spun the combination keys. "We don't know anything about Gloria Buenrostro."

"Haven't you two shared at least one class together every year since third grade? You're telling me you don't know anything about her?"

I shrugged, then looked up through the cracks in the tree line. "If we fail, that's it for us. Jordan won't ever let us recover from this."

Preston clasped his hand on my shoulder. "Then we can't fail."

WE WENT STRAIGHT TO MY HOUSE AND SET up a mini war room in my bedroom. Preston shoved a pile of clothes off my bed to make room for the pizza box. It felt like the right night for a pizza splurge.

"I need a whiteboard or something." Preston snapped his fingers while taking a monstrous bite out of a slice of pepperoni and mushroom. Before I could stop him, he was already pawing through my bookshelf. "Dude. You gotta get rid of this stuff."

He was referring to my painted mini figures, the metal game pieces people use in role-playing games—a little hobby I'd picked up in middle school. I never got into the actual gaming part, but I loved how intricate the pieces were, how much focus they required to paint them well. But it was an expensive hobby. I never owned a complete paint set or a full collection of figures. My personal collection was years in the making, cobbled together from a mixed grab bag of other sets. I used to scour garage sales and hit up the dumpsters behind comic book shops, collecting as many crusty paints and discarded broken figurines as I could get my hands on. When I was younger, I'd spend hours painting, but it had been a while since I'd picked it back up. I couldn't bring myself to throw them away, no matter how much I tried to convince myself I'd grown out of them. I found comfort in the process. The ritual of painting miniatures siphoned all of my concentration. Every stroke had to count—because I couldn't afford to make mistakes. I got good at shutting out distractions, shutting out the world. It was just me and the little piece of metal between my fingers. That was the only thing I had to worry about.

"Can we get back to the actual reason we're here?"

Preston gave me one of those looks like he was staring at a lost three-legged puppy. "One of these days you're going to have a girl in your room and you're going to blow it when she sees those little statues."

"What are you looking for?" I asked, trying to get him focused back on the task at hand. "Something to write on?"

"We need something big so that we can both see it. If we're going to do this, we're going to do it right."

"I'm sure Audrey's got something."

Preston gestured to the door. "Well? What are you waiting for?"

Easy for him to say. He'd never had to ask my sister for a favor in her current state.

I could hear Audrey's pop-punk songs of choice through the door. I knocked once and then again, a little bit harder.

"Enter and die."

I took a chance.

Audrey sat cross-legged on her bed, hunched over her laptop. Her floor was covered in clothes, and I counted no less than eight dirty drinking glasses scattered about. This summer we were about as opposite as siblings could be, but we both shared a hatred of sorting laundry.

"What do you want?" She didn't look up from the computer.

"Can I borrow your whiteboard?"

"What's in it for me?"

"I don't know. I'll do your laundry when I do mine." I'd been dying to throw her hoodie into the wash, but I wasn't about to tell her that.

"Ha. Right. When's that going to be? I need my jeans cleaned sometime this century."

"Tomorrow. I promise. Okay?" I felt like a goon standing in the doorframe, waiting as Audrey considered my offer, her eyes glued to her laptop.

Audrey waved me off. "Yeah, go ahead. Bring it back, though."

"Thanks." I stood there for a moment, trying to think of how best to phrase my next question. "Hey, Audrey?"

"Yeah?" If she was trying not to sound annoyed, she was doing a terrible job at it.

"Have you ever... done something that you thought was kind of messed up, but went along with it anyway because you knew it would lead to something great?"

"That's pretty vague, but I guess it all depends on what the 'great' means."

"Making new friends. I guess."

Audrey's eyes finally broke free from the monitor and met mine. "Friends? Do you trust them?"

That question knocked me back a bit. I didn't really know Jordan outside of his being one of the perfects. You had to know someone before you could trust them, didn't you? That was why I was doing all this.

"Yeah." I figured best to lie and to skip forward to Audrey's answer.

"Then you gotta do it."

"Okay. Thanks." Even with my sister's endorsement, I couldn't shake that tiny little tickle in my gut that something about this wasn't right. But if my best friend was on board and my sister was on board, then maybe I was the odd man out for a reason. Maybe I should tell my inner voice to stuff it for a change.

"The door," she said before turning back to her computer.

I shut it and raced back to my room. Preston suctioned the whiteboard to my closet door and popped the cap off of a dry-erase marker before giving it a deep sniff.

"Will you get serious?" I chucked a balled-up sock right at his head.

"Okay, okay. Let's get started." Tapping the board like a professor giving a lecture, he wrote, *How to Steal a Bracelet*.

Preston stared at me. I could only stare back. "Start spitballing. Anything you got. No bad ideas here." The pen stayed frozen an inch from the board. "Nothing?"

"You don't think I've been trying to come up with something the second we stepped foot out of Poppy House?" I sat on my bed, setting my pizza slice down. My appetite gone.

"She lives around here, right?" Preston whipped his pen out again, poised and ready. "Did she tell you where, exactly? Maybe we can sneak in?"

I wasn't going to be breaking in anywhere and I certainly wasn't about to tell Preston that Gloria lived in a corner store. "No, she never told me. And two, we can absolutely not burglarize Gloria Buenrostro's house or apartment or whatever. I'm not trying to get arrested over this. No way."

"Okay, Mr. Morals, so I guess that leaves blackmail out as an option?"

I shot him my best "get real" look. It was inevitable that I'd have to get my hands a little dirty, but I wasn't going to get slapped with a B and E over a bracelet.

"The way I see it, we only have one option." Preston clasped his hands behind his back and paced like a general dictating to his troops. "You're going to have to steal it from her."

I shot up from the bed. No. Stealing was just as bad as breaking into Gloria's bedroom. I couldn't steal something from her. "And how exactly am I going to steal a bracelet from her? A bracelet she never takes off? No. No way. There's no way I can steal it from her."

I stared at Preston. Preston stared at the empty board. He finally broke the silence by muttering, "This is pathetic. Let's just call it."

He capped the pen before tossing it aside. I hated seeing him like this. He was right—I was the one who put this whole thing in motion. I was the one who decided to march up to Jordan and open my big mouth. We were in too deep and it was all because of me. I needed to muster up that same courage I'd had back in the parking lot if we were going to make it out of this—*I* had to get us out of this.

He started for the door. I knew if I let him go, our friendship would change forever. If I gave up this opportunity, things wouldn't be the same between us. I'd lose that chance at being friends with Jordan and his buddies. Preston would never forgive me. Then I'd have nobody.

"Okay, I'll do it." I stared hard, making sure he looked right back at me. "I'll figure out a way to do it. I'm seeing her again on Monday, remember? I'll come up with something."

Preston didn't look convinced, so I kept going. "Listen. We're not going to have another boring summer. This one's going to be different. We're going to be popular. We're going to be Roosters.

I can feel it in my bones. We're going to make this summer count. This is our time, you hear me?"

"Yeah, whatever."

"Say it. I want to hear you say the words: *This summer is going to be different.*" I grabbed his cheeks and wouldn't let go. I needed him to believe it, even if I didn't.

A smile crept onto his face. He lightly tapped my chest with his fist. "This summer is going to be different."

NINE

IT WAS MONDAY. NOT ONLY WAS I GOING TO be spending an entire day with the hottest girl in school, it was becoming more clear that I was going to have to steal from her.

I didn't feel great about that.

That morning, I woke up earlier than I ever have in the history of all my summers. I showered, brushed my teeth twice, made sure to use mouthwash, and ironed my best short-sleeved button-down. I didn't have a plan on how I was going to snag the bracelet. The best I could do was hope that an opportunity would present itself. I figured the chances of that happening would be in my favor. After all, I'd be spending the entire day with her.

I arrived at the Jig an hour earlier than we agreed. When Gloria came out, cooler in hand and a new set of freshly altered clothes slung over her shoulder, she walked straight up to me. She donned her uniform—chunky sunglasses covering half of her face, and the bill of the ratty baseball cap pulled low over her brow. I caught the glint of the whale charm bracelet.

"You know you can knock on the door, right?"

"Oh, yeah. Sure."

She shook her head like I was a total weirdo. "You want cooler or clothes duty?"

"Uh, whatever you don't want, I guess."

She smiled. "Pick one." There was that dimple she was known for. I directed my attention to the ground or the sky—I can't remember. I just knew that if I looked at the dimple, I'd never be able to go through with stealing that bracelet.

"Cooler, I guess," I said, toeing the ground or staring at some clouds.

Gloria handed me the cooler. "The Jig is always our first stop. Come on."

I jumped and slapped the Jig's awning, as was tradition. Gloria didn't ask questions. She slapped the awning as if it was part of her routine, too.

When I waved to Frogger, I barely got a nod, per usual. But when Gloria waved, his face lit up. I had to duck when he underhand-tossed something to her. Gloria caught it in midair.

"Jorge, no, come on. You're going to get in trouble for this!"

Jorge? So she was on a first-name basis with the corner store guy. Why wasn't I surprised? I was getting the impression this type of thing was Gloria Buenrostro's normal. I guess I had no reason to continue calling him Frogger.

He waved her off. "It's a pack of gum. The owners won't care. And if they do, I'll take it out of my paycheck."

These were the most consecutive words I'd heard from the guy. I couldn't believe it.

"Aren't you the owner?" asked Gloria.

Jorge winked. "So what do you have for me today?"

Gloria shot me one of those "you're up" looks. I suddenly remembered I was holding the cooler. I shuffled to the counter and cracked the lid open.

He rubbed his stubby fingers together as if I had unlatched a chest of pirate treasure. "Roja y verde? What a treat! My best sellers. I'll take all of it."

"Well, I can't give you everything. Some of these have already been claimed."

"I'll take as much as I can get away with." Jorge grabbed bundles, three at a time. "My customers love 'em. Check out that trash bin. It's overflowing with corn husks. I can't empty it fast enough." Tulipán hopped onto the counter, investigating a tamale in Jorge's hand. "See, even Tulipán is a fan!" Jorge fed a tiny piece of tamale to his cat.

Gloria gave Tulipán a good scratch under the chin. "There you go, eating into your profits again."

"What Tulipán wants, Tulipán gets. You want to try denying her one of your tamales, be my guest. Antiseptic is on aisle three." He handed her a thick wad of cash from the register. "And speaking of profits, here's your cut from last week."

Gloria's eyes twinkled. "Wow, thanks. Mom is gonna love this."

"How is your mom doing anyway?" Jorge piled the rest of his tamales, pyramid-style. "How are *you*? Everything okay over there?"

Gloria's smile vanished. Her cheeks reddened as she shot me a glance. "We're fine."

Jorge rubbed the back of his neck. "Your dad stopped by?"

"Yeah, but how did you—?"

"These walls are pretty thin." I got the sense that even Jorge didn't want to be having this conversation. Gloria chewed her cheek. Her fingers went to her whale charm. Even though it had nothing to do with me, I started to get nervous. I thought that maybe Gloria would be more comfortable talking with Jorge freely without me standing there.

"I'll wait for you by the bike," I said, slipping away before Gloria could protest. When they switched to speaking in Spanish, I knew I'd made the right move.

I didn't have to wait for her long. Gloria walked out a few minutes later, hat on, glasses on. It looked like she'd just lost a fight—she gave a quick sniff. One of those "I just finished crying" sniffs.

I wanted to ask her if everything was okay. I wanted to ask her if she wanted to grab some curb and talk about it. And if she needed to spill the details with someone so far removed from the situation that it would make things easier, well then, I could be that for her.

Of course I knew I could never actually say those things, especially to Gloria Buenrostro. Instead I said, "Where to first?"

Gloria pointed east. That was my cue to shove off. She looked relieved that I didn't ask.

GLORIA'S FIRST DELIVERY OF THE DAY ALWAYS

started at the Jig. From there, it was based on a mental checklist in her head. Just like before, my fascination grew with each stop as Gloria interacted with her customers. These were people who probably ate at my mom's restaurant or who I had even served at the county fair. And I never would have noticed them without Gloria.

It was a colorful cast. There was Mr. Ponce in Unit 5, who was always having dress shirts and slacks tailored, but every time he answered the door, he wore the exact same Hawaiian shirt/sweatshorts combo. Gloria was convinced he was a secret agent. Then Ms. Wong, way up on Glenwood, who spent the first ten minutes wrangling her snarly, yappy Yorkies away from the crack in her door. But my favorite customer was Victor Dueñas.

Victor threw open the door, his hands wringing. "Hey, guys. Come in, come in!"

There wasn't much to his apartment. It was pure recently-graduated-bachelor vibes. No artwork hung on the walls. The living room consisted of a single gamer chair and a television set. He used only one bowl, one drinking glass, and one set of silverware.

I whispered to Gloria, "Did he just move in?"

She shook her head. "I wish that was an excuse."

Yikes. Victor owned less stuff than me, and that was saying something.

"Thanks for coming over on such short notice." Victor flitted around the room, picking up half-full chip bags and scooping up crumbs. He checked his watch, nearly dropping a box of cookies. "You got here fast. I didn't think you lived that close."

"Having an extra pair of legs helps speed things along." Gloria raised an iron. I noticed Gloria didn't mention that the Jig was only a few blocks away. "You got an ironing board?"

"I don't need one. I just hang my clothes in the bathroom while I take a shower. The steam gets the wrinkles out." His smile dropped. "Doesn't it?"

"Theoretically. But you really should iron your clothes if you can. Especially before an interview." Gloria filled the iron with water from the kitchen sink.

"See? This is why I go to you." Victor nudged me. "Isn't she the best?"

I nodded.

Victor disappeared into the hallway and came back carrying a wrinkled dress shirt, slacks, and a tie. Gloria grabbed the clothes, shook her head, and handed Victor the iron. "Victor, you're so smart. Any accounting firm would be lucky to have you. You can do this. You just need to slow down."

"How do you know each other?" I asked. He couldn't have just been a customer. Otherwise, why would she be giving him private ironing lessons?

As it turned out, that was exactly how they knew each other. Victor was more than eager to share how he met Gloria—the guy spoke a mile a minute. He was a stuttery, excited, twitchy college grad who couldn't seem to land an accounting job. He had a glow about him. Someone who was completely unaware of how others perceived him. All he cared about was accounting.

He came across the Buenrostros' tailoring service on a recommendation—a good Samaritan bluntly told Victor that he needed to invest in getting his clothes altered to fit his lanky frame. Apparently, Victor was showing up to interviews in clothes that were at least two sizes too big. He was swimming in his dress shirts. His friend sent him to Gloria.

"I would have been lost without Gloria!" Victor said, gesturing to his pristine slacks. I believed him. "Seriously. You should have seen me before. Nothing fit right . . . so I'm told."

"You're fine," said Gloria, handing him his dress shirt. "Now that your alteration situation is under control, we just need to work on your interview face."

"My face?" Victor pulled at his cheeks.

Gloria grabbed Victor's shoulders. "You know you're a good accountant. It's just your nerves. I'll give you the only thing you need to remember to nail this interview."

Victor and I both leaned in. I was no accountant, but I was definitely invested in learning what Gloria's secret weapon was.

"Whatever you have going on in here"—Gloria patted her stomach—"you can't let it show up here." She waved her hand over her face.

"Where did you learn all this stuff?" asked Victor. "Your parents?"

I waited to see if Gloria would have an answer for him.

"Victor," she said. "Your shirt is smoking."

Victor yelped and quickly moved the iron.

I clocked something peculiar that I hadn't noticed before: Gloria never talked about herself. She had an uncanny ability to pull the most intimate stories out of everyone she met, but she kept them at arm's length. Whenever anyone asked a question about her personal life, she found a way to turn it back around to them. And they were happy to continue spinning their own story. She was a conversational magician pulling off an incredible sleight of hand.

Victor disappeared into his room, then came out fully dressed. Gloria cuffed the sleeves of his dark purple dress shirt, making sure that they were wrinkle-free. She straightened his tie and smoothed his collar.

I'd be lying if I said I wasn't a little jealous of Victor's shirt.

"Be sure to *slow down*. If these people could understand what you're saying, they'd realize you're a really smart dude." Gloria pulled a stray thread from his shirt. "I've done all I can do. It's up to you now, Victor. You can do it!"

"God, I hope you're right. I wish I could throw my résumé in their laps and leave. What's the point of writing a résumé if I have to talk to them anyway? It just seems cruel."

Gloria nudged me with her elbow. I was up.

"Do you have lunch plans already?" I asked. "You want a tamale before your interview?"

"Food? Right before the biggest meeting of my life? Are you *trying* to sabotage me?" But as he said all this, Victor fumbled for his wallet. "Oh, all right. I'm gonna be famished if I manage to survive this interview. Gimme one . . . no, two of the green chile pollo."

"Aren't you sick of always getting the same thing?" asked Gloria.

Victor checked himself in the mirror. "Routine. It's all about routine. I can't break routine right now. If I do, it could unravel all of the good work I've done already. No. No, it's best to stay the course. Don't rock the boat. Don't do anything to mess with the Interview Gods. Best to stick to what I know."

We shrugged.

"No, wait, I'll take one more. Make it an even three. Maybe the interviewer will want one. What am I saying? I can't hand her a tamale in the middle of an interview. That'll come off desperate. Two. Better make it two. I'm sticking with my original order. I think."

Gloria ushered me out of the crowded apartment. "Thanks, Victor. Good luck today. And . . ."

"Slow. Down," we said together.

BY THE TIME WE FOUND OURSELVES BACK AT the Jig parking lot, I still hadn't come close to getting the bracelet. I'd completely forgotten about it.

"Hey, Gloria?" It was a miracle I was even able to get *those* words out. She tucked a loose strand of hair behind her ear as she took the cooler from me. "Can I ask you something?"

I was such a coward. Thank God, Preston wasn't around to witness this car wreck.

"Sure."

I willed my brain to spit out the words, *Can we hang out*

sometime? Like for real?, but apparently my brain and my mouth weren't on the same page. "What's with the hat and sunglasses?"

Granted, it was something that was on my mind, but I wasn't prepared to come right out and ask her at that particular moment. I'd have plenty of time to hate myself later for that.

"Oh. Right." Gloria shed both the glasses and the hat. She threw a hand through her hair with a flip. "You're going to think I'm totally vapid and shallow."

"No way. Never." There might have been some point that I believed the rumors that all Gloria cared about was her appearance. But after only spending two afternoons with her, I couldn't imagine that being the case.

"I don't want anyone to see me making deliveries on a bike. I know, it's silly. But I don't want to have to explain to people what's going on. Why I'm spending my summer delivering tamales and altered clothes. God, even saying it out loud makes me sound like a total self-centered, elitist jerk."

"No, it doesn't. I get it." I spun the tandem's pedals with the flick of my toe. "You've come to the right place. I've lived with being broke for sixteen years. Not something you want to shout out to the world." Bile rose in my throat—why did I have to go and share all those details to Gloria?

Gloria nodded. But it was one of those sad nods. She folded and tucked the hat under her arm. "Hey, what are you doing tomorrow night?"

Night? Why did she want to hang out with me at night? Tomorrow night. No, I wasn't doing anything tomorrow night. Tomorrow night was clear. Tomorrow night was good.

"Nothing." I could have said anything—cleaning the gutters, constructing a ship in a bottle, polishing my ice axe for a climb to Mount Everest, but of course I had to say the one word, the only word that implied that I didn't have a life.

"Come over for dinner. We'll feed you. And I can show you how to make tamales."

Gloria Buenrostro's house? Like, going inside? For dinner? She was going to watch me *eat*?

"I'll be there," I said without thinking.

Gloria smiled. That dimple was going to kill me dead in the street before the end of summer. I swore to God.

TEN

I TEXTED GLORIA THAT I'D BE A LITTLE LATE. Scheduled dinners on my mom's nights off were considered sacred. Even Audrey couldn't get out of them. On those nights, we were both expected to be seated at the kitchen table at six. No excuses.

All I had to do was survive this meal—if I didn't make any sudden moves, didn't do anything weird, they wouldn't ask any questions. And to add an extra layer of agony, because of course the universe was against me, Mom made her famous tôm rim. Her boss had ordered too much shrimp, so they let her take a bunch home. Shrimp, or any kind of seafood for that matter, is a delicacy in the Võ household. So it was an extra special dinner.

Any other night, I'd scarf up so much rice, I'd make myself sick, but I couldn't fill up on dinner knowing that I had to save some room for tamales. Fortunately, as the youngest in a family of Viets, I controlled the rice portions. Didn't matter that I was only two years away from graduating high school, I'd had to spoon rice for my mom and sister since I was in diapers. I made sure to give myself a tiny portion. Small enough not to draw attention.

It didn't work.

"What's the matter with you?" asked Mom, bringing her bowl down from her mouth. Mom never changed out of her pajamas on the one day a week she got off. She'd said it was her only real day to relax, so she made a point of taking advantage of it in every way. I thought wearing sweatpants and an oversized T-shirt was her way of rebelling.

"Huh?"

"You're not eating." Mom pressed the back of her hand to my cheek. "You're sick?"

I shrugged her off. "Not that hungry."

Mom laughed. "Okay, that means there's definitely something wrong with you."

Audrey grinned, and I knew I was doomed. "I have a theory about why he doesn't have an appetite. Since he started hanging out with *Gloria Buenrostro*, his stomach has been too full of butterflies."

I sunk low in my chair. I wanted to die.

Mom had that classic mom-twinkle in her eye. "Gloria? Who is Gloria?"

"Some girl," I said. Right. Even I couldn't make that sound convincing.

"Gary, I'm just teasing you. But seriously, you should be owning this," said Audrey. I guess I should have been happy that Audrey was actually speaking to me, even if it was in the form of a brutal roasting. "Gloria Buenrostro is a total ten. She's gorgeous." Audrey turned to Mom. "She's, like, one of the most popular girls in Gary's school."

Mom plucked some shrimp from her bowl and piled them into mine. "In that case, you need to eat more. Get muscles. Girls like that."

It was going to take more than muscles to get through this dinner.

Mom's phone rang. At first she tried to ignore it by letting it go to voicemail, but the second time, she answered. When she started talking in Vietnamese, I knew it was work calling her. Our dinner was about to be cut short.

When she hung up, she shoveled the last bit of rice into her mouth. "I have to go in. They need me tonight."

So much for preserving the sacredness of family dinner. Audrey pushed her chair out and stood up.

"Where are you going?" Mom asked. "Sit. Eat with your brother."

I thought maybe if I flashed my best puppy dog eyes, it would work its sympathetic magic on Audrey. Or at the very least, get a laugh out of her. Maybe with Mom gone, I could fill Audrey in on what was going on with Gloria. Maybe she could give me a pep talk to not make a fool out of myself. Serve up some of that big sister wisdom.

"If you're gone, I'm gone." Audrey picked up her bowl and disappeared down the hall.

Guess that wasn't going to happen.

It was Mom's turn to give me her sad look. "I can be a few minutes late to work. They owe me for all the overtime they don't pay."

"It's fine, Mom. Really."

Mom smiled a mom-smile and sniffed my forehead. "Hopefully I won't be back too late. Do you want me to bring you home anything?"

"Chè if they have any left over." The restaurant makes the best Vietnamese pudding. Well, second best. Mom's chè knocked it out of the park, but it wasn't like she had the time to make it. The fair was the only guarantee Mom would make her famous lychee and coconut cream chè. It was like Christmas in summer in that regard.

"You got it." Mom shuffled down the hall.

And then there was one. It was Audrey's turn to clean the dishes, but I wasn't about to have that discussion. It was fine. I kind of like doing the dishes anyway. I'd have to tell Gloria I'd be a few more minutes late.

ELEVEN

IT WAS ONE OF THOSE BRUTALLY HOT SUMmer nights. One of those nights where stepping outside didn't provide an inch of relief whatsoever. One of those nights when I cursed Mom for letting Audrey keep the only oscillating fan.

The Jig looked different that night. The long shadows cast from the bars on the windows made it look like an impenetrable fortress. All the voices in my head were screaming at me to turn around and go home. Helping Gloria out with her deliveries during the day was one thing, but to actually step inside her house seemed like a whole new level of intimacy I wasn't prepared for.

I was shaking. I had one foot on the pedal, ready to shove off. I could make up some excuse why I was a no-show. A sick grandparent maybe, or I ate some bad catfish.

No, I couldn't bail on Gloria. It seemed more trouble than it was worth to try to come up with a convincing excuse. It was better to suck it up. I did a quick armpit check—not too bad.

As I got closer to her door, I heard a thunderous concoction of trumpets, a passionate drumbeat, and the clattering of dishes. It sounded like a party inside. In the window was a small handpainted sign that read, *The Tamale Tailor*. I knocked twice, but there was no way they could hear me. So I muttered a silent prayer to myself before checking the doorknob. Unlocked. I pushed open the door and stepped in.

That was when I yelped and stumbled backward. I realized I'd almost run straight into a mannequin. She stood in the hallway, posed with her hand on her hip. A partial mustard-yellow romper slipped from her shoulder. I definitely saw mannequin boob. I quickly composed myself and shuffled past the half-naked statue. It seemed silly to shield my eyes, but I did anyway.

I followed the trail of steam and the sound of blaring music down a crooked hallway. The overwhelming smell of seared meat and pungent spices blasted me in the face as soon as I entered. The kitchen was tiny. A cramped, chaotic whirlwind of activity. A window over the sink was propped open by a red transistor radio balanced on its cluttered sill. Dishes stacked high in the drying rack. No dishwasher in sight. A massive steaming pot bubbled on an old stove. And in the middle of it all was Gloria.

"Oh, hey, Gary!" Using the back of her hand, Gloria pushed a sweaty strand of hair out of her eyes. She'd changed into some jean shorts and an old ringer tee with her hair up in a lopsided bun. A colorful array of hair ties wrapped around her left wrist. Her hands were covered in a gloopy white muck. "I was about to come looking for you. I hope Rizzo didn't catch you off guard."

"She has a name?"

"Of course. Rizzo's like family." Gloria hollered out the window, "Mom! Gary's here. The boy I was telling you about."

The screened patio door burst open, and in walked Ms. Buenrostro carrying a pot that was half her size. She was short.

Shorter than me, and that was saying something. Gloria must have shot past her mom by fourth grade. Her hair was long and wild like Gloria's, her bangs plastered to her forehead, and both her cheeks and clothes were streaked with a whitish powder. Once she set the pot down, she reached out her hand, and I shook it. It was wet and covered in something cold and squishy.

"Mom! Wash your hands!" said Gloria.

"His hands are going to be covered in masa anyway." Ms. Buenrostro winked. "Hey, Gary. I'm Gloria's mom."

"Nice to meet you. Thanks for having me over." I wasn't sure why my hands would be covered in anything. What was I getting myself into?

"You two are all set, then? Bueno. In that case, I need to get started on Mr. Ponce's trousers." Ms. Buenrostro turned to me. "I'm the one who sews up all of the clothes that go out—"

"He knows!"

"You see how she talks to me? Okay, I'm leaving. I won't embarrass you anymore." Ms. Buenrostro smooshed Gloria's cheeks and planted a kiss on her forehead, leaving behind a faint lipstick mark. Then laughed as she rushed upstairs.

And there I was. Standing in Gloria Buenrostro's kitchen. The two of us. Alone together.

"Sorry about that." Gloria marched straight to the radio and cranked down the volume. "My mom is *obsessed* with Elvis Crespo. And the rule is, her kitchen, her music." She adjusted a box fan so that the breeze pointed right at us. The bit of wind was a sweet relief. The kitchen was stifling. "We don't have air-conditioning. I know, it's like a furnace in here." Her face flushed red, but I couldn't tell if it was because she was embarrassed or because of the sweltering heat.

"I'm fine." I clasped my hands together, making a point to keep my elbows tucked in as close as I could manage. I wasn't getting out of this place without pit stains. "So, what are we doing here?" I edged over to the sink and washed my hands.

"Right!" Gloria snapped back to the task at hand. "Mom got a huge order in late last night, so now we're behind for tomorrow."

"Lead the way."

She circled back around to the other side of the kitchen island. "You're spreading the masa."

"Masa? What's that?" Seemed like a reasonable question to ask. I was supposed to be in charge of spreading it, after all. "Like, what is it exactly?"

Her brow furrowed. "It's kinda like a corn dough, I think. You know, it's weird that I've never asked!"

I shrugged. If it wasn't a problem for Gloria, it wasn't a problem for me.

At the center of the crowded counter sat a giant bag filled with something pale, cold, and gooey. I rolled up my sleeves, fighting a sinking feeling in my stomach. When Gloria asked me to help her make tamales, I thought I'd be folding neat, tidy little corn pockets. Something clean and manageable. I wasn't prepared to get messy in front of her. Getting covered in corn dough felt like something I needed to build up to. Why couldn't she give me an easier task— something that wouldn't leave me dying of embarrassment?

"You look like you're going to throw up!" She laughed and held out a saucepan. "If you're gonna puke, puke in this."

"I am not!" I said, pushing away the pot. I was lying. I was definitely going to yak.

"There's nothing to worry about. It's easy, I promise. Take one of these, then spread some masa on the bottom part here." Gloria grabbed a spoon and slathered goop from the bag onto some splayed husks. "Then hand it to me, and I'll do the rest. That's it. Nothing to it." She scooped up a handful of cooked pork and sprinkled the chunky flakes. Then topped it off with a strip of speckled green salsa. Gloria tucked her creation into a little pocket and placed it aside. The next tamale, she used seared beef, but with red salsa. She demonstrated again. And again. To me, it looked like pure chaos, but Gloria clearly had a rhythm that worked for her. I was mesmerized. Every tuck, every fold was with purpose. If she ran out of meat, she glided over to the other end of the island and picked up a nicked butcher knife. Her chopping was mesmerizing. I could have watched her all night.

"I'll worry about the filling, you worry about the masa. Got it?"

"I think so."

I had no choice but to plunge my hand into the bag, scooping up handfuls of cold masa. We didn't speak. The minutes stretched on like the dough I was spreading. Every once in a while Gloria would peek over at my progress. Sometimes she'd suggest I add more masa; sometimes she'd use her finger to slide the excess back into the bag.

Eventually I got the hang of getting the portions just right and topping each one off with a bit of salsa with a smooth flick of the wrist. Each time I handed Gloria a finished tamale, I'd steal a glance at her. She never went so far as to sing, but she mouthed along to the music. In my head I begged her to slip and belt out a line or two. I wanted to hear her voice, wanted her to feel comfortable enough to sing in front of me. But she never made a sound. However, she allowed herself to dance. It was slow at first, like she was testing to see if I'd react. I didn't have to wait long before Gloria's hips swayed. Her feet tapped. I even found myself bobbing right along with her. I guess, technically, it was our first dance. Preston would get a kick out of that.

Right. Preston, the bracelet. The whole reason I was here was to get that bracelet.

As I was reminding myself of my objective, I saw it. The whale charm bracelet sat right next to the bowl of masa. When Gloria was focused on wrapping tamales, I could easily palm it without her noticing. I doubt she'd suspect me of taking it.

If I broke up my plan into bite-sized pieces, it almost seemed manageable. I'd take the token, Gloria would think she misplaced it, then Preston and I would find its exact double on Amazon and I'd place it somewhere where she'd find it. Not that bad.

I started to reach for it, but then a knock came from the hallway. My skeleton nearly leapt out of my skin. Gloria pushed past me, rushing down the hall to fling open the front door. Standing in the doorway was a handsome mustached man with wavy black hair. He had to duck under the archway before stepping in. This had to be her dad—he looked exactly like Gloria. It was clear now where she got her height. And her dimple.

"Hi, lucecita." He kissed Gloria's forehead just as her mom

did, but I noticed that she didn't exactly lean into it. She turned her head a bit, crossing her arms. Mr. Buenrostro seemed to notice, too, based on the pained look in his eyes.

"Where is she?" he asked.

"Upstairs," Gloria mumbled, her gaze lowered to the ground. "Sewing."

"How is she?"

"We're a little behind on orders, but she's in a pretty good mood, considering."

He nodded. His eyes were dark and sad. Bags had formed under them like he hadn't slept for days. "What about you? You hanging in there?" He picked up a shirt draped over the handrail and folded it.

"I'm fine."

"Are you eating enough? I keep telling your mom to let me hire a cleaning service, but you know how stubborn she is—"

"We're fine, Dad."

His worried eyebrows didn't look convinced. Neither was I. Her dad peeled out some bills from his wallet and shoved them in Gloria's hand. "This is for you. Don't tell your mom. I don't want you working so hard. This is your summer vacation. You don't get many of those. Take a day off. Get into trouble. Do something other than work." He sighed. "You shouldn't be working in the first place."

Gloria shifted her weight. Her hand went to her wrist, but when she felt that her bracelet wasn't there, she gripped the banister. "I don't mind. Really."

Then he started up the stairs. "Wish me luck."

"Good luck," she whispered. Gloria's dad turned, giving her a wink.

I quickly ducked back into the kitchen and resumed my work. I searched her face to gauge her reaction to seeing her dad, but I couldn't get a solid read.

"Sorry. It's my dad. Did . . . did you hear any of that?"

"Yeah, a little."

We picked up where we left off. Folding. Salsa-ing. I almost forgot that her parents were upstairs, but then the yelling started. Gloria froze mid-wrap, turned down the radio, and stretched her neck out to get a better listen. Even if I could make out what the commotion was all about, it wouldn't have made a difference. The Buenrostros were angry about something, and whatever they were arguing about was entirely in Spanish.

"Is everything okay?" I braved.

There was a shimmer in Gloria's eyes and not the happy kind. "I don't know. Some days I think so."

I kept spreading. There were only a few bits of masa left clinging to the bag. There was more I wanted to ask, but I couldn't bring myself to do it. It didn't seem like my place to pry. What if I said the wrong thing and made her mad? Then she'd never want to talk or hang out with me again. It was better to keep mixing and not risk it.

Turns out, I didn't need to say anything.

"They've been like this for a while." Gloria kept her eyes on the work, folding tamales—she kept up her pace, but I could feel the anger in her folds. "That's why my mom said we had to move this summer. She needed space. I should be grateful that they're still talking."

"Oh." That was the best I could come up with. I worried that if I said something corny, it would take her out of the moment and she'd stop talking. I didn't want her to stop. She needed to get this out, and I was happy to be there for her.

"She refuses to take Dad's money. Not a penny. So that's why we moved out and live, well, here." Using the back of her hand, Gloria pushed some hair out of her eyes. "I don't think my mom really thought it through, but when she's made up her mind, there's no stopping her. I mean, she hasn't worked since she was a teenager. When she married my dad, she didn't need to anymore. She had to figure out how we were going to survive and she tapped into the two things she's really good at: making tamales and sewing." Gloria stopped folding, stopped spreading salsa. She stared out the window. I couldn't tell exactly what she was looking at. Maybe she needed a moment.

The question on my mind was a risky one to ask. I needed to be careful. "Can't you just live with your dad? I mean, if he has all the money—" I caught myself. Needed to course-correct. "I mean, wouldn't it have been easier just to stay? You know. Rather than move all your stuff, all the sewing, and—"

Gloria squinted at me like I'd spit in her cereal. "I can't leave my mom alone. There's no way. Not after what my dad did to her. There's that woman back in Mexico City, and—" She bit the side of her cheek. "My dad made a mistake. A huge one. There's no way I'd leave my mom."

"But at least they're still talking?" I said, trying desperately to find some silver lining. "Do you think they'll get back togeth—"

"They *are* together," she snapped. I had to be careful; I was treading into some dangerous territory. Wetness glazed her eyes. Then her voice got quiet. "They just aren't living in the same house. For now."

Why was she telling me all of this? I got the feeling that she'd been holding it in for a long time, like a shaken-up bottle of pop. I wanted to toss the masa aside, leap across the island, and throw my arms around her. I wanted to promise her that her parents would sort things out. That she had other things to worry about—she should be stressing about things normal high school kids stress about, like college applications and SAT scores.

A door slam jolted us. Followed by more yelling leaking through the walls. I rounded the island to the window and cranked the radio up loud enough so Elvis would drown them out, then returned to my station and held up the bag of masa. "I think I'm finished with my homework here."

Gloria smiled. "I'll be the judge of that." She peeked over and shook her head. "No, you're not done yet. Not even close. You can't waste anything! There's way more masa. You have to dig deep! Get back in there."

Before I could register what was happening, Gloria had plunged her hand into the bag. And that was when I felt them. Her fingers touching mine. Her warmth cut through the cold dough. Her fingertips trickled over my knuckles as if in slow-motion. This wasn't a graze or a brushing. This was a full-on touch. The kind of touch that sucked all the oxygen out of the room. The kind that made you promise to God that you'd never indulge in another sin if it meant getting ten more seconds. I had to keep reminding myself that it would be rude for me to race out of the kitchen and call Preston. No one would believe me anyway. I know I wouldn't.

"I'm doing the masa mash. Ha." God. I hated myself. What was I doing? There she was opening up to me about her parents' crumbling marriage, and here I was making dorky jokes like some sitcom dad. Was this all it took to stop my neurons from firing?

A crash from upstairs made us both jump. Sounded like a plate or drinking glass being thrown against a wall. Even Elvis couldn't muffle that.

There was that silence again. It was killing me. She looked tired, more tired than any teenager should look. She didn't exactly have bags under her eyes, but there were lines that curved underneath that come with stress and exhaustion. I'd seen those same lines on my mom. I had to say something. I couldn't stand there and watch her eyes well with tears.

"Hey, Gloria?"

"Yeah?"

"I'm sorry. I don't know exactly what you're going through, but I'm sorry."

Gloria's hands dipped back into the bag. Through the chill of the masa, I felt her fingers fumble as they grazed my own. Her thumb brushed against my palm, sending chills up my arm. The air caught in my throat. Instead of reeling back in embarrassment, she allowed her hand to remain—touching my own. It may have only been a fraction of a nanosecond, but damn it, it counted.

"You wanna try one?" Gloria said, before finally reeling in her grip. "You have to at least know what you're making. Have you ever had tamales?"

"I don't think so. No. Probably not. I mean, not to my recollection." I hated myself. I wasn't even formulating words. My brain was short-circuiting.

Gloria popped a tamale in the microwave. After about twenty seconds, she brought it out, wisps of steam billowing from the corn husk. "There you go."

I was careful to unwrap it—not afraid of burning my fingers, but of looking like a fool in front of Gloria by opening it the wrong way. I didn't know if it was possible to open a tamale incorrectly, but knowing my record, I would have found a way. I broke off a piece and popped it into my mouth. Of course it was perfect. The pork was tender, practically melting, and the dough delicately crumbled on my tongue. Then came a sizzling wave of heat—not too intense, but not too subtle.

"Well, how is it?" she said, her chin resting on her threaded fingers.

She had to ask me right as I had my mouth full. I chewed with the side of my mouth, mumbled a "good," and finished with a thumbs-up. Real dork-like.

"I'm glad you like them," Gloria said, tucking a strand of hair behind her ear. "You know what's funny? Until now, I didn't even know my mom could cook. Can you believe that? She never had to because we always had someone do it for us. But she somehow managed to conjure up an old family recipe from when she was a kid, and well, look at her now."

I took my time finishing. Chewing and swallowing at a snail's pace. I was worried that if I ate it too fast, then my time with Gloria would be over, and I didn't want the night to end.

TWELVE

BY THE TIME I FINISHED SPREADING THE VERY last dregs of masa, Gloria assured me that she could do the rest herself. I didn't want to leave, but I didn't want to push my luck, either. Besides, I think Gloria was in a hurry to get me out. When I mounted my bike, I could still hear her parents arguing.

I woke up the next morning feeling like I could lift a car over my head. I felt like I could fight a wild grizzly and come out on top. I felt like I could take on the world. Gloria Buenrostro had held my hand. *My hand.* Preston would flip.

Hand-holding aside, it was another business day. Gloria waited for me outside the Jig. She wore her glasses and hat, of course. Sandals strapped to her feet, her freshly painted strawberry-red toenails peeking out. Cuffed salmon shorts. A short-sleeved button-down with lemons (some cut in half, some whole) as the print. I wondered if that shirt was a custom Buenrostro.

"Not a lot of orders today," she said. "Maybe I can take it easy."

I didn't mind the change in routine. Maybe with all the meandering, it'd buy me some time to find a way to bring up last night. Like in a natural cool-guy way. Basically, the opposite of what I'd do.

At one stop, I got the incredible fortune of meeting Aki, the friendliest, fluffiest Akita I'd ever seen. She was supposedly a guard dog that was kept outside, but I didn't sense a bit of "guard" in her. Then we dropped off a knit cap that Gloria had crocheted for Ms. Romano, who was expecting a baby at any moment.

Gloria made a pit stop at her favorite little library—a crooked birdhouse-esque structure packed with mostly graphic novels. "You start your summer reading yet?"

My cheeks reddened. Reading wasn't my strong suit. I hated all the analysis and interpretation. Give me an equation with a straight answer any day.

Gloria plucked a tattered paperback from the shelf and thrust it into my hands.

My fingers brushed the wavy waterlogged cover. It was a collection of Shakespeare plays. Ugh. The Bard. My nemesis.

Gloria smirked. "The specific shade of seafoam green on your cheeks tells me that you're not a fan of William?"

"I can't understand a word of this stuff."

She looked at me from toe to head like she was shopping for a used car. "I think you'd love him, actually. Don't let him intimidate you!" She thought for a moment. "I've got an idea."

Gloria took the front seat. I didn't question where she was taking me—she could have pedaled us directly into the ocean and I would have followed her with gusto.

At some point, Gloria dismounted and we walked the bike under a graffiti-marked tunnel that ran below some train tracks, doing our best to avoid shards of broken vodka bottles and forgotten piles of soggy rags. All the while, I couldn't stop thinking about the feeling of her gooey masa-covered hand on mine.

I wanted to say something, anything to address last night. But even if the courage magically came to me, I couldn't be confident that actual words would spew from my mouth.

A low hum from Gloria's purse snapped her out of her daydream. She checked her phone and frowned. She didn't text back.

"Who was it?" I asked. It couldn't be good.

"My dad. Apologizing about last night."

I gripped the handlebars. "Is everything oka—"

"This is it."

I could take the hint. Dad was a touchy subject.

We emerged from the other side of the tunnel, approaching a secluded park. I was shocked I didn't know about this place—I thought I knew every nook and cranny in this neighborhood. Figured that Gloria couldn't have lived here that long, but she'd somehow managed to find a secret oasis.

There wasn't much to it. A tarnished iron gate stood at its entrance that anyone could easily step over. One look and it was obvious there wasn't a groundskeeper assigned to the plot. Plant boxes sat barren, the soil dusty and dry. The weeds that somehow managed to grow there were so withered that a tiny ember would cause the entire park to erupt into a ball of flames. But I could see why Gloria was drawn to it. It was quiet. And in a city with this many people, solitude was a rare find.

Gloria sat on a bench under a dried-out scraggly tree whose branches provided barely enough shade to justify its existence. "I like to take my lunch breaks here sometimes."

I braved a seat next to her, expecting the sunbleached bench to collapse underneath our weight. "Here? Uh, why?"

She gave me a playful shove. "Don't make fun!"

I looked around, nodding. "No, it's nice. You know, if you're looking for a place to perform a séance."

Gloria waved the book. "Keep it up and I won't help you with the Shakespeare."

I was already nervous about making a total fool out of myself in front of her; the last thing I needed was to pretend that I could untangle language from the Elizabethan era. "No. I can't do this."

"Come on. We can help each other out here. You'll knock a book off your summer reading list and you can run lines with me." Gloria stood up, hands on her hips. "I'm auditioning for *Twelfth Night* next year. I'm going for the role of Olivia."

"Great. Sure. I wish you the best of luck. Break a leg and all that." I clapped. "But I told you, I can't do Shakespeare."

"*Twelfth Night* is a comedy. You'll love it! Look, I'll translate for you."

I sighed. I was starting to learn that when Gloria had her mind set, there was little anyone could do to tell her otherwise. It would be easier to let her have this one.

For the next thirty minutes, Gloria attempted to break down *Twelfth Night* for me in a way I could understand. The book lay splayed out between us. She was so close to me, I had to force myself to ignore the smell of her sunscreen just so I could keep up.

"Okay, how are we doing? I don't see blood gushing from your ears, so I'm taking that as a good sign," said Gloria.

"I think I got it," I said, turning a page. "Malvolio is Olivia's servant, and he's got a total crush on her." I stopped, checking to see if I was on the right path. Gloria nodded, so I continued. "So these other guys play a trick on him by faking a love letter using Olivia's handwriting, telling him to smile, wear yellow tights and cross-garters?"

"But?" Gloria made a "keep going" gesture.

"But she hates all that stuff. So when he confronts her, he's going to look like a total ass."

"Yes! See? You get it!" Gloria grabbed my hands to pull me up. I tried to keep my cool. "Now let's run the scene."

I almost made a break for the exit. "I'm sorry, what? For a second it sounded like you just asked me to act."

"Come on, Gary! No one else is here!" She squeezed my hand. "It's just me and you!"

Oh, she was good. She was really good. She knew exactly what she was doing with that hand squeeze. Eventually I was going to have to find a way to build up a tolerance against this girl. "Let's get this over with."

Gloria handed me the book and then sat back on the bench. "Great! Okay, so you're coming in to meet me, dressed in yellow tights with the cross-garters. You're going to reference the fake letter. Got it?"

"I think so," I mumbled, keeping an eye on the gate entrance. If I spotted anyone approaching, I was going to abandon ship. I cleared my throat. "Um . . . *sweet lady, ho, ho.*"

"*Smilest thou?*" Gloria straightened up. "*I sent for thee upon a sad occasion.*"

"*Sad, lady! I could be sad. This does make some obstruction in the blood, this cross-gartering; but what of that?*" I peeked up from the book. First to check and make sure that we were still alone.

Then I checked on Gloria. Her eyes twinkled; she was eating it up. Her eyes were twinkling because of *me*. I had nothing to lose. Maybe I could play the part a little longer, really get into it. "*If it please the eye of one, it is with me as the very true sonnet is, 'Please one, and please all.'*"

Gloria rose, marching toward me. "*Why, how dost thou, man? What is the matter with thee?*"

"*Not black in my mind, though yellow in my legs.*" Without even thinking about it, I thrust my foot onto the bench, stretching my leg out. I glided my hands up my imaginary tights. I caught Gloria fighting back a smirk, her hand covering her mouth. Whatever I was doing almost made her break character . . . and I loved it. I had no choice but to ham it up. "*It did come to his hands, and commands shall be executed. I think we do know the sweet Roman hand.*"

Gloria placed her palm on the back of my head. "*Wilt thou go to bed, Malvolio?*"

A sweat broke out as I read ahead. "*To bed? Ay, sweetheart, and I'll come to thee.*" I slammed the book shut. The line had to be drawn somewhere. "Okay. I think that's enough for today."

Gloria collapsed onto the bench, tears in her eyes, clapping. "I'm sorry, I'm not laughing at you, Gary. I swear. I'm only laughing because you're good! Really good!"

My neck burned. "I think you're enjoying this a little too much."

"I am." She grinned, hand on her chest. "I really, really am. You better prepare yourself. I'm going to make you audition with me next year."

It felt good seeing Gloria laugh, even if I had to act like a fool to make it happen. Maybe escaping to the land of Illyria was enough to break away from whatever was going on at home. "It's getting late, Olivia. Should we get going?"

Gloria nodded. We picked up the bike and walked it back through the tunnel. A gust of wind blew through, kicking up bits of trash and dried leaves. There was something still bothering me and if I didn't ask, the opportunity might be gone forever. "Was everything okay after I left last night?" There really wasn't a softball way to get into it.

Gloria stared ahead. "I'm really sorry you had to hear that. It's so embarrass—"

"I guess what I really meant to ask was, are *you* okay?"

"Nothing that a broom and dustpan couldn't take care of. We always had too many drinking glasses anyway."

I forced a chuckle, but Gloria didn't follow.

"I'm fine," she continued. "That fight between my mom and dad wasn't exactly something new. Unfortunately." We kept walking. "Gary, do you believe in second chances?"

Her question caught me off guard. "I mean, it depends on . . . all kinds of . . . variables . . . I guess."

A deep wrinkle formed between her eyebrows. "So you know that my dad had been seeing this other woman. Had? Has? God. I don't even know if it's still going on. That's what that whole fight was about. It's what it's always about. Mom only found out about it last year. When she did, she told me to pack my things. Next thing I know, I'm donating all my stuff because there isn't enough room in our new place."

Gloria's pace quickened. "There are nights when I can tell my mom misses him. It's always the times when she has a chance to relax. The nights when the apartment is cleaned, we make a decent profit—you know, when the planets align. She's got a lot on her plate. The less my mom and dad have to check in on me, the better the moods they're in, the more likely they'll play nice. You get it?"

"Yeah, I think so." No wonder Gloria was hyper-focused on everything being buttoned up, all neat and tidy. Another piece of the Gloria Buenrostro puzzle was falling into place.

"So, do you?"

"Do I what?" I asked.

"Believe in second chances."

I considered this for a moment. I wasn't sure how I really felt, but at that moment, I needed to say what Gloria needed to hear. "Yeah. I do."

THIRTEEN

GLORIA'S PHONE RANG. WE PULLED TO THE curb so she could answer it.

It was a new day with new orders. Gloria and I didn't speak again about her parents. I thought talking about it had sapped all of her energy, and I didn't want to push her to reveal more to me than she already had. I got the gist of it—things weren't going great with the Buenrostros.

"Mom? What is it? Okay, calm down." Gloria's face lit up, but her smile quickly diminished to a panicked frown. "No. Seriously? No, Mom. No. Please don't make me. I'll sell a hundred more tamales. I'll work weekends." She puffed her cheeks in defeat. "Yeah. I know. Okay. Okay, fine. Yes. Bye."

Gloria stuffed her phone into her back pocket. She didn't look happy.

"What's going on?" I asked.

She shook her head. "A big order just came in. Huge."

I wasn't sure why she looked like she'd just come back from a funeral. "That's great! Payday!"

"No. It's not, Gary. The customer is someone ordering from Acorn Crest."

"I'm not following..."

Gloria threw off her baseball cap. Her black hair tumbled down. "I haven't been there since last summer. Back when I was a member."

Acorn Crest was a ritzy country club on the other side of town. Everyone called it the Club, for short. Every summer, kids from my school flocked there. It seemed to have everything—a sprawling golf course, polished basketball courts, a renovated exercise gym, and of course the main draw: their massive pool. Not a bad way for a high schooler to eat up three months of freedom. Preston and I wasted so many hours daydreaming of what we'd do if we ever got a chance to spend a day there. We'd only have to strike an oil well first.

"Oh."

"I can't go back. Not like this." She gestured to her outfit—black shorts and a faded blue vintage tee that had the words *Mini School* splayed across her chest. I didn't see the problem. "Everyone will be there."

I wasn't used to Gloria being rattled. She was the most beautiful girl in school—a title that had gone undisputed since elementary school. Everyone I knew wanted to be her. What did she have to worry about? I wanted to tell her that she, of all people, had nothing to worry about. I wanted to tell Gloria that every girl sunbathing under the cabana shade didn't hold a candle to her. She was Gloria Buenrostro. How could she not wield all of her power with confidence?

"You won't be going alone. Come on."

IT WAS TRICKY LOADING ALL THOSE TAMA-les onto the back of the bike. I discovered that with enough bungee cords anything was possible. For not being here that long, Gloria had an expert knowledge of the neighborhood. We slalomed through side streets and secret alleys, making record time.

It was only eleven, but the sun was already out with a vengeance. Acorn Crest Country Club was built on top of a winding mountain with a famous driving range that looked over the cliffside. I rarely got to see mountains. I could admit that I still got chills standing at the bottom of the drive and staring up at them looking majestic when the sun hit the clubhouse just right. The Club's main building was quite a ways up from the main road, so naturally I thought we'd bike there. I quickly realized that wouldn't be the case—Gloria wasn't in the saddle.

"I can't go up there on a bike." Her cheeks flushed. "I know it's ridiculous. But you don't know these people like I do, Gary."

I thought about all the rich kids I knew who had memberships at Acorn Crest. I would have given about anything to have an excuse to breach the Club. I would have worn a potato sack and been happy to take a steam in their legendary sauna. But this was Gloria's first time being on the other side. My side. I had to follow her lead. "How do you want to do this?"

Gloria bit her bottom lip, scanning the area. "Here. Let's ditch the bike behind this bush."

Couldn't exactly blame her for wanting to ditch the old tandem. I looked up at the long drive winding to the main building—and then I remembered how heavy the tamale order was. It wasn't going to be easy. I emptied my threadbare backpack holding our lunches and water bottles before stuffing the pack full of the rest of the tamales. Gloria got the bag, I got the cooler. "After you."

The walk wasn't too bad once I made peace with the fact that there was nothing I could do to keep from being a swampy mess by the end of it. It was actually kind of pleasant. The smell of fresh-cut grass swirled around us. Gloria and I patiently waited as a couple of the Club's peacocks crossed in front of us. Only the hypnotic sound of synchronized lawn sprinklers filled the air.

I couldn't believe how much greenery the place had. Rows of towering palm trees accentuated with cactus and rare desert flowers lined each side of the long, winding driveway. They had grass. Actual grass. I'd been stuck in my neighborhood for so long, I forgot that with enough water you could grow anything. I was used to being surrounded by dust and concrete. My street didn't even have trees on it. The closest thing resembling a tree on the street was the sporadic crooked telephone poles. Trees? Natural shade? That was a luxury.

Our stroll up to the country club was so nice, by the time we reached the front entrance, I'd almost forgotten what we were there to do. A sprawling mansion with more windows than I had time to count. That was when I turned and noticed Gloria wasn't keeping up with me. "Please don't make me go in there," she said. She actually looked ill.

"It'll be easy," I said. "In and out like a couple bank robbers. We keep our heads low and don't make any direct eye contact; no one will notice us." Not like anyone noticed me anyway. It was Gloria I was worried about. She drew attention the moment she stepped foot in a room.

Before I realized what I was doing, I threw an arm around her. Gloria leaned her head into me, laughing. I couldn't believe I'd done that. And that she didn't flinch or shove me away. She'd actually *leaned* in. Gloria's head rested on me for like a solid ten seconds.

Then she took a breath, snapped on her sunglasses, and pushed the doors open.

The lobby was massive. Workers with crisp uniformed polo shirts and radios hooked to their belts bustled behind the front counter. Guests occupied every table scattered throughout—sipping on coffee while reading the morning news from actual newspapers. I was suddenly very aware of how thirsty I was when I caught sight of glass tanks of ice water with slices of fresh cucumber and strawberries bobbing in them. There was a faint scent of peppermint and rosemary everywhere. Everything was so shockingly white that I almost asked Gloria to borrow her glasses.

"Can I help you?" chirped the receptionist. She looked only

a few years older than us, probably my sister's age. Probably a college student back home for a summer job.

Gloria checked her phone. "I have a delivery here, but there's no name. It says, 'Deliver to Guest Six-Five-Six'?"

The receptionist squinted at her computer. "Oh. He's by the pool. You're going to head down the hall here and—"

"I know where it is," said Gloria. "You coming, Gary?"

I did my best to keep up with her. She marched through the Club like she was on a mission. Maybe she was used to being in a place like this, but I wasn't. I didn't even like basketball, but I would have gladly taken it up as an excuse to step out onto the gleaming freshly waxed courts. Walking through a place like Acorn Crest made me feel important. Like I mattered.

"How does it feel to be back?" I asked.

She bit her cheek. "Weird. Weirder than I thought it would be."

As cool as the inside was, nothing could prepare me for what was outside.

The lush golf course lawns seemed to spread for miles. They were so beautiful, they almost made you forget about the millions of gallons of water wasted on them every year. Shiny polished golf carts buzzed to and from the putting greens to the clubhouse bar. Mysterious-looking shaded mini tents peppered the poolside. And the weirdest part was, everyone there was beautiful. I didn't see a crooked smile or a misshapen nose or ears that stuck out a smidge too far. I was convinced there was something in the drinking water, and it wasn't just sliced fruit.

"How are we supposed to find this guy?" I asked.

Gloria peered over her glasses. "Oh no."

"What?" I scrambled to get a look at whatever she'd spotted.

Gloria nodded. I turned, looking where she was looking. There he was. Waving his hand high in the air, beckoning for us to come over. Guest 656.

Jordan Tellender.

FOURTEEN

"COME HERE, COME HERE! SO GLAD YOU CAME."

Gloria flashed a look at me, then back at Jordan. "How did you know about . . . this?"

I could feel the warmth tingling on the back of my neck. Would Jordan rat me out?

Jordan placed his sunglasses on top of his head. "Word gets around. I'm told these tamales are legendary. Everyone's buzzin' about them."

Jordan was lounging on a pool chair. His arms behind his head, his legs kicked up. His short-sleeve palm-tree-patterned button-down was open, exposing his bare chest. When we got closer, he swung his legs to the side and slipped into a pair of sandals. "These are the tamales, right? They smell incredible. You can set them over there. I had the staff bring out a table for this event. Here, I'll help you."

I didn't know what kind of game Jordan was playing, but I was part of it, whether I wanted to be or not. All I knew was that I was responsible for revealing to Jordan what Gloria had been up to. I was so excited about the Rooster meeting that I didn't even consider that Gloria may not have wanted her summer activities to be exposed to her friends.

Gloria nodded. She did a quick glance to make sure no one else was looking. Hands on his knees, Jordan leaned forward. A little too close for my liking. "Gloria? Is that you? Kind of hard to tell with those dark glasses on."

She hesitated for a split second before bringing her sunglasses down to her chin.

"There she is!" Jordan grinned. "It's been too long. Almost didn't recognize you."

"How's it going, Jordan?" she said, unloading the cooler.

"It's going fine, just fine. We've missed you. I've missed you." Jordan winked at me. "Gary, you doing all right?"

"I'm good." I wasn't sure what my move was. Was I supposed to play it cool and act like we didn't know each other? Or was Jordan expecting me to pretend that we'd been acquaintances after all this time? I thought best to keep my responses short. One slipup from me and I'd blow the whole Rooster operation.

Jordan pulled out his wallet. "What's the damage?"

Gloria's eyes stayed on her phone. While she plugged numbers into her calculator app, Jordan snuck in a smile. Best I could give was a noncommittal nod in return.

"Fifty bucks."

"Cool. I've been looking forward to these. We all have." Jordan pulled out a silver money clip and handed a stack of cash to Gloria. Fifty bucks for lunch? And he didn't even flinch. My knees nearly buckled. "This should cover it and then some."

"Thanks." Gloria kept a cool poker face as she pocketed the money. From what I could tell, it looked like a lot. Like *a lot* a lot.

Jordan cupped his hands around his mouth. "Food's here!"

Within seconds the pool emptied. All the beautiful people swarmed the table, snatching up tamales. "Look at these cute little pouches!" and "What are these?" and "How are you supposed to eat it?" were some of the sound bites I plucked from the crowd.

Gloria grabbed my wrist and pulled me back toward the main house. She wanted to sneak out while the attention was on the tamales.

"Gloria! Is that you?" It was Jessica Krebs, followed closely by Eliza Kennedy and Nicole Warren. I hadn't seen them since the parking lot night over at Circus Burger. Gloria's best friends.

"Oh, hey, guys." Gloria shed her glasses and hat. Her disguise hadn't done its job. She was completely exposed now. "How's it going?"

"Does this mean you're back?" asked Eliza, her eyes aglow. "To the Club, I mean?"

"I don't think so. Not this season anyway. Maybe next year." I could feel the embarrassment radiating from her. "I should probably get going, though. Mom keeps texting, asking where I am."

"It's not the same without you" came a voice from behind us. It was Jordan again. "How many orders do you have left for the rest of the day? No, you know what? Doesn't matter. Just tell me how much you make on an average day and I'll double it. Kick off and hang out with us the rest of the afternoon. Of course that goes for you too, Gary."

Nicole lit up. "That's perfect! You can borrow one of my swimsuits! I have an extra one in the cabana."

"Come on, Gloria! Lunch is on me."

Part of me hoped Gloria would accept Jordan's offer. Staying could have been another way in—and maybe they'd let me off the hook with the whole stealing-the-bracelet thing. I imagined Gloria introducing me to everyone, her vouching for my reason to be there. And after I'd won everyone over, I'd find a way to get Preston in as well.

"I can't," she said.

My heart sank. And not just because all hopes I had of getting to hang poolside with the cool kids were instantly dashed. It was a lot of cash to walk away from. Not only did she need the money—she needed a day goofing off at her old country club. No, she didn't just need it . . . She deserved it.

Jessica, Eliza, and Nicole started to protest, but Gloria plowed through before they could change her mind. "The rest of these orders were placed ahead of time. People are expecting me."

"Maybe next time," said Jordan, putting his sunglasses back on. He unwrapped a tamale, broke off a piece, and popped it into his mouth. "Man, these are delicious. You'll have to show me how to make these sometime."

My jaw clenched at the thought of Gloria's and Jordan's hands together in a bag of masa.

Eliza waved goodbye. "I'll text you later, okay?"

I followed Gloria toward the front with the empty cooler.

When I looked back, I saw Jordan raising his arm in the air. He gestured to his wrist.

The bracelet. Right.

"HEY, WILL YOU WAIT A SECOND?" I SPILLED out of the front doors, practically running down the driveway. I guess I could officially add "speed-walking" to Gloria's ever-growing list of accomplishments.

Gloria spun to face me. There was a storm of fury and sadness in her eyes. "I'm so embarrassed."

Being the food delivery girl to your rich friends must have been a specific kind of humiliation. I mean, I would have been happy to do it, but then again, I wasn't Gloria.

Before we shoved off on the tandem, Gloria leaned over. "Have you ever been to a country club before? Not counting now, obviously. I mean as a guest."

It took everything in me not to laugh in her face. Me, at a country club? "What do you think?"

She nodded. "We're going back. I don't know how, and I don't know when, but you and I are getting back there."

At that moment, looking in her eyes, I suddenly understood why Gloria wanted to return. It was about reclaiming a bit of her old life. The life where she didn't have to worry about how her membership was paid for and she could blow off an afternoon without worrying about the repercussions. She didn't want to be called to the Club by Jordan. She wanted to go back on her own terms. And if that was what Gloria wanted, I wanted to help her get it.

FIFTEEN

THE NEXT FEW DAYS, WE CONTINUED THE delivery route. I kept waiting for Gloria to bring up Jordan, or how she was planning on getting us memberships to the Club, but she acted like none of it had ever happened.

Our rides always started at the Jig for Gloria's pack of gum and her daily gossip with Jorge. On one slow morning, Jorge laid out a sampler for us of every snack in the store. We were supposed to taste each treat and give it a rating—the only rule was, we had to try everything no matter what. Which meant Gloria and Jorge got a good laugh watching me choke down the coconut flakes in some kind of candy bar. Then it was my turn to cackle when Gloria chugged an entire Gatorade, trying to cool off her tongue after downing an Atomic Fireball. Even after trying everything, Gloria stubbornly stuck with Bubbaloo, while I had the pleasure of being introduced to the brilliant innovation that was a chocolate marshmallow bar with strawberry filling. After that, whenever Gloria got her gum, Jorge always set aside a Jolly Boober for me.

Gloria and I took the same route and saw the same people—I was starting to put faces to names and remember their stories.

Ms. Romano invited us in to meet her new baby boy, Petey, who just so happened to be wearing Gloria's knitted cap. Another day, we brought Victor Dueñas a bouquet of the Jig's finest convenience store snacks to celebrate landing his first job. At the height of a sizzling two-day heat wave, Gloria had the brilliant idea to dig out an old sprinkler from Mrs. Espinosa's apartment building basement, and we spent the lunch break cooling off by leaping through its waving spray. Mrs. Espinosa even kicked off her fuzzy slippers to join us.

Sometimes I'd catch Gloria singing show tunes. She rarely hit her notes, but there was an earnestness in the way she punctuated the lyrics with a sway that oozed with a specific Gloria-charm. No wonder she always landed the lead roles. I could listen to her all day.

Some days were better than others. There weren't really any "bad" days, but by the end of the week, Gloria was always on edge. On the days Gloria's dad was scheduled to visit, we always worked twice as hard. The bar for perfection was set high— Gloria wanted to bring in a nice chunk of change at the end of the day and have enough time to shower, clean the house, and help with dinner. Anything Gloria could do to remove a spinning plate from her mom, the better.

I kept waiting for Gloria to blow up about her dad, but she never said a bad thing about him. I didn't understand how she could keep it together—it was his affair that had caused her family to crumble, to strip her life away as she knew it. He'd messed up. Big-time. Why didn't she let him have it? I didn't understand. But then again, there were a lot of things I didn't understand about

Gloria. And about dads in general, I guess, since I never knew my own. She kept reassuring me that her mom and dad would find a way back to each other. I had a feeling it wouldn't be as easy as all that, but I wasn't about to say that to her. All I could do was hold on to that hope for her, too.

Gloria wasn't the only one clinging on to a flimsy hope—I still wasn't any closer to getting that bracelet and becoming a Rooster. I could only ignore Preston's texts for so long. But the opportunity would come sooner than I'd realized.

On Saturday morning I heard a sharp knock on my door.

"Go away," I hollered, covering my head with my pillow.

"Well, good morning to you, too," said a voice from the other side.

That got me up. It was Gloria. Right outside my bedroom. Gloria Buenrostro was going to look inside *my bedroom.*

"Wait. Geez. Give me a second!" I scrambled for the nearest pair of shorts and any shirt within arm's reach. I shoved a pile of dirty laundry into the closet, then ditched a used rice bowl and three empty Coco Rico cans into my nightstand.

"Are you decent yet?"

"Yeah, um, sorry. Come in." The yearbooks from that night with Preston were still out—still opened to the pages featuring Gloria. I managed to kick them under my bed as the door clicked open.

Gloria was in my doorway. Practically in my bedroom. She wore her bee-patterned sundress—a standard outfit in rotation that had quickly become one of my favorites. Her baseball cap was nowhere to be found, and with her hair down, it flowed to her lower back. Her cheeks held a trace of pink, as if she were the one with a reason to be embarrassed. "Sorry, your sister said you'd be up by now."

Audrey. I was going to kill her.

"I'm up. I'm up."

Gloria took in my room. When she stopped in front of my bookshelf, I knew I was in trouble. I forgot to stash my mini figurines.

"Whoa. These are awesome," she said, poking an ogre who was missing an arm and holding a broken club with the other. "Did you paint all these?"

I rubbed my nose. The one time I didn't listen to Preston was coming back to haunt me. "Just a corny hobby."

"I think they're beautiful. Must have taken you hours." Gloria plucked a dark elf archer from the party. "She kinda has my eyes. Have you named her yet? Maybe Gloria the Ravenous?"

"How about we workshop that one?" I scooped the figurines and dumped them into my desk drawer. "So what are you doing here? I mean, you're always welcome here, of course, but, like . . . why?" I didn't care how bad I was stumbling. It was Saturday morning and I wasn't a Saturday morning person. Not to mention the one major fact that Gloria Buenrostro was in. My. Bedroom.

Gloria tossed a bundle at me. "Your uniform. Only thing I couldn't get was a pair of khaki shorts. But I know you have a pair. We'll need them. Also, don't forget to pack some swim trunks."

I unfurled the polo shirt. There on the breast pocket was a small stitched emblem of an acorn surrounded by a pair of oak leaves. "You made this?"

"Picked up the polo at a thrift shop, but that little crest there was all me. Not bad, eh?"

"When you said we were going back, I thought you meant that you'd work some connections or something. You're seriously considering—"

"Wearing these uniforms and pretending that we're club employees so we can spend a whole day goofing off? Yeah. I am seriously considering it."

I shook my head and shrugged. "I need to find my shorts."

ONCE AGAIN, WE FOUND OURSELVES AT THE bottom of the winding stretch of concrete leading to Acorn Crest. The sun wasn't kidding around. It was a cruel joke. It was the kind of nasty, stifling, choking heat that never let up. There wasn't even a bit of wind to provide any scrap of relief. We had to pedal faster just to get any kind of breeze.

"Let's get into these uniforms before anyone drives up," said Gloria, shouldering the backpack.

"Right," I said, searching for somewhere, anywhere I could use for shelter to strip down to my undies.

Gloria paused for a moment. "Uh. Do you mind? You're supposed to be the lookout." She made a "turn around" gesture.

"Of course. Sorry." I turned and rubbed my nose. She had to

have heard my heart thumping. The entire club should have. It was pounding like a jackhammer. Gloria Buenrostro was changing right behind me. How could I not freak out?

"You're up," she said.

When she didn't turn immediately, I made the same "turn around" gesture.

"Sorry." Now it was her turn to blush.

We looked the part. I wasn't surprised that Gloria somehow managed to look stunning even in a polo and khakis. Now the only thing left was to make the trek up the long drive. With each step, I felt like throwing up. But before I could suggest we turn around and forget the whole thing, Gloria beat me to it.

"Forget it. Let's bail." She stopped walking as if paralyzed at the thought of the "crime" she was about to commit. "I know this was my idea and all, but I didn't think this through. I mean, we're talking about breaking into a private establishment. Could we get in serious trouble for this? This was a bad idea. I'm sorry I dragged you into this."

The quiver in her voice told me that she needed me to be brave for both of us. Even though I shared her exact same reservations. Gloria didn't want to walk through those doors, but she needed to. And I needed to be right there next to her.

"Gloria, look at me. We're in this together."

"If my parents find out . . ."

I backtracked to where she was left frozen in place and made a point to look her in the eyes. "Then we won't get caught."

I must have masked the fear in my own voice, because Gloria nodded. We made our way up the walk, step by step. When we reached the front door, I checked to see how Gloria was doing. She was shaking. I led her back to the fountain.

"Just like a bank, remember? We just can't go in there *looking* like we're trying to rob a bank," I said. "Let's walk through this plan and I'll poke any holes in it." I scanned the courtyard. "Do we need to worry about being spotted on camera?"

Gloria shook her head. "Acorn Crest doesn't have security cameras. At least not in the areas we're going. Members voted them down years ago. Said they would disrupt the ambiance."

"What are the chances that any of the staff will recognize you? Your family had a membership there for years, right?"

"Low risk," she said. Some of that confidence was back in her voice. "When we were here last time, I didn't see anyone from the old days. The turnover is pretty high."

"Okay, what about the guests? What if Jordan, Eliza, Nicole, or Jessica are back?"

"I thought about that. If they happen to be here today and they do see me, it's not like any of them are going to snitch on us. This place is big enough—we'll just have to be where they aren't."

I was impressed. Gloria had an answer for everything. I guessed I shouldn't have been surprised—this was the girl who had already cemented her place as our class valedictorian.

"That's all I got. You feel better?" I asked.

"You know what? I actually do. Okay. Let's do this." She attempted to flatten my hair. Gloria Buenrostro's fingers were thrumming my scalp. I had to force myself to focus on her words and not on the fact that my knees could buckle at any second.

"Don't look at the receptionist. But don't look like you're not looking at her."

"You're losing me."

Gloria cleared her throat, shook off her nerves. "We'll walk right past her. You have to remember that there's a hierarchy here. Trust me, it's a whole thing. Reception doesn't pay close attention to the grunts. Once we're past the front desk, we're free."

I could only nod. All of my brain energy was focused on trying to make my limbs not shake like a leaf—I'd used up all of my nerves talking to Gloria. I gripped the Acorn Crest–branded beach bag containing our clothes and swimsuits.

"Showtime." Gloria pushed open the doors.

SIXTEEN

LUCK WAS ALREADY ON OUR SIDE. THE RECEP-tionist at the desk wasn't the same girl as before. She barely even glanced at us as we strolled right on by. I turned to sneak a smile at Gloria, but she never once broke character. It wasn't until we reached the front of the locker rooms that she spoke.

"We did it, Gary. We did it! See, I told you not to be nervous," she said with a wink. *She'd* told *me*? Unbelievable. "Ditch the clothes and meet me at the pool."

Gloria shoved me through the double doors of the locker room.

I immediately got why Gloria risked going through with this whole ridiculous scheme. The room had the most elaborate setup I'd ever seen. Everything seemed to have a glow to it. It looked like everything else I'd seen so far in this club—brand-new. Even the grout between the tiles seemed to sparkle. There wasn't one big communal place to shower like the community pools I was used to. Here there were enough individual stalls for everyone. Next to the sinks sat baskets bulging with lotions, razors, shaving cream, and mini sticks of deodorant. I'd never seen anything like it before. I didn't even know where to begin.

How was I supposed to act in a place like this? Was there a protocol I should be following?

"They're free." A voice jolted me out of my stupor.

"What?"

"They're free, son," said the man standing next to me. He splashed some cologne onto his wrinkled cheeks before popping a piece of peppermint candy. "Your membership pays for it."

"Oh right. Of course."

I waited for him to shuffle out of the room before I gargled some mouthwash and helped myself to as many packs of gum, deodorant, and razors I could stuff into my pockets. Why was it that the people who could easily afford this stuff got it for free? The world didn't make sense.

As I was shutting my locker, my phone buzzed. A text from Preston.

> Dude. Bracelet update.
>
> Come on.
>
> Jordan's asking.
>
> Tell me you're getting it.

The bracelet. I'd almost forgotten. Normally, I'd shoot a text back to Preston right away. But instead I turned my phone off and shut the locker. He was going to have to wait. I wanted to enjoy this day.

Stepping out into the pool area, I scanned for Gloria. Even though there wasn't a single empty beach chair and there was a long line for the high dive, I felt alone. Exposed. I didn't belong here. I was surrounded by fresh haircuts, expensive poolside loungewear, and beauty.

I became very aware that I should have retired my only swim trunks years ago. They used to be Preston's, but we'd agreed for a while to trade shorts since we each only owned a single pair—better to swap and keep up the appearance that we both could afford a variety of swimwear. Not only were they two sizes too big for me, but Preston had accidentally spilled bleach on them, so there was a weird orange splotch smeared across the front.

But when I watched as Gloria emerged from the dressing room, suddenly I forgot all about my ill-fitting shorts. Her one-piece was patterned with fruit—bananas, pineapples, kiwi, and halved papayas. She was stunning. Not exactly shocking that Gloria fit right in with the rest of them.

I made a point to close my mouth. The stinging of my eyeballs alerted me to blink.

"Did you make that swimsuit, too?" I asked, trying to keep my voice from going full falsetto.

"Yeah. Well, kinda. My mom helped. What do you think? I sort of messed up the left strap here and I don't know if I got the—"

"It's nice. You look nice. Really . . . nice." My eyes flitted away. At that moment, I understood what Gloria meant when she said you needed to look like you weren't looking. Staring directly at Gloria in a swimsuit would be like looking into a solar eclipse. I made a point to check out the high dive, the golf course, my bare feet.

"Thanks," she said, looping her arm through mine. "Now, come on. Let me show you how it's done."

And just like that, the pool was different. I wasn't craning my neck searching for the nearest exit. Instead I stretched my neck, rolled my shoulders. I didn't feel like a poor Viet kid lost in a sea of privilege—not with Gloria at my side.

The day was ours. We spent most of the morning in the pool. We somehow managed to secure our own personal mini tent and from there, I watched as Gloria performed perfect swan dives into the deep end. When it was my turn to test out the diving board, she squealed every time I cannonballed too close to her. Occasionally we'd point out someone from school and for a second I thought we'd get caught, but no one seemed to notice. Maybe a couple sneaking glances or hushed whispers. In any case, no one was raising a fuss about us.

"Hey, play this pool game with me." Gloria launched herself up to the edge of the pool. "Trust me, it's fun."

"Sure," I said. She had to have known that at this point I would have given her my right kidney if she asked.

Gloria grabbed my hands, pulling me toward the deep end. I still wasn't used to her holding my hands and wasn't sure if I ever would be. "I'm going to shout a word at you underwater and you have to guess what I'm saying."

I guess my poker face needed some work because Gloria flicked water at me. "Don't be too cool for this."

"I've never been too cool for anything," I said, wiping my face.

"Okay, I'll go first." She dove under before I had a chance to clarify the rules. I sucked in a breath and went in after her.

Underwater, Gloria's hair flowed outward like untethered seaweed. Anytime I floated away, Gloria reached out and pulled me back. We held hands, anchoring each other. She tried to stop herself from laughing as she shouted her mystery word over and over, large bubbles floating from her mouth to the surface. Sometimes her legs would bump into mine and we'd blush and Gloria would mumble, "Oops, sorry," which was surprising because Gloria was rarely shy about anything. There was no way Preston would have risked being seen playing a babyish game like this, especially in a place like the Club. And for the first time, I saw Gloria in a way I never had before. There were times she was visibly self-conscious, fiddling with her whale charm bracelet whenever she was unsure of herself. But there were times when she wasn't worried about what anyone thought, even if that meant jumping into a pool, holding hands with a complete nobody. Gloria wasn't some celestial being from another planet. She was a goofy, silly teenager trying to figure it all out just like the rest of us.

"*Gary!*" she said, splashing me with water. "I was saying *Gary!*"

A couple things hit my mind at that moment. One, I found it amusing that out of all the words she could have chosen, she'd picked *Gary*. Second, I wondered why she picked my name out of all the words she could have chosen.

We played her guessing game for a few more rounds. It was almost impossible to translate underwater. *Kitty cat*, *Tamale Tailor*, and *bubbles* were just a few of the words that neither of us could make out. At the end of every turn, we came up sputtering and laughing. We could have easily kept going for a few more hours.

We called it quits when Gloria came up, gagging on water.

"Are you okay?" I asked, actually worried she'd managed to get pool water in her lungs.

"I think so," she said, shaking the water out of her hair. "I just really, really wanted to guess your word. Was it *pocket*?"

"It was *pickle*," I said, laughing. "Hardly worth drowning over!" I climbed out of the pool and pulled her up. "How does it feel being back amongst your people?" We made our way to our pool chairs, tucked in the very back—away from the main thoroughfare.

Gloria wrapped a towel around herself. "Weirder than I thought it would be. Acorn Crest was such a big part of my life. Practically my second home. It's what we'd do on weekends. Whenever Mom would wake me up and tell me we'd be spending the day there, the first thing I'd do was check to see if Eliza, Nicole, or Jessica needed a ride. Dad would golf. Mom would sit out here by the pool with a book. And then we'd grab lunch at the clubhouse. And now we . . . don't."

She shivered under the towel. "You should have been here with me. You would have loved it."

"Me? Here? There's no way. Are you forgetting something?" I rubbed my fingers together—the money gesture.

Gloria blushed, forgetting my sad economic standing. I didn't blame her. The Club was like Neverland—it made you forget about the real world. "Sorry. I didn't mean to—"

"It's fine. I mean, look, I know I could be a lot worse off. A lot worse. We own our house. It's not much, but at least we have that, you know?" I stopped myself, remembering that Gloria and her mom rented their duplex. Now it was my turn to awkwardly spit out an apology for being insensitive. "Sorry."

Gloria shook her head, telling me it was okay. "Keep going."

"There was a point where we were in danger of losing the house. I don't really remember all the details too well. Audrey told me about it much later. For the longest time I didn't even know we were, you know . . ." I still had trouble saying the word out loud. "My mom did a pretty good job keeping it from us. I thought we were just like everyone else."

Gloria inched forward. "When did you know?"

I tossed my towel over my chair and leaned back. "You ever try Maggi sauce? Little brown bottle with a red-and-yellow label? No? Wow. You're missing out. That stuff is liquid gold. And it's not even all that expensive, but in our house, it was a luxury. If we were lucky, we'd find some in our Christmas stocking. Audrey and I used to fight over it all the time until my mom couldn't stand it anymore and got us our own bottles. To make sure I'd know which one was mine, I used to take a marker and write my initials on the bottom left corner of the label.

"Do you remember in third grade, Mrs. Duval was big on those food drives? That year Audrey and I went around our house, barely filling up a shoebox. I still had one of my unopened bottles of Maggi that I wanted to donate.

"A couple weeks later I came home from school and saw a box sitting at our front door. It was full of canned corn, boxed mashed potatoes, that sort of thing. Then I saw it. My bottle of Maggi sauce. Right there on the label were my initials. That's when I knew. And suddenly everything made sense. There was a reason why Audrey and my favorite game to play growing up was pretending that the green utility box outside our house was a pirate ship. *We* were the poor family."

Gloria watched as some kids were getting yelled at by the lifeguard for playing a game of chicken. I couldn't tell if she was listening to me or if she was lost in her own thoughts. "I had no idea you were going through that. Isn't that sad? We've been in, what, four classes together?"

"Five," I said. "If you count us having the same lunch hour."

I thought that might get a smile out of her. It didn't. She kept looking at the game of chicken—the one team finally knocking the other into the pool.

"Does it ever get easier?"

"What? Being broke? I'll let you know when I strike it rich." I smiled. This was supposed to be our day and I was ruining it with all this downer talk. "You want a soda or something? My treat?"

"I think I swallowed too much pool water thanks to you," she said, standing up. "Gotta run to the bathroom. Try not to blow our cover!"

When she disappeared into the main building, I noticed a glimmer reflecting off something underneath her towel. After making sure Gloria wasn't on her way back, I peeled up a corner of the towel and took a peek. There it was—the whale charm bracelet.

It was right there. All I had to say was that someone must have taken it when I went to the bathroom myself. It would be the only chance I was going to get to nab it. I thought about how happy it would make Preston if we were initiated as Roosters. I'd have a group of friends to call my own. Like Preston said, my last two years of high school would be epic. For the first time in my life, I'd be a hero.

Besides, this thing between me and Gloria—whatever it was—couldn't last. It was a miracle she'd had me stick around as long as she had. But the Roosters? These guys were a club. A group that had each other's backs. The Roosters were the safer bet.

I turned my phone back on, in case Mom or Audrey tried to get a hold of me. Nope. Just another text from Preston. The guy had a sixth sense.

> Gary.
>
> Buddy.
>
> Call me back.

This was the only chance I was going to get. This was what I'd spent weeks waiting for. I couldn't chicken out now. And if I thought too far ahead, weighed too many of the consequences, I would have blown my only window.

I snatched the bracelet and stuffed it into my pocket.

SEVENTEEN

I KEPT REPEATING TO MYSELF THAT I WAS going to give it back, that I wasn't stealing it, that this was all temporary. Once Preston and I were initiated, maybe we could pull a reverse heist and get Gloria's bracelet back to her. Anyway, that was a future-problem.

When Gloria came back, the first thing she did was check under her towel and then underneath the pool chair. "Have you seen my bracelet?"

I shook my head. My guts were burning. "Bracelet?"

"The one I always wear. I thought I put it under my towel, but it's gone. Maybe I left it in the locker room . . ."

I needed to change the subject. Get her talking about something else. Anything else. "Yeah, maybe check there, or I'm sure we can ask the front desk later to see if it turned up. Anyway, I'm starving. How about you?"

Her eyes lit up. "I could eat. This is the best part. Come with me."

I nearly collapsed. Too close.

Turned out that was the exact distraction I needed. I followed Gloria to a small building right on the border of the golfing greens. We waited at the window for a few minutes before someone emerged from the back. It was Sophia Guzman, a girl I recognized from student council meetings, balancing two serving trays.

"Sorry, guys. I'm the only one on duty back here and... Gloria? Is that you?"

My heart dropped. We were caught.

Gloria lowered her sunglasses. "Sophia? Oh my God. How are you?"

Sophia practically dropped her trays of food and vaulted over the counter before wrapping Gloria in a hug.

"Where have you been all summer?" asked Sophia. "Every day I look for you."

"Working," said Gloria.

"Tell me about it." Sophia nodded toward the trays of food.

"Do you know Gary?" Gloria always took an open opportunity to change subjects when she saw one.

"How's it going?" said Sophia, with a nod. I offered a small wave, happy to slink into the background. I stood back and listened as the two friends reconnected and caught up on country club gossip. They would dip in and out of Spanish to English. Sophia asked about Gloria's parents (a topic I noticed that Gloria was happy to breeze through) and Gloria asked how Sophia's summer job was going. At some point, Gloria told her about the day Jordan had called in the tamale order.

"No offense, Gloria, but I don't know why you hang out with that guy and his crew. His parents are total cheapskates." Sophia rounded on me. "And if someone's parents don't tip, what does that say about them?"

Was she expecting me to answer? I was trying to formulate some kind of response when Sophia whipped back to Gloria. "Anyway, does this mean you're back as a member or what?"

Gloria blushed a bit. "Not exactly. Gary and I... we kind of... well, snuck in."

Sophia's eyes twinkled before she gave Gloria a playful jab to the shoulder. "Look at you going all rebel! I didn't know you had it in you. I like this new Gloria." She winked at me. "He must be a good influence on you."

Gloria nodded with a simple smile. "We make a good team!"

Her words ricocheted in my head. I couldn't even look at her. My hand reached for the whale charm tucked in my pocket. Did she know?

Sophia picked her trays back up. "I better get back to work before I get yelled at again. How about a couple burgers? Manny's on the grill, so you know he'll hook you up with extra fries."

"Sounds great!" Gloria pulled out a wad of tamale money, when Sophia's hand covered it.

"Your money's no good here." Sophia smirked. "This one is on the Tellenders."

My eyes grew as wide as Gloria's.

"No way, Sophia. I can't let you."

"You think they're going to notice a couple burgs and fries on their platinum credit card bills? Come on. Let me do this."

"Only if you give yourself a nice tip," said Gloria.

There was part of me that felt guilty for ripping off Jordan's parents.

But only a small part.

I didn't even know they made burgers that big. They were the biggest I'd ever seen—a patty as thick as a book, crispy lettuce, juicy tomato slices dripping with condensation, and crunchy sweet pickles. We stayed at the end of the bar, away from prying eyes, where we noshed on our burgers, dunked steaming steak fries into ramekins of thick ranch while watching the hazy sun start to dip over the golf course. We washed the burgers down with sparkling lemonade. I didn't even know lemonade could sparkle. I was so surprised by the bubbles, I nearly choked. Sophia even managed to sneak us a couple ice cream sandwiches. And not standard ice cream sandwiches, but fancy ones made with real oatmeal cookies and pistachio ice cream with chunks of actual pistachio. I'd never eaten like that before in my life. And my mom worked at a restaurant.

When we polished off dessert, I suggested we leave. We'd been lucky to evade capture so far, but I wasn't about to push that luck. Gloria agreed. After changing in the locker room, I found Gloria standing outside a set of double doors, right near the entrance.

"I want to show you something before we go." She pulled me inside.

It was a library—something straight out of an old murder mystery novel. Bookshelves from floor to ceiling. The fresh oil emitting off of the leather chairs stung my nostrils. "This is the best room in the Club," she said. "When I wasn't swimming, I was in here. Check it out. They keep their own version of a yearbook."

She pulled a stack of books off the shelf and flipped through them. She pointed out a picture of the Buenrostros. Smiling. Mr. Buenrostro had his hand on Gloria's shoulder. Ms. Buenrostro draped both arms around her husband's thick neck. "This was the last picture we took together here. I remember I didn't want my picture taken because I had just gotten out of the pool." She looked at the picture for a little longer before filing the yearbook back on the shelf. There was that smile I'd been waiting for.

Gloria grabbed another book and flipped through it. But then she frowned.

"What is it?" I asked.

"This is weird. My picture is gone."

There, where her picture was supposed to be, was a square hole. Someone had taken scissors to it. It didn't take me long to put two and two together. The picture in the Rooster's cigar box was a black-and-white photo.

"Why would someone do this?" She looked ill. Kinda scared. Then she looked at me. Straight into me. Pleading me to come up with some kind of explanation. Suddenly my pocket felt heavy. Very heavy. I almost came right out and told her.

Then Sophia barged into the room.

"You guys have to get out of here. Someone must have ratted you out, because security is looking for you." Sophia raised her walkie-talkie. "You're all over the radio."

The color drained from Gloria's face. "I can't get busted. If my parents find out . . ."

I wouldn't let us get caught. Especially on a night when her dad was visiting. That wasn't an option. "Is there a way out of here that isn't the front lobby?"

"No," said Sophia. "Everyone is on the lookout for you two now."

I rushed to the double doors and peeked at the lobby. The receptionists were on their radios; someone got up from the desk and headed toward the pool. That was when I spotted something useful. The cleaning crew. "Can you bring over one of those giant garbage cans?"

Sophia's eyes lit up. "I'm on it."

She slipped out and returned a few minutes later rolling a trash tub right up to the door. She waved us over and mouthed, *Quick, get in.*

Gloria hopped in first. I swear I caught a glimpse of a smile. "I can't believe we're doing this."

I crawled in next. We lay down as flat as we could at the bottom of the cart.

Sophia layered enough trash bags to cover us. Then she rolled us out of the room.

Gloria was smushed. I was smushed. Her knees dug into my ribs. I kept blowing strands of her hair out of my mouth. It would have been kind of hot if we weren't gagging on the sickening chemical smell of fermenting soda sludge that sloshed at the bottom of the bin.

"Oh my God," Gloria said, holding back a laugh. "I think my elbow is right in the garbage juice."

"Well, don't get it on me!" I laughed back.

"I can hear you two giggling like a couple of schoolkids!" hissed Sophia. "Are you *trying* to get caught?"

Of course nothing made you laugh even harder than when

you were trying not to laugh. It was a miracle we didn't get busted. Gloria and I snorted and snickered, trying our best not to choke on our own spit.

Sophia rolled us right out the back door. No reason to suspect she was escorting a couple stowaways safely off the premises. She was just another low-wage worker taking out the trash.

EIGHTEEN

AFTER OUR NARROW ESCAPE, GLORIA AND I sprinted down the drive, trying to catch our breath—not easy, seeing as we couldn't stop laughing the entire way down.

"Well, I say that was a pretty successful day. What do you think, partner?" she asked.

I rubbed my neck. It was warm to the touch. From shame or sun? Hard to tell. "We probably should have planned for sunscreen."

"Next time for sure," she said. "And might I suggest a better escape plan. I'm going to take an extra-long shower tonight. I swear there's more popcorn kernels in my hair. Do you see any?"

I took a moment to pick out the remaining kernels from her head before getting on the tandem. The entire ride home we replayed our narrow escape. It was a damn near perfect day.

At the Jig, Gloria climbed off the bike and started inside.

"Hey!" I called. "Isn't your dad coming over for dinner tonight?" Normally, on the nights when her dad was coming over, Gloria was a nervous wreck. But she hadn't even mentioned him once.

Gloria smiled. "I had a good day today. I'm going to choose to take that as a sign. Later, Gary!"

BY THE TIME I GOT HOME, THE STREETLIGHTS were already on. Audrey was sitting on the front steps when I pulled up to the sidewalk. I thought she'd be looking at her phone, but she had her elbows on her knees, looking out at nothing. A blank stare on her face. She hardly acknowledged me as I rolled up on the tandem.

"You got guts riding that hunk of metal around," she said, watching as I pulled open the garage door. "Still can't believe you got mom's bike up and running."

"It wasn't in that bad of shape," I said. "When was the last time Mom rode a bike?"

"Wait, do we even know for sure if Mom knows how to ride a bike?"

"That's a good point." I rolled the bike in, shoving it wherever it would fit. Normally, I would have gone straight to my room, but I decided to press my luck with Audrey. See if I could get her talking. Maybe Gloria was right: Maybe a good day was a sign of more good to come.

I returned from the garage and sat down next to Audrey. "Is Mom at the restaurant?"

She nodded. "She said she's going to be late. We're on our own for dinner."

I straightened up a bit. "You wanna go get something?"

"I'm not that hungry. I'll figure it out later." She stood up and started to head back inside.

I could have let it go and left her alone, waited a few more weeks before trying again to get answers. But I was feeling bold, like I could get away with anything. "Audrey, what's going on? You've been acting weird ever since you got back from school."

"Yeah, I know." Her fingers strummed on the porch railing. "There's just a lot going on. Something I have to deal with."

"What is it? Can I help?"

"There's nothing you can do. Don't worry about me, okay?"

"Yeah. Okay."

I felt a jab to my shoulder. "If anyone's changed this summer, it's you. You wanna fess up about where you've been all day?" She pinched my cheek. "Looks like you got some sun there, Gare Bear. Let me guess. Soaking up rays with Gloria Buenrostro?"

"Is it that obvious?" I pushed her hand away, fighting back a grin.

"If you could see the dorky smile you've got on right now, you wouldn't be asking that." Audrey started back inside. "Also, Preston stopped by. He seemed pretty pissed. What's that all about? You guys cool?"

I wasn't sure how to answer that. My hand went to my pocket. He might be mad now, but that was only because I hadn't told him I had Gloria's bracelet on me. One call telling him I got it, and I'd be back on his good side.

"I don't know if we are. Hard to tell sometimes."

"Yeah, well, maybe that's for the better. I've never liked that little snake-weasel anyway."

"Come on, Audrey. That's my best friend you're talking about." Audrey had never been the biggest Preston fan. Anytime he came over, Audrey made a point of being anywhere else.

Audrey shook her head, looking at me like I was a lost cause. "I don't want to tell you who to hang out with, but I think you could do a lot better than Preston Trương. He'd trade you in for scrap metal if he thought he could make a profit off it."

"I think you're being a little harsh." I could feel my cheeks get warm. I knew Audrey thought Preston was obnoxious, but she'd never come out swinging like this before. Where was all this coming from?

"People like Preston might be fine. He'll probably be successful. He might go through life without his shittiness catching up to him. But I'm telling you, wherever he goes, he's going to get there by climbing over people. Trust me on that." Audrey turned her attention to the street again. "Make sure you really know who you let in. That's all I'm saying."

Before I could ask Audrey to elaborate, the front door swung shut.

It was the most Audrey had spoken to me all summer, but I wouldn't say it was the most fulfilling conversation. I thought talking to her would give me some insight as to what was going on with her, but I was left with more questions.

Oh well. At least she was talking to me.

I followed Audrey inside. The house was dark. She didn't bother to turn on any lights. I checked the fridge to see what I had to work with. Not sure why I even bothered. As usual, there was nothing promising. I hoped the monster poolside burger I'd had for lunch would tide me over until morning. Besides, I was totally wiped after swimming all day long under a blistering sun. I'd take a bath and call it an early night.

I woke up to my phone vibrating on my nightstand. I had fallen asleep with my clothes still on. It was a text. But not from Preston.

It was Gloria.

> You up?

> Yeah.

> My parents are fighting. It's bad. Real bad.

I shot up in bed. I was fully awake now.

> Are you okay?

She didn't write back right away. I could only watch the digital ellipses loading while she typed. The wait was agony.

> Not really.

I checked the time. Eleven. Blood pumped through my fingertips as I hammered out a response. I hit send before I had a chance to chicken out.

> You want company?

I stared at my screen until my eyeballs went dry. What was I thinking? Why did I think that was a reasonable thing to ask?

Then came her response. I wasn't prepared for it.

> I'm already here.

I ripped open the blinds and there she was waving at me. In her baseball cap, a plain tank top, a pair of running shorts, and a backpack.

I was frozen. I needed to give my brain a few moments to boot up. I opened my window and gestured to her to come in. Gloria hesitated, as if wanting to make sure I was being serious. I waved her in again. She handed me her bag and I pulled her inside.

Both of her eyes were red and her cheeks were flushed. Could have been from the bike ride or from crying. My gut told me that it was the latter.

"You think I'm some kind of freak stalker now, don't you?" she said, sitting cross-legged on my bed.

"I guess that makes us even." That got a smile out of her. I lived for those moments. "How long were you waiting out there?" I asked.

"Ten minutes. As soon as I got here, I almost turned right back around. I didn't want to wake you. Did I wake you? I did, didn't I? You were totally sleeping and I woke you up."

"It's fine," I said. "What's going on with your parents? Was it bad? That's a silly question. I guess it would have to be pretty bad for you to walk all the way over here."

"Worse than bad. You didn't hear them? Dad had just come over and they were already getting into it. I set all the food out even though I knew it wasn't going to get touched. So I went to my room and tried to finish this scarf I've been working on. They got so loud, I actually had to cover my ears. When the doors started slamming, I knew I couldn't stay there. Told them I was staying the night at Eliza's. They could still be going at it, for all I know."

So she hadn't eaten.

"You hungry?" I asked.

"No," she said. "Well, a little. No, I'm fine."

I rolled my eyes and got up from the bed. "Come on, follow me."

We crept to the kitchen. I really didn't need to be so cautious—once Audrey was in her room, she wasn't coming out for the rest of the night, and Mom didn't wake up for anything after she pulled a late-night shift.

I quickly scrubbed the skillet I'd left soaking in the sink. "All right, I need you at the fridge. Call out anything and everything you see in there."

Gloria pulled out crisper drawers. "I'm not seeing much . . ."

Normally, I would have died of embarrassment knowing that Gloria was seeing just how little food we kept in the house. But I had a friend to feed. "That's normal. What am I working with?"

"A carton of milk, a bunch of condiments, a takeout box of leftovers . . ."

My nose wrinkled. "Eesh. That creamy alfredo is from last week. Better not risk it."

Gloria chucked the takeout into the trash. "There's about half a bag of spinach here? Some of the leaves look a little slimy though."

I snapped my fingers. "Perfect. Yes, that'll work. I swear I saw an onion over here the other day and yes, here it is. Still good. Any fish in the freezer? Shrimp?"

Gloria shook her head.

"Okay, that's all right. That's okay. Nothing a little extra splash of fish sauce can't help. Which, let's be real, no respecting Viet would let themselves run low on." I pulled a bottle from the pantry. "What did I tell you? Would you mind starting the rice? The cooker is on the bottom shelf there."

"I had no idea you could cook." Gloria moved to the sink to rinse the rice.

I grabbed a knife from a drawer. "My mom works all the time, so it's pretty much up to my sister and me to fend for ourselves. After school one day I just couldn't choke down another Triscuit cracker smothered in pasta sauce. If I wanted to eat real meals on a regular basis, I needed to figure it out myself. Thanks to the internet, you can find a bunch of ways to get creative. And the best part is, Viet cooking is so easy. Like, minimal ingredients. And the ingredients cost nothing."

"Can you show me?"

I felt like I'd hit a milestone. Finally I had something I could teach Gloria. She stuck by my side and watched as I lopped off the rotten part of the onion using my mom's nicked cleaver. I filled my favorite dented pot with water from the tap while Gloria separated the good spinach leaves from the ones already turning.

"How's it taste? Think it needs more fish sauce?" I asked, raising a spoonful of broth to her lips.

Gloria thought for a moment. "Maybe another glug?"

When the soup hit a rolling boil, Gloria sat at the table while I hopped up onto the counter. Which gave me the opportunity to ask Gloria something that was on my mind. "So why did you come here?" I stopped, realizing it had come out worse than intended. "I mean, I'm glad you did, but I'm sure Jessica or Eliza or any of your other friends would have come and gotten you."

Gloria poured a bit of salt on the table, pushing it around with her finger, building a small mound. "I haven't told them about any of this. They don't even know I've moved." Gloria fiddled with the salt-and-pepper shakers, rolling them in her palms. "When Mom told me we were going to live here, I didn't tell anyone. I thought it'd just be a few weeks, you know? Mom and Dad would figure it out like they always have and Mom and I would go back to our old house. What was the point of having that conversation? Well, those few weeks turned into a few more weeks. And a few more after that."

I rubbed my nose. If Gloria didn't want her best friends knowing about her living situation, she certainly didn't want Jordan or the other Roosters knowing, either. But now they did, and it was all because of me. It was only a matter of time before it got back to her.

We were both keeping secrets.

Only mine were way worse.

While we waited for the rice to cook, letting the broth simmer, Gloria asked me about my sister. I never talked about Audrey, even during all of our time spent biking together. There wasn't much to say, seeing that she wasn't ever around. But we had time to kill, so I filled Gloria in (as much as I could) on whatever it was that was going on with Audrey—how she came back from college and had been stonewalling me ever since.

Gloria listened the entire time. Like, really listened. She didn't check her phone or have that glazed look of someone who was just waiting for you to wrap it up (something Preston had perfected over the years). That'd never happened to me before.

"If there's a silver lining to my dad gambling away all of our money and leaving us completely broke, I guess it would be that Audrey and I had no choice but to be close. We didn't have tablets or phones or TV or the internet to escape to. Not a ton of toys to play with. It was just me and her together all the time, making the best of what we could. She was my best friend. But now I don't know what's going on with her."

"I'm sorry," she said. "You have all this going on with your sister and here I am feeling bad for myself—about how I don't want anyone to know that I'm living in your neighborhood. That's not cool of me."

The rice cooker beeped.

I waved her off. "I get it. I mean, it is what it is. The truth is, you really shouldn't be walking alone around here at night. Even Audrey doesn't do that." I filled two bowls with steaming rice and dolloped the broth on top. Gloria followed me to my room. "Maybe things will go back to normal when school starts again."

"Maybe."

Gloria settled cross-legged on my bed. I took a seat at my swivel chair, careful to shift my body to cover up the bits of duct tape. I watched in awe as Gloria attacked her bowl. Even the way she shoveled in rice and slurped broth was mesmerizing. She somehow made eating look enchanting. It almost didn't seem real that Gloria Buenrostro was enjoying something that I'd made with my own two hands.

She froze mid-bite. "What? Do I have spinach on my face?"

"No," I said. "You're good. What do you think? Usually this soup has shrimp in it."

"I don't understand how you can get this much flavor out of spinach and onion." She swallowed another mouthful. "This is incredible, Gary. It's so, so good. You're a wizard. Why didn't you say anything about how you can cook? How long have you been holding out on me?"

"I've never cooked for anyone but myself before."

"Can you show me more recipes?"

"Anytime." I pulled open a drawer and tossed something to Gloria. "Got room for dessert? This isn't my doing, though. Had to call in some favors for it."

Gloria snatched it from the air. "Grape-flavored Bubbaloo! Oh man! You shouldn't have."

"I had a feeling it might come in handy to have an emergency reserve stashed somewhere."

She tore the packaging open with her teeth and offered me a purple candy disk. "Do you want to know what they were fighting about?"

"Only if you want to tell me," I said, and shrugged.

"I think my dad started seeing that other woman again."

"Whoa." I wanted to say something profound and meaningful. It was the only thing I could come up with.

Gloria shook her head, the moonlight creeping through the

cracks in the blinds casting a shimmer on her eyes. "I thought things were getting better. That there might be a chance they'd come around.

"I'm doing everything I'm supposed to do. I get the grades, I get the awards. I stay out of their way, I'm self-sufficient. I could take myself out of their equation and they could focus on their marriage. I figure if I'm a good daughter, they wouldn't have to worry about me. One less thing to fight about. Am I making *any* sense?"

"Yeah," I said. "You are."

"Doesn't matter." Gloria reached for her bracelet, but remembering it wasn't there, started to rip the gum wrapper into tiny bits. "It's not working. Nothing I'm doing is making things better."

I swiveled in my squeaky computer chair. From what I'd learned about Gloria, she was someone who thrived on control. She was used to getting what she wanted if she only worked hard enough. "It sounds like whatever is going on with your parents has nothing to do with you."

But it was like she wasn't even listening. Maybe she didn't need me to cobble together a bit of advice. Maybe she just needed to say it out loud. "Everything I did, everything I *do*, is for them, and it doesn't even matter."

I could only stare at the last bits of rice floating at the bottom of my bowl. There was nothing I could say or do for Gloria, no matter how much I wanted to. There was nothing I could do to fix this for her, just like there was nothing she could do to fix her parents.

I checked my clock. It was almost one in the morning.

"It's pretty late." I grabbed her empty bowl and stacked it on mine. "I'll ride with you home."

Tears welled up in Gloria's eyes as she crossed her arms against her chest. "I can't go back there."

I knew there wasn't anything left to be said. I wasn't going to talk her into going home if she didn't want to. What I wanted was to throw my arms around her and promise that I could make all of this go away. Of course, that wasn't an option. So I had to do the next best thing.

"Where are you going?" she asked.

"I'll be right back."

My heart was beating so fast that I was worried the thumps would wake my mom. I breathed a sigh of relief when I saw that Gloria was where I'd left her—on my bed, bathed in a combination of desk lamp and moonlight. She was beautiful. More than she normally was. And that was saying something.

"We're in luck," I said, setting down my prize. "I found one of these babies from my childhood!" A dusty old oscillating fan. A fan in a summer like we were having was worth its weight in gold. Especially on a sweltering night like this. I thought Audrey had the only one.

"Jackpot!"

I unfurled my ancient mustard-yellow sleeping bag next to my bed. "You're cool to stay here if you want. You don't have to worry about anyone busting us. My mom always sleeps in on weekends and my sister never leaves her room. But the walls are paper thin, so . . ." I made a "keep it down" gesture.

"Are you sure this is okay? I'll set my alarm right now and I'll be out of here before you know it." Gloria tied her hair up. "And I can't let you sleep on the floor. I'll take the sleeping bag."

"I actually kind of like sleeping on the floor. Reminds me of when Audrey and I were kids. All we needed was a comforter on the ground and a comforter on top and we were set."

We lay together for a long time. The only sound the rattling whir of the fan. It was an exceptionally suffocating, sticky night. I didn't know why I had even bothered getting the sleeping bag—there was no way I was sleeping in that heat sack. Each time the air from the fan passed over me, it was like a breeze coming directly from heaven.

"Gary? You awake?"

"Yeah." I stared at the ceiling, my hands folded on my chest.

"Can I ask you a question?"

"Of course."

Gloria rolled over the side of my bed, peeking down at me. Her hair tumbled down, the ends nearly brushing my cheeks. "You ever have a girlfriend?"

I snorted. "No."

I expected Gloria to be laughing along with me, but she only stared back. Not a hint of a smile. "What's so funny?"

"I could be wrong, but I'm pretty sure that before you get a girlfriend, you have to go on a date."

"You've never been on a date?"

"No," I said, half laughing. I could feel the heat rising from my neck. "Have you?" I already knew the answer. It was universal knowledge that Gloria Buenrostro didn't go on dates. I guess I wanted to hear it from her.

Gloria shook her head.

I decided to push my luck a little further. I was already staring down the precipice. Might as well swan-dive. "Haven't you ever wanted to date? Boyfriend? Girlfriend?"

"Yeah, of course," she said. "I guess I hadn't found the right person."

I kept my eyes locked onto my ceiling. I didn't dare look over and risk her catching something on my face. And although I couldn't confirm it, from the very corner of my eye, I swore I could feel Gloria staring right at me.

For a minute neither of us said anything. We lay in the dark, listening to the sounds of cars zooming down the nearby interstate. Her words hung out there, waiting to be grabbed. The right person. Could I ever be the right person? I thought she might have been asleep, but then she broke the silence.

"I had fun today."

"Me too."

She held her arm up, inspecting her wrist. "Never found my bracelet, though."

Oof. The bracelet. If it hadn't been so hot, I would have crawled deep into my sleeping bag to wither away. I wanted to fast-forward past this part. I wanted to tell Gloria if she could just wait a few more days, I'd get the bracelet back to her. But that wasn't an option. Not yet.

"Can't you just buy another one?" I asked. Meanwhile, I was praying that Preston was right about that.

"I mean, yeah, technically, but it wouldn't be the same." Her fingers touched her bare wrist. "My dad got it at a gift shop in Monterey. When I was a kid, I had this thing with whales and begged my parents to use one of our vacations to go whale watching. It was, like, the last big trip we all went on together." She raised her wrist. "Anyway. I've talked your ear off long enough. Thanks for . . . listening to me."

"You'd do the same for me." Listening was nothing. That part came easy to me. I'd been listening all my life. And listening to Gloria? Pff. I could listen to her talk for an eternity.

A few minutes later I could hear a soft snore from above. "Gloria?" I sat up, crept over, and looked at her. My stomach melted. Gloria had one arm around my pillow, the other arm dangling over the side of the bed. I could make out her chipped Creamsicle-colored nail polish. Her long legs barely fit on my measly twin bed. A single bead of sweat dripped down her forehead. Her hair spilled out from her messy top bun—splayed out on my bedsheets, wisps curled from the humidity. Gloria Buenrostro was asleep in my bed, somehow looking perfect and not perfect all at the same time.

And it was at that moment I felt my brain finally catch up to my heart.

I was falling in love with Gloria Buenrostro.

A perfect day in itself is a phenomenon. But sometimes, if you're lucky, a perfect day will add up to something even a little more magical—it takes a pair of crackling bare wires and shoves them straight into your heart. It gives an extra jolt to those particular feelings, those feelings you're too afraid to admit you have, because once you acknowledge their existence, it's already too late. A perfect day will take those feelings that are buried deep down hidden in the crevices of your guts and force them to the surface.

And Gloria and I had had a perfect day.

Well, almost perfect.

There was only one pesky thorn keeping the day from reaching perfect status.

I pushed the knob on the back of the fan to stop it from oscillating—the blades trained on Gloria so the air would only blow on her side. I slid open my desk drawer and pulled out the bracelet. I let it hang from my hand. Feeling the weight of it.

I couldn't do it. Not after this day. Not after this night. Not after knowing what that bracelet meant to her. I'd have to deal with Preston and the Roosters later. My chance at being popular, at being one of the perfects, of being part of something, would have to wait.

I slipped the bracelet into her backpack and somehow, eventually, managed to fall asleep.

WHEN I WOKE UP, GLORIA WAS GONE. THE rice bowls were nowhere to be seen, and my bed was made. If

Mom or Audrey saw that, they'd know something was up. I had to mess it up again to cover up the evidence, but I appreciated Gloria's thoughtfulness. At some point during the night, she'd adjusted the fan to have it pointing at me.

I checked my phone. There was a series of texts from her.

> Thanks again for everything.

> I hope I didn't get you in trouble.

> My mom talked with me.

> It's official.

> They're getting divorced.

NINETEEN

I TEXTED GLORIA RIGHT AWAY, BUT I DIDN'T hear back. Not that I blamed her. I even biked past the Jig a few times, hoping that she'd see me and come running out. But from what I could see, there was no movement in the Buenrostro household. The curtains were closed. It was quiet, and not in a good way.

On Monday I was sure that Gloria wouldn't be up for her delivery route. But surprisingly, I got a text from her asking if I'd be up for joining her. I was a little nervous about seeing her. I wasn't good with words. What could I say? What did you say to someone whose parents had just announced that they were breaking up for good? But for Gloria, I needed to find the words. I needed to show up for her. Even if whatever I managed to say turned out to be a garbled mess of the English language, I could trust Gloria not to laugh at me.

She shot me a simple smile before mounting the back of the bike. The first thing I noticed was that she wasn't wearing her cap or sunglasses. Maybe that little detail was insignificant, but it stuck with me the whole day. Gloria had been thrown off her axis.

"You want to hang for a few minutes before heading out?" I

asked. "My parents haven't been together for a long time and I actually don't think they were right for each other, but there are still times I wonder—"

"We should get moving." Gloria strapped the cooler to the rear rack. "A lot of orders to get through today."

"Do you wanna talk about what happened?"

Gloria's eyes dropped to her handlebars. "I don't really feel like getting into it, if that's cool."

"Sure."

I thought that Gloria would open up if I gave her enough space and time. A day or two at most. I guess I didn't need Gloria to tell me she was hurting, because she showed me in other ways. Little changes at first. Gloria didn't feel like taking a detour to pet Ms. Wong's pooches. Our visits to the Jig were strictly business only. I could tell Jorge missed his meandering banter with Gloria. He'd sneak me a look that said, *What's going on with her?* and I could only shrug in return. We stopped jumping in sprinklers.

On another slow day, I suggested we eat an early dinner at Gloria's secret park. I hoped maybe a different location would shake things up a bit, jolt Gloria out of her funk.

The park was empty. I kicked an empty McDonald's bag aside and handed Gloria half of my bánh mì after picking off the jalapeños for her. The sunset was exceptional that day—it splashed the city in a hazy mix of purples, pinks, blues, and oranges meshed together. Old Gloria would have reveled in a moment like that, but she didn't even look up at the sky.

"Hey," I finally asked. "Is everything okay? I know you said you didn't want to talk about your parents and all and I totally get that. But it's been a few days and well, I just want to check in."

"I hate baking," she finally said.

I wasn't sure what to make of that. "Okay . . ."

She didn't turn to face me, like she was having a conversation with herself. "You know the thing about baking is that it's precise. The measurements have to be perfect. The timing of when you put it in the oven has to be perfect. The timing of when you pull it out of the oven has to be perfect. You mess up once and it's all ruined. Everything has to be perfect."

I struggled to see where this was going. This was coming from the girl whose cherry bakewells and cobblers won awards. As a sophomore, she'd had her own column in the school newsletter. It was the most popular section.

"And I hate studying and I hate writing essays and I hate student council."

"But . . . you're a straight-A student. You're a great writer." I couldn't wrap my head around why someone would hate the things they excelled at. I'd sell my own sister out to be good at any one of those things. Hell, to be good at *anything*.

Gloria stared out at nothing, her mouth a thin line, brushing the baguette crumbs off her overall shorts. "It doesn't matter anymore."

A candle inside Gloria had been snuffed out. Something had changed in her. And there was nothing I could do about it. The best I could do was sit and listen. I had to hope that was enough.

That wasn't to say those days were all doom and gloom. I taught Gloria how to improvise a tasty stir-fry without letting the leftovers go to waste (the magic of Maggi), and she showed me how to properly order from an elodero, one of those guys in cuffed jeans and cowboy hats pushing along street carts fashioned with bicycle bells. We'd each splurge on street corn "con todo," which included a side of wagon wheel pork rinds, and polish it off with ice-cold pineapple Jarritos. We had our bike route nailed down to peak efficiency, even going so far as to avoid the streets where the gag-inducing stench of evergreen pear trees bloomed.

Before I met Gloria, I would skip lunch during the summer—I trained myself like a camel and could make a bowl of cereal stretch till dinner. But that summer, I ate like royalty. Gloria always kept me fed. On the days when she said she was sick of dipping into her own supply for lunch (I never got sick of the Buenrostros' tamales, but I faked it for Gloria's sake), I'd pack us some simple white bread sandwiches stuffed with pork floss and we'd grab a patch of sidewalk curb to eat them. Sometimes her mom would whip us up something and we'd all eat together in the Buenrostros' mini backyard garden among the unruly wildflowers and crooked tomato cages. If we finished our deliveries early, we'd ditch the tandem and wander around downtown or watch the skaters attempt rail slides at the skate park.

On the rare occasion that orders were slow, Gloria's mom would send us on a mission to scope out the vintage clothing stores. We never left empty-handed. Gloria was like a textile bloodhound whenever she stepped foot in the door, always able to track down the best fabrics that weren't already picked over. There were times she'd get excited when she found something really special, but then I'd discover a small hole or a tear or some other blemish in it. It didn't matter to Gloria. We'd buy it and find a park with some shade where she would teach me how to sew. I got pretty good at mending minor patches.

When the weather got unbearable, we'd hide in the library, soaking up the free air-conditioning while catching up on our summer reading list. On one such library afternoon, Gloria and I found a table directly under the air-conditioning unit. I was nearly finished with *Twelfth Night* when I slammed my copy shut.

Gloria looked up from her book. "Everything okay over there?"

"You said this play was a comedy."

"It is."

"Oh yeah?" I opened the book again and slid it across the table. "Act Three, Scene Four."

Gloria tucked her hair behind her ear and read.

I strummed my fingers, waiting for her to react. "Well?"

"Well, what?" she said. "I don't get what you're so upset about."

I stomped around to her side of the table, picked up the book, and put on my best Malvolio. *"By the lord, madam, you wrong me, and the world shall know it: though you have put me in darkness and given your drunken cousin rule over me, yet have I the benefit of my senses as well as your ladyship."*

When I noticed most of the library patrons were staring at me, I lowered my voice. "They do Malvolio so dirty! Maria, Fabian, and even that jester guy, Feste—they all trick him into thinking Olivia loves him and have him thrown in prison on the basis of insanity when he makes a total ass of himself. And then that's it? His story is over?"

Gloria flipped ahead, scanning. "I guess you're right. Huh. I never realized that."

"So I ask you again, how is this a comedy?" I watched, hands on hips, as Gloria tried to hide her smile. "You're laughing at me, but I'm asking a serious question!"

"Maybe you're right. Maybe it's not a comedy. Maybe it's something in between...," Gloria said. "But look! I got you debating Shakespeare with me!"

I was not amused.

Shakespeare wasn't the only thing Gloria was opening my eyes to. Every day, I was picking up on things that I hadn't noticed before. I found myself thinking about funny things she'd say, corny jokes from candy wrappers and Popsicle sticks that would crack her up. I'd wake up in the morning and find myself looking forward to spending another day with her—stalking the best fruit cup carts and snacking on spears of mango and papaya drizzled with lime juice from a squirt bottle and dusted with tart Tajín powder. Some days we'd skim a portion of the profits and buy groceries to drop off at Gloria's community fridge. Lots of afternoons were spent reading in our secret park. Before I'd met Gloria, my summers were spent in my room, hiding and waiting for another school year to start back up. With Gloria, I was seeing my neighborhood for the first time. At night I'd reflect on our day, squeezing every detail into memory so I could recall them whenever I felt alone. Whenever I thought about school starting back up, a pit formed in my stomach. Would she forget about me?

TWENTY

WHAT WITH GLORIA AND THE DELIVERIES, with Preston and the Roosters, I'd almost forgotten the most important event of the summer. The annual summer county fair was upon us.

The county fair was a big deal for my family. On that single weekend, we made most of our money for the whole year. Since before I was born, my mom had rented the same booth every year, hocking "Asian" food. She started off selling authentic Viet food—spicy green papaya salad, little individual dishes of bánh xèo, and chả giò deep-fried mini rolls stuffed with pork and veggies. Eventually she got tired of having to explain that chả giò aren't the same as egg rolls. And they certainly aren't deep-fried pickles. Besides, she learned that she could make more money selling the more familiar chicken chow mein (actually made from soy sauce and spaghetti), fried rice (boxed rice mixed with ketchup), and sweet-and-sour chicken sticks (skewered chicken nuggets) . . . that sort of thing. There was lots of money in these faux-Asian-style dishes, and as a dutiful son and member of the Võ family, I was expected to do my part.

Mom kept selling chè, though. Audrey and I wouldn't let her

take that off the menu. The night before the fair, after dropping Gloria off, I turned down my street and hit the brakes. Someone was parked in the driveway. A Protege. Preston's Protege.

The fair also marked the middle of summer vacation. We'd be back roaming the halls of high school before we knew it. I shouldn't have been surprised to see Preston. I knew he was getting antsy for answers on the bracelet.

When I walked my bike up, Preston greeted me with open arms. "He lives!"

I rubbed my nose. "Hey, man. Sorry. I know I haven't gotten back to you. I've been a little—"

"Busy. I know." Preston grinned, wagging his finger. "I figured I'd save you the trouble and swing by to see how my best buddy was doing."

I could hear it in his voice. I could see it in his smirk. He'd come for answers.

Mom came out of the garage. "Dinner's ready. Oh, hi, Preston. Have you eaten yet, con?"

Preston looked at me. I stared back. It was an unspoken challenge.

"No, not yet."

"Come on inside. Let's go, boys." Mom waved us in.

We kicked off our shoes and sat at the table. Steam puffed from the rice cooker. I grabbed Preston a bowl and a fresh set of chopsticks.

Mom always took the weekend off for the fair. It was tradition that the night before, we'd have a big meal together. Kind of like troops getting warm chow before they went into battle. "Preston, are you joining us at the fair tomorrow? Gary hasn't mentioned anything about you needing work this year."

"Thanks, but I decided to take a break this time. I'll be wandering around, though. Save some chè bà ba for me?"

From across the table, Audrey raised an eyebrow at me. Preston never passed up a chance to work the fair—he was happy to walk away with a nice wad of cash in his pocket at the end of the long weekend. Rather than working up front with Audrey and me, Preston always chose to work in the back alongside my mom, chopping vegetables and boiling noodles, because he worried about someone from school recognizing him. Maybe with the potential of joining the Roosters hanging by a thread, he didn't want to take the risk of being spotted.

"The offer is still open if you change your mind," said Mom, plucking a chunk of catfish from a clay pot and dropping it in my bowl. "How's your mom doing? I haven't heard from her in a while."

Preston helped himself to a heaping spoonful of the seafood-pineapple soup. "Seems like everyone is preoccupied this summer." He winked from over his rice bowl. "Mẹ is khỏe though. I'll remind her to call you."

I shoveled rice into my mouth. The sooner I could finish, the sooner I could get rid of Preston. He only busted out his Vietnamese when he was trying to get on my mom's good side. I wasn't sure what he was trying to get at, but I didn't like it.

Mom continued. "You haven't been around much this summer, either."

"I'm afraid I've been forgotten," he said, through a mouthful of broth. "Not that I blame Gary. I mean, if it were the other way around and Gloria Buenrostro asked me to spend every waking hour with her, I'd be gone in a second."

I felt a little kick from under the table. Audrey knew that something was up. She mouthed, *Say something*. I shook my head.

"Oh, the popular girl?" asked Mom.

Preston smirked. "She seems to have put quite the spell over him. I've never seen our boy so entranced before. It's almost as if—"

"Okay, Preston, we get it," Audrey said. What was he trying to do? I expected this kind of ribbing from a grouchy sister, but not someone who was supposed to be my best friend. And here, Audrey was the one defending me.

"Xin lỗi. I'm joking." Preston raised his arms. "Anyway, since you don't have a date tonight, Gary, why don't you come with me?"

"Where?"

"There's a little get-together tonight. A little party," said Preston. "Nothing too serious."

My eyes narrowed. What was he playing at?

"A party?" My mom set down her chopsticks, patting my arm. "You should go, honey."

Audrey almost leapt from the table. "What? No way. Gary was supposed to do the trailer this year."

"Audrey, come on. Do this for your brother. This kind of thing doesn't happen very often—"

Let me tell you how cool I felt at that moment to have my mom come out and admit she thinks I'm a loser. "It's fine, Mom. I promised I'd pack the trailer."

"I forgot," said Preston, sucking the last bit of catfish from the bone. "You always were great about keeping your promises."

I ate my rice in silence for the rest of the meal. I was worried that if I spoke up, I'd only be walking into a trap.

Thankfully, Preston declined dessert. When I walked him out, I turned to face him. "What the hell was that?"

"Yikes. Language. Is this the kind of influence Gloria has been on you?"

"What are you doing, Preston?"

"Tomorrow is the fair. And maybe you've forgotten, but summer is halfway over. We don't have a lot of time left here. Where's the bracelet?"

"On her wrist, probably," I said. Preston stepped back, shocked at my abrasiveness. I was a little shocked, too. I'd never spoken to him like that before. Maybe I needed to retract my claws. "I'm sorry, man. I know I said I'd help you, but I'm not going to steal from her. There has to be another way. Look, you know that I want to get into that club just as much as you—"

"No. No, you don't." Preston climbed into his car. "We started off this summer wanting the same thing, but now I don't know what you want. Maybe you love spending your weekends alone with your little painted models. Maybe you like the feeling of asking a girl to a dance and wondering if she's saying yes out of pity or because she was dared to. Maybe you like being invisible. I used to think you wanted a crumb of something better than what we have, but clearly I was wrong about that."

Maybe Preston didn't know what I wanted, but in that moment I knew exactly what I wanted to do—slam my fist into his face. I was mad, but I wasn't mad at Preston for his accusations. I was mad at him for being right. I was the one who'd gotten us into this mess and then I'd changed the rules on him. It wasn't fair.

"All right. Let's go to the party."

Preston turned the ignition. "I was lying. There is no party, Gary. At least not for us. And you know why a couple of losers like us were left off the invite list, right? Because we're not Roosters."

"I'm sorry, man. I—"

"You're stuck, Gary." He shoved his finger in my chest. I didn't bother pushing his hand away. "And you're always going to be stuck. By the time you wake up and realize that, I'm not going to be there to pull you out." He revved the engine. "See you at the fair."

As I watched Preston peel away, a low, rumbling feeling of guilt settled in my stomach. My anger at him morphed into shame. Maybe I was being selfish. If Preston needed a little boost to get to that next rung on the social ladder, then shouldn't I be doing everything I could to help him? Especially if I was the one holding him back. He was my best friend, and I was treating him like he was a stranger.

I felt a tap from behind and nearly leapt out of my skin. It was Gloria.

"This whole sneaking-up-on-me at night thing can't become a habit," I said, clutching my chest. "My heart won't be able to take it."

"I tried texting you. See?" Gloria pocketed her phone. "Who were you talking to?"

"Preston. He stopped by."

"Is everything all right?"

There was nothing I wanted more than to tell Gloria what was going on. I was sure she would have some sage insight on how I could save my crumbling friendship. But I couldn't exactly tell Gloria what the argument was about. So I lied. It was becoming a disturbing trend of mine.

"It's nothing," I said. Gloria looked a little hurt that I didn't want to tell her. "Seriously, it's nothing. He came by for dinner and then had to leave."

Gloria followed as I walked back to my driveway. "So what's with the surprise visit? I thought you'd be stuck at your place getting ready for your first fair weekend."

"Mom and I finished up early," Gloria said. "Oh, put those eyes back in your head. If you don't think I went over my to-do checklist at least three separate times this week, you don't know me. Pots and pans are polished and packed. Sewing machine is stocked with extra needles. We have enough food to feed a small army. We're ready."

"I should never have questioned you, Princess of Preparedness," I said with a bow.

Gloria returned with a bow of her own. She closed her eyes and massaged her temples. "I'm not only royalty, but a soothsayer." She opened an eye. "Did you know that?"

"I didn't, but I'm not surprised."

"I'm seeing a boy who is in desperate need of decluttering."

"Wow, you're good," I said, getting a grip on the garage door handle. "Well, you might want to keep those eyes closed. What you're about to see may shock you." I yanked open the door and the sound of a hundred metal poles clattering on the cement rang throughout the neighborhood. Gloria gasped.

We stood in front of a sea of heavy tent poles, crumpled tarps, two moving dollies, an old freezer, toolboxes, and coolers of all different sizes.

"You're telling me all this"—Gloria gestured around her—"has to fit in that?" She knocked on the side of the tiny trailer parked in the driveway.

I nodded. "My uncle somehow manages to do it every year, but he's out of commission on account of the gout—"

"Wait, wait. I'm sorry, you can't skip over something like that. Did you say *gout*?"

"It's a Vietnamese thing. Or maybe a Vietnamese uncle thing," I said. "Anyway, I'm sure he's keeping his foot elevated and ignoring doctor's orders by inhaling baked squid with a side of Heineken. Which leaves the task up to me, and as you can see, I'm nowhere close to figuring out this Tetris puzzle from Hell."

Gloria puffed her cheeks. "I don't envy you. Good thing you have me around."

"You really don't have to do this to yourself. I wouldn't wish this on anybody."

"Of course. I got you."

Then Audrey came out of the house, her car keys twirling on her finger.

"Where are you going?" I asked.

"Out."

Gloria nudged me. "Ask her to help."

"No way."

"Why not?"

"You know why," I said, trying to fold up one of the giant pieces of tarp. Gloria knew it wasn't as simple as my walking up to Audrey and calling her out directly—we didn't have that kind of brother-sister relationship. "She's going on one of her drives. She's not going to spend her night combing through all this junk with me. She hates me."

Gloria watched as Audrey opened the car door. "Wait here."

"No, Gloria, come on . . ." I didn't know why I bothered trying to stop her. I knew by now that Gloria was going to do what Gloria was going to do.

Gloria caught up to Audrey before Audrey could turn over the engine. As Gloria leaned into the window, I held my breath, trying to listen to their conversation. I couldn't hear a word Gloria was saying, but whatever she said must have worked because Audrey stepped out of the car. Gloria followed Audrey back up the driveway, flashing me a secret thumbs-up.

Audrey surveyed the mess. "This pile seems to get bigger and bigger every year."

"I don't even know where to start." I looked at Gloria, who mouthed, *Ask her*. "I know you're busy; you don't have to stick around."

"It's fine. I've seen Uncle Tri do this a hundred times. It won't take us long." Audrey grabbed the tarp from me and began rolling it up. "The trick is to roll the tarps, not fold them. Then you stuff them into coolers to save on space. The other problem is that you put the poles in first. You want them to go in last. Here, help me get these out of the trailer . . ."

Audrey was right. With her help, we managed to stuff everything into the trailer within a half hour. While we worked, Gloria suggested Audrey pull the car up and play music through her radio. I even caught Audrey singing along. Gloria told Audrey all about the Tamale Tailor and Audrey even put in an order for one of Gloria's custom medium-weight jerseys. There was magic to Gloria's gab. It was the most I'd gotten to see Audrey all summer.

After I'd managed to somehow squeeze in the last remaining cooler, Audrey returned to her car. "Catch you kids later."

"What did you say to her?" I asked, totally astonished.

Gloria locked eyes with me, something that used to make me uncomfortable. "I told her that you were a little overwhelmed and that you needed help this year with the trailer."

"That was it?"

"That was it."

Gloria must have noticed my jaw drop. "People will listen to what you have to say, Gary. I promise. But they won't know what you want unless you speak up."

TWENTY-ONE

THERE WAS NOTHING LIKE WAKING UP AT FIVE in the morning to a pair of pot lids crashing together like percussion cymbals inches from your face. That distinct headache-inducing reverb came around once a year, which meant only one thing. Fair day had finally arrived. Mom never missed a moment to wake me up in her signature fashion. Audrey and I were at odds this summer, but at least we could both find common ground in our mutual hatred for being woken up while it was still dark out.

We arrived at the fairground right as the sun was coming up. With my uncle out of commission, it was up to Audrey and me to set up the booth. But because we had packed the trailer together, we knew where everything was. There wasn't so much chaos and confusion this time around. We cut our setup time in half.

Within minutes of the fair opening, a long line of customers had already formed at our booth. Audrey took her usual post at the cash register while I manned the drink station. All morning I kept hoping there'd be a lull so that I could find Gloria and see how the Buenrostros were faring, but the customers kept coming. I got yelled at more than once by Mom to keep focused on the drink orders.

Right after the lunch rush, Audrey and I got the okay to take our breaks. I was about to ask Audrey if she wanted to take a walk around the fairgrounds and say hi to Gloria, but she was already gone. I guess we needed more than one night of packing the trailer for us to get back to normal.

It didn't take me long to find the Tamale Tailor stall. I thought that our line was long but the people lined up for theirs were almost double. I was happy that the Buenrostros would be making money, but my heart sank knowing that Gloria couldn't afford to take a break. Still, I wanted to at least wave hello and show my support.

I had to push and squirrel my way through the crowd, assuring every annoyed customer that I wasn't trying to cut the line. I found Gloria furiously spreading masa and folding tamales. Towering piles of golden corn husks were stacked neatly next to her workstation. Ms. Buenrostro was at the sewing machine, sweat soaking through her purple bandana, working on a pair of jeans. There was another woman at the cash register and another elbow-deep in sudsy water, using an open cooler as a makeshift dishwasher. They both shared Gloria and her mom's curly dark hair, so I could only assume they were Gloria's aunts.

I stood among the sea of fairgoers, watching from afar, not wanting to interrupt Gloria's flow. It only took a minute or so before she looked up and locked eyes with me. Her iconic dimpled smile spread across her face as if seeing me was like opening a gift on Christmas. And for a moment, a fraction of a fraction of a second, I caught something in her look that I hadn't seen before. Maybe I'd stumbled into some alternate universe where Gloria Buenrostro felt something toward me. Something more than friends. Was the blazing sun playing some cruel mirage trick on my eyes? Was that look all in my head?

Before I could give it a second thought, Gloria hollered something. I couldn't make it out over the crowd shouting out orders.

"What?" I yelled back.

Gloria waved me over. "Come inside!"

I looked around, trying to find some semblance of an entrance. The line to order snaked around the entire tent and was only getting more unruly. "How?"

"Hop the counter!"

I wasn't about to embarrass myself in front of all these strangers by trying to hop over anything. I circled the tent until I found an opening.

Gloria used her arm to wipe her forehead. Her custom-made cotton-candy-blue tank top clung to her skin. Her hair tie was working overtime, trying to contain a mess of thick curls. Her shoulders glistened. She somehow made sweating look cute. Nothing about Gloria surprised me anymore.

"I've been keeping an eye out for you," she said, folding a perfect tamale without even looking down at it. "You guys must be busy!"

"Not as busy as you are. Have you seen the line you have forming out there? I've been working this fair since I was in diapers and I promise you I've never seen anything like it."

"My mom can hardly keep up with the alteration orders. And

my wrists are already throbbing from folding a thousand tamales. I'm so glad she convinced my aunts to come down and help out. We would have been totally screwed."

It was at that moment I got that tingly sensation you get when you feel like someone is watching you. From the corner of my eye, I saw them. Jordan and the rest of the Roosters waiting in Gloria's line. They were goofing around, shoving each other out of line, giving each other playful punches to the gut, and cracking jokes. Then I caught sight of Preston. Standing with them.

That was when they saw me. More laughs. Some whispers. Jordan gave me a little wave and then pointed to his wrist.

I turned back to Gloria, realizing I hadn't caught a word she was saying. "Sorry, what did you say?"

"I said, I probably can take a break after the dinner rush if you want to take a walk around. I haven't had a chance to see anything yet."

"I'll come back around eight."

"Save me some of that pudding!"

"Already hid a cup for you."

As I headed back to my own booth, someone leapt out and grabbed me by my lapels, pulling me into a tent alley.

It was Preston.

"Dude! What is wrong with you?" I said, shoving him off me. He yanked me so hard, I had to retie my loose apron strings. "You almost ripped my head off."

"Okay. You need to listen to me." He was out of breath. There was that familiar gleam in his eye. Whatever he was about to say next wasn't good. "Things have changed."

No kidding. But I had a feeling he wasn't referring to our rickety friendship. "What are you talking about?"

"The Roosters, man." He laughed, practically giddy. "Jordan is offering us another way in."

I frowned. "I can't talk about this again. I'm not going to steal—"

Preston shook his head. "And you won't have to. Forget about the bracelet. It's over. I talked to Jordan and the guys about it and they're willing to let it go, but . . ."

"But what?"

"Well, the ante goes up." Preston scratched the back of his neck. "Like, up, up."

Now he had my attention. "What is it?"

Preston rubbed his hands together. "This one you'll like. I promise. In fact, you're pretty much halfway there."

"The longer it takes for you to come out and say it, the more nervous I'm getting."

"Okay. Here goes." Preston took a deep breath. "You gotta kiss her. You have to kiss Gloria Buenrostro."

It was my turn to laugh. Hard. Like, so hard that I had to grab onto the nearest tent pole to keep my knees from buckling. When I finally came up to catch my breath, I checked on Preston.

"You're not laughing."

"Because I'm serious." He did look serious. "Ever since you two showed up at the Club, people have been clucking. No girl spends this much time with a dude unless they're expecting something."

I guessed I should have been elated at hearing Preston's words of affirmation, but something didn't seem right. "So, what? The Roosters suddenly don't care about the bracelet?"

"Talked 'em out of it. Told them all about you and Gloria. I mean, you get why scoring a kiss with Gloria Buenrostro is better than a keepsake, right?" Preston was pacing the sidewalk now, working himself up. "No one has ever gotten this far with her. And for a newly initiated Rooster to have been her first kiss and they get to claim it as theirs? That's way more than any little trinket."

I swallowed. "Okay, so what if I just lied about it? The Roosters wouldn't know."

Preston nearly doubled over. "You? Lie? They're gonna see right through that. They're gonna want details."

I guess I should have taken that as a compliment, but Preston had no idea that for a few short hours, that bracelet was mine.

"Look," said Preston. "Conrad Pritchard is throwing a rager at his place tonight, dude. And the Roosters can get us in."

I rubbed my nose.

"No, no, no. What's with the nose rubbing?" said Preston, knocking my arm away. "You only do that when you're having second thoughts about something, and a party at Conrad Pritchard's isn't something you have second thoughts about. I don't need to remind you who Conrad Pritchard is, do I?"

"No, you don't." I sighed. "I know who Conrad Pritchard is." If high schools had tiers of social hierarchies (which they all did, let's be real), and Jordan Tellender ruled the sophomore class, then Conrad Pritchard was S-Rank of the entire school. He ticked off all the boxes of a Build-a-Beautiful-Boy checklist—his hair was always neatly cropped, never out of place, his shoulders broad, and he had a set of perfect teeth paired with a superhero smile.

You couldn't help but stare at the guy, wondering how it all came together. One of those kids who you knew already had his successful future laid out for him. Like Gloria, Conrad had his own rumors that swirled around him. Some people believed that his parents had bought him a penthouse apartment in New York that was waiting for him after graduating from Vassar. His parties were legendary. Attending one of those soirees had always been a big item on Preston's and my bucket list.

"Then what's the problem? I thought you'd be excited about this. Do you like her? No, wait, don't answer that. I already know the answer." Preston looked around, making sure we were truly alone. "Kissing Gloria Buenrostro is something you already *want* to do, isn't it? And something she wants to do with you, anyway. So why not? The way I see it, this is a win-win! You don't even have to steal anything. You and I will be living the high life until we go to college and you'll get to say you kissed Gloria Buenrostro. No one can take that away from you. You'll hit god status!"

I wish I could have said that everything Preston was pitching was total BS. But I had to be honest with myself—it wasn't like I hadn't thought about what it might be like to find myself in the unlikely scenario in which Gloria Buenrostro actually wanted to kiss me. Even taking the kiss out of the equation, I'd been wanting to say something to Gloria about how I felt about her before the summer was over. What if the Roosters' offer happened to line up with what I was planning to do anyway? This could be the shove I needed to find my courage and see if Gloria had the same feelings as me. Preston and I would be instant celebrities.

Preston would get to go to the party of the century. Everyone would get what they wanted.

"Yeah," I said, trying to mask any uncertainty in my voice. "I mean, if she'll kiss me back."

Preston looked to the sky—a blended, melty mesh of purples and oranges. "We're on track for a beautiful night, brother. It's the first night of fair weekend. This is the night miracles happen."

TWENTY-TWO

THE REST OF MY SHIFT WAS A BLUR. IT WAS the hardest I'd ever worked a fair before, and the only option was to put my brain on autopilot to cut through the swath of seemingly never-ending customers. But even as I was slinging Viet iced coffees, my mind kept going back to Preston, the Roosters, and Gloria and their new proposition. I kept flip-flopping—I wanted to kiss Gloria, I could be honest with myself about that, and maybe the perfect opportunity had fallen into my lap. But if it was so perfect, why couldn't I ignore the faint blinking twinge of guilt? I'd sneak looks over at the Tamale Tailor booth and catch Gloria hard at work. If she started to look up in my direction, I'd quickly refocus on my own task at hand.

Eight o'clock came before I was ready. I couldn't hide behind a stack of soda pop syrup boxes forever. I asked my mom if I could take my big break.

"To see that girl I saw you with earlier?" she asked. "Is that Gloria?"

"Yeah."

The twinkle in her eyes was blinding. "You're smiling a lot more these days. Don't think I haven't noticed. This girl is special?"

"Yeah, she is." It felt refreshing to be honest for a change.

"Go," she said, swiping a twenty from the till and stuffing it in my hand. "Have fun."

"Mom, I can't take this." A twenty may not seem like a deal to most families, but that was real money, serious money, in ours.

She clicked her tongue against her teeth—the Vietnamese sign that the discussion was over. There was no use fighting her on this. I stuffed the twenty in my pocket, kissed her on the cheek, threw off my apron, and tried my best not to sprint all the way to Gloria's tent.

There was still a line at the Tamale Tailor, but it wasn't as long as before. I scanned for Gloria. My heart went in my throat when I finally saw her. She was standing to the side of the cash register, talking to Eliza, Jessica, and Nicole.

What were they doing at the fair? Maybe they were just waiting for their tamale order. Or maybe Gloria's mom was finishing up an alteration. I stood and waited. And waited. I watched as Gloria laughed. I watched as they laughed with her. They were Gloria's friends, that wasn't news, but something about seeing them and seeing Gloria connect with a slice of her past life caused an uneasiness to wash over me. This summer it had just been Gloria and me. And deep down, I knew that it couldn't last forever. I knew that she had friends and a life beyond me. But I wasn't ready to admit that my time was up. At that moment, I knew—I was losing her.

I was about to sneak away back to my booth when Gloria's eyes met mine and when they did, they grew wide. Her gaze was like a tractor beam—I couldn't pull away even if I wanted to.

"Gary! Come over here!"

I should have run in the other direction, but I was trapped now. I rubbed my nose and walked toward the booth.

"Hey, guys, you remember Gary, right?"

God. Why would she ask that?

Jessica nodded. Not a very convincing nod. "Yeah, of course." Not a very convincing answer, either.

"Hey," I mumbled. Eliza and Nicole waved to me with forced smiles. I was used to the vacant stare of someone who couldn't quite place me.

Gloria threw her arm around me. "This was the genius who was with me that day at the Club. It was his idea to sneak us out in the garbage bin."

Eliza brightened. "Oh yeah, now I remember you. That was hilarious."

Okay. So maybe it wasn't the end of the world to get recognized. "Too many prison break movies, I guess."

"I didn't think you had it in you," said Jessica, turning back to Gloria. "Oh, come on, Gloria. Don't give me that look. It's not like you're some badass rebel. It's what we love about you. You're the dependable type. Sort of like a—"

"A goody-goody." Nicole picked something from a rack and stepped behind a curtained-off area inside the tent. The Buenrostros had set up some kind of traveling dressing room. "When we heard what happened, none of us believed it was you. How you managed to pull that off. You caught a lot of attention from all the right people."

Gloria blushed. "Come on, guys." The hair on the back of my neck tickled. *All the right people?* What did she mean by that?

Eliza chomped into her waffle cone. "So we heard you've moved to the east side?"

My stomach flopped. This was inevitable. I knew it was only a matter of time before Jordan told them. But did he rat me out, too?

"How did you—"

Jessica stepped up, giving Gloria a hug. "Why didn't you tell us?"

That was my cue. I took a step back, hiding in the shadow of the tent, letting Gloria catch up with her friends. I watched as they laughed and joked and traded stories. I should have been happy that Gloria was happy. It had been weeks since I'd seen deep crinkles form in her eyes whenever she laughed hard. The first time since her parents announced they were getting divorced. And now Gloria was back with her people. This was where Gloria was meant to be. Not with me.

Finally it looked like the girls were wrapping up. Nicole came out of the tent holding up a rainbow-striped tank top—it was one of my favorites. I'd even helped Gloria pick out that fabric. "This is really cute. Probably need to take it in a bit."

"Thank you," said Gloria. "That's one I made."

"No way. You can sew?"

"Mm-hmm. I'll alter it for you," said Gloria, taking the tank top. "I can text you when I finish it."

Then Jessica turned around, walking backward. "We'll see you at the party tonight. You're not going to bail on us again, are you?"

Gloria hollered back. "I said maybe! Maybe!"

Party? Oh no. What was going on?

Gloria whipped out a rag stuffed in the back pocket of her jean shorts to wipe the counter. "Sorry. Didn't mean to keep you waiting."

"I didn't think they'd be caught dead at the fair."

"Why not? We always used to go to the fair together. Every year." Gloria hung Nicole's tank top on a rack next to the sewing machine. "It was a nice surprise seeing them. They stopped by the booth and got a couple tamales. Can you believe our pool break-in made waves?"

I was still thinking about this party Gloria was invited to.

"Waves! Pools!" Gloria snapped her fingers an inch from my face. "Come on, puns are usually your department. What's going on?"

"Nothing," I said. I didn't want to spoil the night. "Need help cleaning up or anything?"

"No, I'm good until closing time. Let's get out of here." Gloria waved to her mom as she cast off her apron.

I shoved aside all the weirdness I felt watching Gloria gab with her old friends. My petty jealousy was quickly overshadowed when I remembered what was at stake. The Roosters, Preston, the new proposition. Time was ticking. I had to make a decision before the night ended.

So all I had to do was make sure the night didn't end.

Gloria and I only had about forty bucks between us and that doesn't come out to much when converted into fair currency. We paid too much for candied apples and deep-fried elephant ears, which left only the reject rides for us to afford. I almost lost my shoe in the haunted house when Gloria jumped out from behind a mirror and scared the life out of me. We somehow managed to stay behind and sneak an extra ride on the Gravitron.

Gloria checked her phone after stepping out of her malfunctioning bumper car. "Oh man. I gotta get back before the park closes. There's so much cleaning up to do."

"I'll help," I said, following her.

With all of us working together, we tidied up both the Buenrostros' and my family's booths in record time, securing them for the next day. I could see that Mom and Audrey were both completely wiped out, so I offered to stay behind to finish loading the trailer. By now the park was an hour past closing time and we were the few vendors still closing up shop. The din of the crowds faded, and all that was left were the sounds of pickup trucks rumbling off the lot and the caws of a few hungry crows searching for scraps. We circled the empty fairgrounds, slurping spoonfuls of chè.

"Your booth was mobbed today," I said after swallowing a mouthful of taro. "You must have made out all right?"

"I had no idea we'd get so many customers. You weren't kidding—the fair is the place to make money! We could barely keep up. I guess it was kind of silly of us to sell both tamales and do on-site alterations, huh? Did you see my mom, though? Haven't seen her that happy in a long time."

"Can't have one without the other. You are the Tamale Tailor." I hit the halfway point of my dessert and switched cups with Gloria so I could finish the lychee flavor. "So your mom's doing okay? Considering everything . . ." I trailed off.

"Better than I thought she'd be. She's dancing around the

apartment, singing. It's like I'm the only one that cares that Dad isn't ever going to be in the same house with us again. Why am I the only one mad about this? I mean, they're getting divorced. It's all so... final. Why doesn't she care?"

"I don't think you're weird for not being super hyped that your parents are splitting up," I said.

"Whatever. Maybe it's a good thing. I guess I can stop trying to please everyone now. In hindsight, it didn't really matter what I did anyway, right? I used to lose sleep wondering how to make them happy. I tried to be the best I could be for them. You do all the right things and where does it get you?"

I didn't know how to respond. It wasn't like I was an expert on two-parent households. It killed me to know that Gloria thought her behavior would have any effect on her parents' marriage. I wanted to say something, but when I looked up, I knew I wouldn't have to.

"Gloria. Gloria." I tapped her. "You're not going to believe this. Look."

There, perched right on top of the merry-go-round was a bird. A white bird with a yellow mohawk. Sir Ivan himself.

"What do we do?" Gloria lowered her cup to the ground.

"I don't know! I've never had to catch a bird before. You're the one who knows him!"

"It's not like we're best friends!" Gloria scanned our surroundings. "Okay. There's an empty box right next to that dumpster. Grab that. I'll watch the bird."

I returned with the box. Sir Ivan was still there, cooing and enjoying his view of the fairgrounds.

"Now what?" I asked.

"There are some barley pearls in the chè. Do birds like barley? It seems like birds would like barley. You think I can coax him over?" Gloria climbed on a painted frog wearing a saddle. "Give me a boost."

I gave Gloria the push to get her on top of the carousel, then tossed up the empty box. I watched as she crept over to Sir Ivan, her hand outstretched.

"Wait, wait!" I said. "How do we know it's him?"

Gloria looked over the edge, eyebrow raised. "How many loose bright green red-beaked parakeets do you think are hanging around?"

"I'd feel better if we knew for sure!"

Gloria rolled her eyes, then called out. "Ivan, it's me. Your buddy Gloria."

"Sir Ivan. Sir Ivan."

Gloria raised a hand. "Sorry, my mistake. *Sir* Ivan."

Sir Ivan returned with a squawk. That was our bird all right.

"Okay," I said. "Go for it!"

Gloria reached her hand out, presenting the barley pearls. "I have some yummy treats right here I think you'll like. Mmmm. Barley."

Sir Ivan eyed her palm. I didn't think there was any chance that this bird was going to take the bait. That was when I learned never to underestimate Gloria Buenrostro. Sir Ivan flew straight to Gloria's hand. That settled it. Even birds couldn't resist her.

"Gary, if I move, our royal friend here might fly off. Can you get up here?"

I managed to scramble my way to the top. I took my time, holding the box as I inched my way over. I was right above him.

"Now?"

"Now."

I couldn't believe I'd managed to snag a parakeet. I guess I could check that off my bucket list. Gloria and I climbed back down and only opened the box once we got Sir Ivan into Gloria's mom's car.

"I'm exhausted, but, like, my blood is pumping too much for me to feel sleepy." Gloria cracked a bottle of water, guzzled, and then tossed it to me. "Who knew capturing an escaped parakeet could be such a rush?"

"We make a good team," I said. We walked across to the Scrambler and plopped our tired bones in an empty cart.

For a few precious minutes we could sit together and enjoy the peace that comes after a day of working the chaos of a carnival. Preston's prediction was right. The stars shone at their brightest. The cool breeze felt good against my sweat-dried skin. The sweet scent of straw that lay scattered over the fairgrounds filled the air. One of those summer nights they write about in poems. We didn't have many more nights like this. Summer was almost over. Well, halfway anyway. But my time with Gloria was almost up. What would it be like once we were back at school? Would she forget about me? I shut my eyes, trying to force the thoughts from my head so that I could enjoy a perfect summer evening.

But of course my brain wouldn't let me enjoy anything. My head kept swirling about Preston, the Roosters, and their deal. I looked over at Gloria, leaned back with her arms around the rear of the carriage, trying to catch a breeze. I knew I couldn't go through with it. I wanted to kiss her. I really did. Who wouldn't? But I couldn't bring myself to go through it knowing that the Roosters would own it.

No surprise, Gloria sensed that something wasn't right with me. "You're quiet. More than usual, I mean."

"Oh," I said, trying to play it casual. I was still thinking about the invite to the party, too. I didn't want her to go. I didn't want her to remember her old life. I wanted her to sit with me in this squeaky old carnival ride cart forever. "I heard Jessica say something about a party. Whose party is it?"

I knew that it was Conrad Pritchard's party, but I wanted to hear her say it. Maybe there was a sliver of a chance I could have been thinking about something else.

It took Gloria a moment to catch on. "Huh? Oh. I guess Conrad Pritchard is throwing something at his parents' beach house tonight."

"Are you going?" There was that deep dread slinking up again.

"Yeah. I was thinking about it. Wanna go with me? Might be nice to go to a party for once."

"You've never been to a party?" I said, with a hint of bite.

"Not this summer."

I snorted. Gloria hated being laughed at, but I couldn't stifle it this time. I wanted it to sting. She was leaving me for them and I felt like being a baby about it.

"What? What's so funny?" Her eyes turned to slits.

"I'm sorry. I'm a little surprised that you ... that Gloria Buenrostro isn't going to parties every weekend."

She frowned. "You *know* what I do every weekend."

I knew that my next words would hurt. "What? Like you don't have friends."

"You know, Gary, I really don't." She pushed up the cart's safety bar and stood. "And before you try to throw Eliza, Nicole, and Jessica back at me, they haven't exactly been around. Not since I had to move. You know this."

"Oh, come on. You can't tell me those are your only friends. Everyone knows you. Everyone wants to be you. You're *Gloria Buenrostro*." I rose to meet her.

"Being the most talked to is very different than being the most talked *about*." She stepped out of the cart. "Forget it. I thought you knew me better than that."

Apparently I wasn't the only one throwing low blows that night. I couldn't let her get away with that one. I did know her, and she knew me, but maybe that wasn't enough compared to her rich, popular friends and their fancy parties. "That's not fair," I spit. "I know that you . . . I know that you say your favorite book is *Little Women* because you know it's what everyone expects you to say, but actually your favorite book is *The Sisterhood of the Traveling Pants*. I know that you'd trade in a Michelin-star tiramisu for an eighty-five-cent pack of grape gum without batting an eyelash. I know that you consider eight in the morning the ideal time to wake up, but secretly you wish you could sleep in until at least noon. I know that if anyone deserves a break, it's you, but you'll never let yourself take one because you feel like you'd be disappointing someone, and you'd rather work yourself into a messy puddle before letting yourself give into a single second of relaxation. I know that you blame yourself for whatever happened to your parents even though deep down, I know there's a part of you that realizes it was completely out of your control, and I wish that your dad or your mom knew the kind of torture you put yourself through trying to make their relationship work and that they saw the toll it was putting you through and—"

That was when Gloria stomped back to me. "Come here," she said, her voice low, but not quite a whisper.

I couldn't have fought it if I wanted to. I was weak. Before I knew what I was doing, I leaned over the rail. Gloria cradled my head and pulled me in.

And before I knew it, Gloria Buenrostro was kissing me.

It couldn't have been longer than two full seconds. It wasn't a peck and yet, it wasn't a full-blown make-out. But the details I could recall made it seem like it lasted so much longer. Her hands trickled their way to my jawline, brushing my cheeks. I could taste the stickiness of her strawberry lip gloss. I felt a softness I'd never known before. A glowing warmth trickled to my toes, then surged to the top of my scalp. Suddenly I became very aware of my breathing. Was I breathing too much or too little? I tried to remember every single second so I could replay our kiss in my head whenever I wanted, but at the same time, I wanted to empty my brain so I could simply enjoy this moment. My first kiss.

When she pulled back, I realized I had been gripping the safety bar of the cart so hard that my palms hurt.

She held her gaze on me before I had to turn away. "Thanks for saying all that."

"Wow, okay. Well, maybe I don't know you as well as I thought I did," I managed to choke out.

Gloria shuffled her feet, shadowboxing. "I'm keeping you on your toes." Then she cleared her throat and dug into her pocket, twirling a set of car keys around her finger. "I've got a wild idea. Let's keep the night going. My mom got a ride home with my aunt. Which means I got mom's car tonight. Come on. Let's go to that party."

She couldn't be serious. After a kiss like that, she still wanted to go to Conrad Pritchard's beach house? Why wasn't it enough to just be with me?

"No, thanks." At least my brain had thawed enough to allow my mouth to squeak out those two words. "Why do you want to go over there anyway?"

Gloria backed up and spun around with her arms stretched out wide. "I don't know . . . I guess it might be fun to do something a little different. Come with me! Let's ride this wave. Mix it up!"

I felt like I could take on the entire world. But I didn't want to share Gloria with anyone else. Why couldn't it just be us? I wasn't about to hold her back, though. "I'm pretty tired."

The disappointment in her gaze was thick. So much so that I couldn't look back at her. She offered me a ride home and I accepted. My brain still wasn't back to full operating power by the time she dropped me off. We said our usual goodbyes, neither of us acknowledging the kiss.

"Are you sure you don't want to come with?" she asked as I

stepped out of the car. "I'm going to swing by Mrs. Espinosa's to drop off Sir Ivan, but if you change your mind, text me."

I wanted to beg her to stay with me. That she didn't need that party. That she didn't need the others. "Nah, I'm good. But you go. Have fun. Be safe." I meant the safe part. Not so much the fun part.

She smiled her trademark smile—the one where she didn't show her teeth, the smile using one side of her face to produce one dimple, and nodded her Gloria nod and then she was gone.

I went inside, dropped onto my bed, and thought about Gloria. My innocent crush, which I hadn't wanted to admit was real, had become all-consuming. She'd kissed me. My whole life I'd wondered what my first kiss would be like. I never would have dreamed that it would have been with someone like Gloria. And I certainly wouldn't have believed that it would be perfect.

Did it mean she had real feelings for me? It had to, right? She'd kissed me.

Suddenly all I could think about was the party. What would she be doing there? Who would she be seeing, be talking to? Then I thought about Preston. I was shocked that he hadn't flooded my inbox with texts. I hadn't kissed Gloria, Gloria had kissed *me*, but something told me that the Roosters wouldn't take me to task over that technicality. All I had to do was tell Jordan about the kiss and all my problems would be over. That was when Audrey walked in.

"What are you so giddy about?" Audrey leaned against my doorframe, her arms crossed.

"Nothing."

"Bullshit. You're grinning like a total goon."

I didn't want to get into the whole kiss with Audrey, but this was a rare opportunity to get some of the insight from her that I'd been craving all summer.

"Can I ask you something?"

"I'm here, aren't I?"

"I have a chance to make some friends this summer. Like, real friends. But they're part of this exclusive group, I don't know how to explain it . . ."

"What? Like a frat or something?"

"Something like that."

"Well, so what? Are they asking you to kill someone? They aren't forcing you to chug an entire bottle of Wild Turkey while running a mile in your underwear or something dangerous like that, are they?"

"No, no, nothing like that."

"Good. I know you're not that dumb." Audrey checked her phone. "Look, Gary, if you want my advice . . . I say you could use a little thrill in your life. You always play it safe. High school is going to be over before you know it. Do something bold and stupid, but nothing so stupid that it will get you killed." She paused and turned back to me. "You sure you won't get killed?"

I shook my head.

"Okay, then I say go for it. Hey, if you found some genuine friends, do everything you can to hold on to them. Don't make the same mistake I did."

Before I could thank Audrey or even ask her to explain what she meant by "mistake," she was already back in her room. Our little chat hadn't gotten me any closer to enlightenment. How could I know for sure if the Roosters were genuine? From the outside, it looked like once you were in, you were part of a tight-knit group. That seemed genuine enough. Maybe I could be part of that. Part of something.

Even though I clicked off my desk lamp, I knew I wouldn't be able to sleep. And it wasn't because the adrenaline from the kiss was still pumping through my veins.

Gloria Buenrostro had kissed me. The very thing that would get Preston and me initiated as Roosters. The hard part was over. Technically, it was all her, but I'd kissed her back, hadn't I? With one little text, I could make everyone happy.

And at this very moment, she was over at Conrad Pritchard's. I grabbed my phone and fired off a text.

> Preston. I did it.

> Come get me.

> Let's go to that party.

TWENTY-THREE

I COULD HEAR PRESTON'S WHEELS SQUEALing as he pulled into the driveway. He leapt out of his car with the engine running and sprinted to meet me.

He grabbed my shoulders. "Can I kiss you? Or are you all tapped out for the night? Come on, plant one on your old pal Preston!"

"I'd prefer you didn't." I shrugged him off.

He took a step back, eyeing me up and down. "Let me get a good look at you. Do you feel different? You look different. You definitely got a glow about you." Preston opened the passenger door. "Your chariot awaits. I'm taking you to the ball, Cinderella."

I rolled my eyes and buckled in. Preston got back in the car and hit the gas. "Okay, I need to hear you actually say the words. You kissed her?"

"Yes."

"Yes, what?"

"Yes, I kissed her."

Preston cupped his ear. "You kissed who?"

"Gloria Buenrostro."

He shut his eyes like he was a maestro conducting an orchestra and waved me in. "Okaaaay. Now put it all together."

"I kissed Gloria Buenrostro. Well, actually, if you want to get technical, she was the one who—"

"You're shitting me."

"No, sir. I am not." I actually put my hands behind my head.

"Oh man, oh man." Preston whipped out his phone; his fingers flew across the keypad as he kept one hand on the steering wheel. I should have told him to keep his eyes on the road, but I was too busy squeezing the handle that hangs above the car door.

"Jordan's already there. He just texted me back. They're going to want to hear all about this." Preston careened onto the freeway, nearly sideswiping the concrete wall. "You're not lying, are you? You know those guys can sniff out a lie. Because if you are, you have to tell me now."

"It happened."

Preston zipped me in the arm. I tried not to wince. "I knew it. I *knew* you had it in you."

WITH HIS PARENTS' WINE TASTING IN NAPA, of course Conrad had no choice but to throw a rager at the family beach house. Although Conrad's parties were so notorious that I would have been shocked if his parents didn't know about them and were happy to turn a blind eye. I would have bet they actually encouraged it to give him a leg up on networking.

Shiny new cars were packed tightly together, bumpers kissing bumpers, all the way up Conrad Pritchard's driveway and all up the narrow side streets. It took us a good fifteen minutes to find a place to park.

When Preston said that the house was on the beach, I didn't think he meant that literally. We had to pass through a security gate before making our way down a winding path of stairs leading directly to the sand. The Pritchards' second house was bigger than both mine and Preston's combined. The two-story vacation home was more like a gaudy vacation fishbowl—it was mostly made up of giant windows. Flames from the scattered tiki torches illuminated teens on the second-floor deck playing beer pong and sharing cigarettes. A group hung around a sizable bonfire on the beach. Someone busted out a guitar. Almost everyone had a red plastic cup in one hand while checking their phones in the other.

I was totally out of my element.

Preston pranced down the steps like he was straight out of a Fred Astaire movie. "You smell that, Gary?"

"Smells like a campfire. I'm not sure what the other smell is, but I'm guessing that whatever it is, it's still illegal in thirty-one states."

"That's the smell of our new lives. You and me, buddy. We're not just a couple of Viet nobodies anymore. We've made it."

As we maneuvered our way inside, Preston and I didn't make

it past the veranda before getting stopped by Scottie Cook. He raised an eyebrow, attempting to place us.

"You guys know anyone here?"

Before I could remind Scottie that we were in the same social studies class during my freshman year (on account of him needing to repeat the class), a voice called out from the back.

"They're cool. Those two are with Tellender."

It was Conrad Pritchard. The host himself. He wore a perfectly tailored breezy beach shirt with the two buttons on top unbuttoned. The shirt was wrinkled, but, like, perfectly so, as if he wanted to give off the impression that he'd thrown it on as a last-minute decision, but not messy enough to come off like a slob. His bare feet exposed the tan lines on his ankles. A pair of expensive sunglasses perched on top of his fresh crew cut. He was objectively handsome and he oozed charm, and I hated him. Conrad took a swig of beer, then wiped the foam from his mouth with a swipe and flick of his middle finger. He even made wiping away beer foam look cool. "Tellender is around here somewhere. There's a keg upstairs and another by the bonfire. Only use the bathroom on the first floor. Any doors that are closed are off-limits. Oh, and if you break anything, I'll kill you."

Preston looked as scared as I was. There was a sparkle of mischief in Conrad's eye.

"Guys. I'm kidding. Relax. It's a party." He reached his hand into a nearby cooler and tossed us each a beer. "Have fun."

Damn it. I really didn't want to like this guy.

How an underage minor like Conrad was able to secure a keg,

let alone two kegs, was beyond me, but I'd learned that rich kids could get away with anything if they set their minds to it.

As Preston cracked open his can, he was practically frothing at the mouth. "Thanks for having us, Conrad. Seriously. This house is great, man. Really great."

Conrad winked, turned, and rejoined his people. That was when I noticed the circulation in my arm was getting cut off. It was Preston squeezing it with glee. A couple senior girls I recognized came in from the outside, wet bikinis clinging to them as they squeezed past us. I was worried Preston's head might actually fall off from the amount of swiveling it was doing. "We haven't been here for more than five minutes and already I could die a happy man. *We're Roosters.* Come on. Let's check out that keg and find Jordan."

It took us a solid ten minutes to make it to the balcony. There were kids playing some drinking game involving cards and stacking cups in the kitchen. Some were dancing in the living room—twisting and contorting their bodies in ways that made me blush. Others were snatching up armfuls of chips and salsa and other snacks before racing back to the beach. It was hard to imagine that they would be *my* people.

A pit formed in my stomach—what if they ran out of beer? What if they asked all of us to pitch in to refill the keg? What if Conrad expected everyone to throw in some money to cover all the booze? I didn't have any cash on me. Hell, I didn't have any cash at home, either—or anywhere else, for that matter.

Before I could spiral any further, Preston doubled back to drag me along. He made a point to say hello and to flash finger guns at anyone he recognized (whether they recognized *him* was another story). I mumbled a greeting when it felt appropriate, but for the most part I was happy to linger behind Preston. I craned my neck, searching the pockets of people, trying to find Gloria. Maybe she'd decided not to come after all. I started to worry. Where was she?

Before I could peel off and search for her, Preston was pushing me over to the keg.

There they were. The Roosters. Jordan nodded and Charlie closed and latched the double doors leading back into the house. Then he raised a plastic cup, foam sloshing down the sides. It took a nudge from Preston for me to realize that the cup was for me.

I took a sip and had to force myself to keep a straight face as I gulped down a bitter, hoppy mouthful. This wasn't like the cheap, clear, might-as-well-have-been-hose-water beer that Preston and I snuck from his uncle's stash—this was dark, thick, expensive rich-people brew.

"To the man of the hour!" Jordan raised his own cup. The others followed. I wasn't sure who we were toasting to, but I held my cup up anyway. Everyone laughed. I quickly lowered my hand, terrified I was already doing something to humiliate myself in front of these guys.

"Gary, they're talking about *you*, man. See? This is why this guy is the best." Preston pulled me in and planted a kiss on my cheek.

They weren't laughing *at* me. They were cheering *for* me. I could get used to this.

Jordan polished off his cup and pumped himself another.

"It's my great pleasure to welcome you as official Roosters. This is what it's all about, gentlemen." His hand slapped my back. "Look, we knew asking you to get that bracelet was a near impossible feat. We knew that. I want you to know we knew that."

The guy was slurring. His eyes were bloodshot. Jordan was hammered.

"But you endured," Jordan continued. He stumbled his way toward me. He was right in my face. I could smell the sharp sting of peppermint schnapps on his breath. "You found another way. A better way. The best way. You did what no other man could do."

That was when Preston hoisted me on top of the keg.

"Let's hear it!"

"Don't leave out any details."

"It must be good! Look, he's blushing!"

I didn't think anyone had ever shaken my hand or given me a high five or slapped my back besides Preston. Standing on that keg, I took a moment to soak everything in—the bass from the music inside rattled the windows, the glow from the roaring bonfire was calling my name, and everywhere I looked there were people laughing and smiling. Jordan, Blake, and Charlie stared up at me, beaming as if we'd been childhood friends. Sure, they were all sloshed off keg beer, but I was one of them and for the next two years, maybe even longer, these guys would be my people. My buddies. Everything was falling into place. And none of this would have been possible without one special girl. That was when I raised my glass. "To Gloria!"

"To Gloria!" crowed the Roosters.

The second gulp of beer didn't taste as bad. My brain was

swimming—from a cocktail of beer and adrenaline. I felt like I mattered. I was important. I was powerful. I was a king.

As I pulled the cup away from my lips, I heard someone calling my name from down below.

"Gary?"

Gloria's voice pulled me out of my trance. Did she hear us crowing her name? I regained my balance and turned and looked over the side of the railing. There was Gloria, far below, yelling up at me from the beach. Jessica Krebs, Eliza Kennedy, and Nicole Warren were there, too. And by their side was Conrad.

She planted her hands on her hips, shaking her hair from her face. "So you decided to come after all?"

Whew. The sound of crashing waves must have muffled our cheers.

"I've been looking all over for you." I raised my phone in the air. "Check your texts!"

"My phone was on silent!" she hollered back. "We're taking a walk down to the other end of the beach. Come with us."

My instinct was to leap right off that balcony to join her. Then a voice hissed in my ear. "Maybe we should get her up here and hear all the juicy bits straight from the source." It was Jordan.

My smile faded. I almost forgot that I was still standing on top of a keg. The flames of the tiki torches illuminated Gloria's smile. I could barely make out her dimple in the flickering shadows. She was my key to instant popularity. My stomach churned as I realized that my friendship with her had started all because I was trying to use her as a way in. What was I doing? I was about to share the most intimate details of the best thing that had ever happened to me to these guys. The kiss wasn't theirs. It was mine. And I was going to keep it that way.

"I'll catch up with you later," I hollered back.

I watched as she continued down the beach with the others. Then she broke from the group and dashed toward the ocean, kicking off her sandals along the way. She stopped once the waves reached her knees, then plucked something from the sand. A sand dollar or a bit of sea glass, probably. Gloria turned back and raised it in the air to show it to me, proud of her find. Even though I couldn't see what she was holding, I could feel her smile.

Blake came up to the other side of me, shoved two fingers into his mouth, and let out an ear-piercing whistle. That jolted me out of my thoughts. Not to mention that it got a laugh out of everyone. If Gloria heard it, she didn't act like she did.

"That girl knows how to work a pair of jean shorts," Jordan said, peering over the railing. He was so wobbly, I was scared he might flip over the balcony. He deserved it. "Enough stalling, let's hear about the kiss."

My back was slapped. My shoulders were jostled. My arm was playfully jabbed. Someone even ruffled my hair. I stared at a sea of smiling faces, eager for me to spin them a story. I understood what Preston had been trying to tell me all this time. I caught a glimpse of what the next two years of my life would be. Weekend hangouts at the infamous secluded watering hole down by the river that only the elite knew how to find, cannonballs off the diving board at the Club, lounging on the hoods of cars, goofing off while watching the stars. Maybe I'd even have the guts to ask someone to prom.

And then I realized that I already had all that stuff, with someone who actually gave a damn about me.

I felt ill. And not just because of Blake's creepy catcall whistle.

"I can't do this." I climbed down off the keg. I caught Preston's glare; he looked like he wanted to throw the keg at me. "I didn't do it. I didn't kiss Gloria."

The cheering instantly turned silent. Jordan took another pull of his beer. "Say that again?"

"I only said I did it because I wanted to come to the party tonight."

Preston raised his hands. "He's kidding, guys. He's nervous about having to rehash all the juicy details—"

Jordan swatted Preston's hand away, his eyes trained on me. "I don't like being lied to. Both of you need to leave. Now. Before we have a problem."

That was fine by me. I set my keg cup on the railing and squeezed past the other Roosters, keeping my focus on the door. I didn't wait to see if Preston would join me.

I shoved through a crowd of my classmates as I made my way outside. No one said goodbye. No one noticed me or acknowledged my existence. Why would they? I was a stranger in a strange land. There was no way that anyone outside of that balcony could have heard what had happened, and yet it also felt like everyone wanted me out.

I wasn't sure what my next move would be. So I sat on the driftwood steps leading up to the main road, waiting for Preston. I didn't have to wait long. I rose to meet him.

"Sit." He wouldn't even look at me. "I'm only going to ask you this once. And as your supposed best friend, I think you owe it to me to answer. The truth. Did you kiss Gloria Buenrostro?"

I swallowed and looked out at the beach, wondering if Gloria was out there. "I swear to you it happened."

Preston sighed, looked in the same direction I was looking. "Then why—No, forget it." He walked past me like I wasn't even there.

"Where are you going?" I felt a panic creep its way up my throat.

"Nowhere apparently." He nodded to the beach. "Ask your new bestie for a ride back."

He got into his car and peeled away. I didn't think he'd actually do it. But he did. He really left. I wondered if that would be the last time I saw the Protege.

I fired off a text to Gloria.

> Got kicked out of the party. I need to talk to you.

While I waited for a response, I could hear shouts and laughs coming from Conrad's. I could still make out the bonfire in the distance. I kept checking my phone every ten seconds, waiting for Gloria. The beer buzz from my two seconds of fame had evaporated. I almost considered texting Audrey for a ride, but before I pulled that trigger, my phone dinged.

> Weh where
>
> R
>
> u
>
> Where are you?

Uh-oh.

I told her where I was, and eventually Gloria found her way to me. Or I should say, staggered her way. And she wasn't alone. Conrad was keeping her propped up. She tripped coming up the stairs.

"Whoa. First time getting your sea legs, huh?" I asked, trying to help her up, but Conrad beat me to it.

"I'm fine," she giggled. The fall caused one of her sandals to break loose. She grabbed onto me for balance as she ripped the other sandal from her foot. "I paid like seven bucks for these. What did I expect?"

"How much has she had to drink tonight?" I asked Conrad. He covered a smile with his hand, amused at Gloria's sloppy stature.

"I'm definitely not driving anywhere, if that's what you're asking." Her slur was not lost on me. "Hey! You got any grape gum?"

"You really want some?" Conrad squeezed her hand. My stomach dropped when I saw Gloria squeeze back. "If you promise to stay another half hour, I'll run to the corner store and get as many packs as you want. Gary, what's your poison? I'll pick up something for you too."

An agonizing five seconds went by before Gloria responded. "I better not. My mom's going to be waiting up for me."

"Are you sure? There's nothing I can do to convince you to hang with us for a little longer?"

"She's fine," I said.

"What he said," said Gloria, tossing me her purse. I fished out her car keys.

Gloria steadied herself on me and we started up the stairs.

Conrad pulled out his phone. "Let me at least call you a ride. I got a guy who can be here in ten minutes."

"I can drive." Couldn't this guy take a hint? We didn't need his help.

"Gary, at least take my number down. Text me to make sure you got her home all right. That's precious cargo right there." Conrad, with one cool-guy hand in his pocket, waved goodbye and then strolled back to his party.

Lucky for us, Gloria's car was parked right up front. "It was nice of him to move the car for me," said Gloria, tumbling into the passenger seat.

"Conrad did that?"

She nodded. The guy was a real American hero.

"You know I only have my permit, right?" I said, sliding the keys into the ignition.

"It's fine," she said with a wave. Old Gloria wouldn't have been so quick to let someone without a license drive her mom's car. But this was Post-Parents-Separated Gloria. Anything was on the table.

As we headed east, I kept looking over to check on her. She rolled down her window, the warm summer air tossing her hair in all different directions. Her eyes shut, a smile on her face.

"Do you mind if I plug in my phone for some music?" she asked.

"It's your car. Go ham."

As soon as she found her music, she was in a different world. She swayed in her seat, arms in the air, and sang—well, screamed, along to some Carly Rae Jepsen. Gloria couldn't hold a note, but the way she belted out the lyrics without caring was endearing. For the first time in a long time, Gloria was laughing again.

That was why it killed me to do what I was about to do.

I'd spent my whole summer tangled up in a stupid lie. And I was tired. Tired of lying to her.

"Why aren't you singing? You love Carly."

It was true. Gloria and I had been known to belt out some CRJ during our bike rides together.

"Hey, Gloria?" I said. She was so into the music, she couldn't hear me. I reached over and turned down the volume. "Gloria!"

"What?"

"Before I drop you off, I need to show you something."

Gloria stopped giggling, sitting up in her seat. That might have been enough to sober her up. "You sound serious."

"I am."

"Yeah, sure."

TWENTY-FOUR

MOSQUITOS DANCED IN FRONT OF THE headlights as I pulled up to the end of the cul-de-sac. A soft wind pushed patches of clouds covering the half-moon. Crickets hiding in waist-high weeds of the overgrown yard chirped all around us. I hadn't been back to Poppy House since I'd first learned about the Roosters. And here I was, about to dismantle it all.

"You're not bringing me to this murder house to kill me, are you?" asked Gloria, unbuckling her seat belt. "Gary? Hello? That was a joke."

I wasn't in the mood for a laugh. Instead I forced a dry chuckle and circled to the trunk. "Will you help me find your emergency kit?"

"Okay, now I really am nervous."

"I need a big flashlight—we could use our phones, but it's completely pitch-black. There's no electricity." I wasn't sure how I was going to explain all of this to Gloria.

By the time I'd unlocked the cellar and we'd made our way up to the living room, I was still praying that the perfect sequence of words would come to me. How could I hope to explain this to her? Gloria was going to hate me forever. Was there any way to prepare myself for that?

I reached up into the fireplace to extract the cigar box. She stared at me for a moment before accepting it.

"I don't understand."

"Open it," I blurted, before giving myself a chance to chicken out.

She gingerly unlatched the lid. Her eyes wide in confusion, trying to process what exactly she was looking at. Her brow furrowed. She plucked each one of the tokens from the box and dropped them onto the coffee table. The pottery, the phone charm, the sock, and the retainer.

"Gary, what is this?"

I struggled to find the words. I couldn't. My tongue refused to cooperate.

Her voice trembled. "Gary?"

"It's a secret club. They call themselves the Roosters. It was started by Jordan Tellender and his buddies. I only found out about it at the beginning of the summer when Jordan asked me and Preston to join."

I braved a glance at Gloria. Her eyes stared back, unblinking. They had that sheen to them, the kind of glossiness that alerted you that the waterworks were inevitable. I could feel the sting in my own eyes. I turned away. If I was going to get through this, I couldn't look at her.

"It started off as a stupid game," I continued. "Over the years they've collected things from the prettiest girls in school. They call them 'tokens.' It's like a contest—who can contribute the best one. They offered to make me a member if I stole your whale bracelet."

Gloria fiddled with the bracelet around her wrist. A deep wrinkle formed between her eyebrows as she scrambled to catch up with everything I was throwing at her. I couldn't blame her—trying to explain it to someone, listening to my own words, none of it made sense. "Wait. So that day at the Club, I didn't actually lose it . . ."

"Yeah. That was me." It was all I could manage to choke out. I turned my head to one of the dust-smeared windows rather than look at the tears in her eyes.

I fought every instinct to reach out and hold her. I didn't dare. Maybe I should have slowed down, given her time to let each new piece of information sink in. The thing was, I knew that if I didn't get it all out, I would never be able to. "There's more. This afternoon at the fair, Jordan said he'd let me into their club if I . . . if I kissed you."

I waited for her to say something. To say she hated me. To say she never wanted to hear from me or look at me ever again. I wouldn't have blamed her for spitting on me. But Gloria stayed silent for a long time and somehow that made it so much worse. She gave me nothing. Her face was stone.

"Is that why that happened? Were you trying to get me to like you?"

"No. God, no." I could feel my heart thumping, as if it would break through my chest. How could I prove to her that the kiss had nothing to do with the Roosters and that it was all a matter of horrible timing? "I was never planning to—I wasn't going to—Gloria, you're amazing, and so beautiful, and..."

"Stop. Just stop."

I shut up. We were together in the uncomfortable, agonizing silence. Well, we were in the same room, occupying the same space, but we weren't together. That was when I noticed the first tear. Then another. Followed by a steady streaming down her round cheeks. Gloria sat at the edge of the coffee table, staring at the cigar box balanced on her knees.

"I hate that word. *Beautiful*. I never want to hear the phrase 'you're so beautiful' ever again. I'm so, so tired of it. My whole life, that's all I've ever heard. It's the first thing people say to me, it's the last thing people say to me... and I'm pretty sure it's the *only* thing people say *about* me.

"If no one ever looked at me again, I'd be ecstatic. Over the moon. It'd be complete bliss. Is anything I'm saying making sense? Do you get it, Gary?"

I wanted to say, *Yes, I think I do*. I wanted to spill my guts, tell her that I couldn't stop thinking about her, and that kissing her was the best thing that had ever happened to me. But I'd said enough. There were some moments where the right move was to shut up.

She sat for a little while longer. I stood there, unsure what to do with my hands. I would have stayed there all night if I had to—I wasn't going to make the first move.

Finally Gloria cleared her throat and wiped her tears with

both palms. I kept wishing I could be the one to wrap my arms around her and use my thumbs to push those tears aside. Tears that I had caused.

She held up a small square bit of paper. The clipped-out photograph from the Club's yearbook. "So here's where that picture went."

"Yeah."

Gloria placed Marissa's dish, Shelby's retainer, Bristol's phone charm, and Allison's sock back in the box and tucked it under her arm. To this day I still have no idea what she did with all that stuff and I never asked. She started back to the car. I waited for her to get a few paces ahead before I followed.

Gloria rested her chin on her palm and stared out the window as I drove back to the Jig. Occasionally she'd push the hair out of her face, but other than that, she didn't move. I snuck a few glances, hoping to catch a change in her facial expression, some kind of sign that we'd be okay again. I didn't think I'd ever gone this long without seeing Gloria smile. She never looked at me. When I finally parked the car in the Jig parking lot, I mustered up the courage to utter my first words since the confession.

"Will I see you tomorrow?"

She looked down at the cigar box in her lap. "I'll probably stick around the booth." I followed her as she stepped out of the car.

Sure. She needed some space for a day. That was reasonable. I held out the car keys. "What about Monday? You want some help with deliveries?"

She reached for the keys and let her hand settle on mine. For a moment I was back in the Buenrostros' kitchen, my hand in a bag of cold, gooey masa, Gloria's fingers wrapped around mine.

Then she pulled the keys away. "I think I can handle the route by myself for a while. I'll let you know if that changes, okay?"

I rubbed my nose as a lump formed in my throat. I prayed my voice wouldn't crack. "Sure."

Gloria walked around to the back of the car and popped the trunk open. She rooted around for something, found what she was looking for, then circled back around to the car's side mirror. The glint of the streetlights reflected off of something grasped in her hand—a pair of fabric shears. She bent over to look at her reflection and before I realized what she was doing, she had snipped her hair. A pile of long dark curls mounded on the street. And her hair—now a jagged, uneven bob—stopped at her chin.

Gloria checked the mirror one last time, admiring her work, and without saying another word, she disappeared inside.

It was only a few miles back to my house. Not too bad. I could use the walk anyway.

TWENTY-FIVE

I DIDN'T HEAR FROM GLORIA THAT WEEK. Not a call, not a text. It felt like I was checking my phone every other minute, hoping that the next text would be the one. She never stopped by our booth during the last day of the fair. The next day I told myself I wouldn't ride by the Jig or follow the delivery route hoping to catch her.

It took about four days for me to break that promise.

There was an emptiness riding solo on the tandem. I was used to Gloria shouting directions behind me or repeating an eye-rolling joke that she found on the back of her gum packaging. I wondered how Gloria was making her routes. Maybe her aunt let her use the car. Or maybe she'd pulled the trigger and bought herself a new bike—with the Tamale Tailor success, she probably could afford a trendy fixie by now. But at each one of the usual stops I passed, I never spotted a bike leaning on a building or chained to a rack.

On a hunch, I dropped by Gloria's park. It was empty, as usual. On the bench was a book. I knew what it was before I even picked it up. The book of Shakespeare's plays. Maybe she left it there by accident, but I doubted it.

I figured my best shot at getting the scoop on Gloria would be through Mrs. Espinosa. After the series of locks clicked open, a crack opened in the door. A familiar pair of lens-amplified green eyes peered back at me.

"Who are you?"

"It's Gary. Gloria's friend?" At least I hoped I still was.

"Gary? Oh yes, yes, yes. You brought Sir Ivan home!" The door flung open. Sir Ivan was perched on her shoulder. I was prepared to grab him in case he thought of attempting another escape. "¿Cómo te sientes? Shouldn't you be in bed? Is that what you're supposed to do with shingles? I have no idea. How do you cure shingles anyhow?"

"Shingles? I don't have shingles."

"Shingles. Shingles," Sir Ivan repeated.

Mrs. Espinosa placed a hand over her heart. "Oh, that's good news. I wonder why Gloria would say such a thing?"

So Gloria was telling her customers I had a form of herpes. I guess I deserved that. "Did she, by any chance, make her delivery today?"

"Same time she always does."

"Right." I nodded. So Gloria *was* making her rounds. Without me.

Mrs. Espinosa whistled. "I heard the Buenrostros were doing well, but not that well. When did that girl get a new set of wheels?"

"I guess she couldn't ride with me forever. Must be some kind of bike, huh?"

"Bike? Honey, this was no bike. I'm talking about a real nice piece of metal with a European engine."

I shook my head. A car? Maybe Gloria's aunt let Gloria borrow the car for a few days, but it wasn't exactly anything to whistle about.

"Come on, you must know," she continued, seeing my face twist in confusion. "A red Porsche? You can't miss it."

Red Porsche. Conrad Pritchard's car.

Was Gloria seeing Conrad Pritchard? Was I the only one who didn't know? I wondered if Preston had gotten wind of this new development. Preston kept tabs on everyone; he had to have known. But he wasn't speaking to me, either.

Mrs. Espinosa put her hand on my shoulder. One of those "I'm so sorry" hand-on-shoulders. "Is she doing all right?"

For a second I felt some hope. Maybe Gloria had opened up to one of her favorite customers. "What? Did she say something?"

"No," said Mrs. Espinosa. "That's the problem. She doesn't say anything anymore. I miss our chats."

"Me too," I said.

Mrs. Espinosa brightened up again. "Hey, I tell you this, though. You're much better-looking than that guy."

"Thanks, Mrs. Espinosa."

She pulled me in for a hug. It was something I didn't know I needed, but it made me feel a little better. Even if her old-lady perfume made me feel dizzy.

"Listen to me. Whatever happened between you two, just apologize. Make this right."

How could I explain that fixing this was going to take more than a simple apology? Gloria needed time and space—that I could give her. But there was someone else I needed to settle with.

"I KNEW I'D FIND YOU HERE." IT WAS FRIDAY night and Preston never missed washing his car on Friday night.

Preston trained his hose on the windshield. His car looked clean enough to me, but knowing Preston, he wasn't going to finish until it was beyond sparkling. "Where else would I be, Gary? I'm not going anywhere. Clearly."

"Look, I'm sorry, all right? I'm sorry. You have to believe me. I really am. I know how much being a Rooster meant to you, but I couldn't go through with it. Not like that." I sucked in a breath. "I had to tell her."

"Of course you did." He moved to the other side of the car. He would have clipped me if I didn't step back.

I knew it was over for me and the Roosters. I knew that when I straight up lied to them. I'd hoped that maybe there was still a chance for Preston.

"So Jordan and the other guys must be pretty pissed, huh?"

Preston scoffed. "I wouldn't know. No one is responding to

my texts. They've probably moved on, Gary. Why would they care about us now? They offered us an in and you spit in their faces. We didn't deliver. And if you don't deliver, you don't matter."

"Well, now Gloria hates me, too." I stared at the sliver of sun dipping below the tree line. "If that makes you feel any better."

He tossed the garden hose aside. "You still don't get it, do you? Why would that make me feel better? If anything, it makes me feel worse. Wanna take a crack at why that might be? No? Well, I'll tell you. Now both of us are losers. Neither of us gained anything from all of this. You get it, man? You have *nothing*, Gary. Your white-knighting was all for nothing. She hates you. The Roosters hate you. And now I—"

Preston caught himself. I was going to make my oldest, best friend finish that sentence.

"You hate me, too?" I focused all my energy onto not making my voice tremble. He didn't need to say anything; his eyes told me everything I needed to know.

"Was she worth it?"

"You don't know her."

Before I could register what was happening, Preston was right up in my face. An inch between us. My body tensed, preparing for him to clock me across the jaw.

"I know her." His spittle sprayed across my cheek. I didn't dare wipe it off. "I know her type. They're all alike. You ever stop to wonder why a girl as hot as Gloria Buenrostro hasn't ever been on a single date? Girls like her don't give a shit about guys like us. Never have. She never talks to anyone, too distracted with her own reflection in the mirror—she's the very definition of stuck-up. How can you not see that? Because you think you're the exception? That you're special to her?" He nodded toward the tandem. "She used you, man. She used you for free labor. We have a measly four weeks left. She cheated you out of a summer, and now that it's all coming to an end, she's done with you. People like her don't give a shit about people like us. We're stepping stones to them."

"So what? We're supposed to be like Jordan Tellender?"

Preston tapped his temple. "Yes. Exactly. It's a race to the top and if you're lucky enough to make it, you fight to stay there. It's that simple."

"They're jerks, Preston. And don't tell me you can't see it."

"Yeah? And?" said Preston. "They're winning and we're losing. So what if I want what they have? You wanted it, too. But you're lost now."

"Doesn't mean we have to be like them!"

"God, Gary. When are you going to wake up and see the world for what it really is? Yes, that's *exactly* what we have to do. You're what they call a perfect target. You're a total sucker."

I swallowed. I was cornered. Out of ammo. "You don't know what you're talking about."

Preston dunked a sponge into a bucket and attacked the custom-made rims of his tires. "From what I hear, she's spending a lot of time with Conrad Pritchard lately. She got someone else to help her with her route, someone with a car. So let me ask you again, was she worth it?"

My heart sank. My jaw clenched. My guts shredded. As I mounted the tandem, I could hear the last words Preston would ever say to me.

"I'm done trying to throw you a life preserver. You gotta save yourself."

TWENTY-SIX

I DIDN'T SLEEP WELL THAT NIGHT. SO WHEN Audrey yanked open my blinds, causing sunlight to pierce through my eyelids, I was less than enthused.

"What's going on?"

"Get up." She waded through a pile of my laundry, then chucked a pair of shorts at me. "Dude, seriously. Do some laundry sometime."

"What's going on?" I mumbled, scrambling for a T-shirt.

"I'm taking you somewhere. It's a secret."

Why not? It wasn't like I had anything else on my agenda. Preston and I were done. Gloria wanted nothing to do with me.

Audrey stayed true to her word. After the fifth time she refused to answer me when I asked her where she was taking me, I decided to give in to the ride. I kept searching for landmarks, trying to guess where we were headed. We were almost downtown. Not a place I would have been able to bike. What business did Audrey have downtown? Or better question, what business did *I* have downtown?

Then Audrey pulled down a side street and parked. Not quite in the thick of the financial district or the glitzy shopping centers. We were right on the fringe of where all the action was. The part where if the street cleaners were to skip a week or two, nobody would care.

"Audrey? Come on. What is this?" I said, stepping over a frothy mud puddle choked with cigarettes and a half-submerged soda bottle. This wasn't the kind of place you wanted to hang around after the sun went down.

"No hints, I said. Now, come on. It's this way."

I followed Audrey down a narrow alley packed with shops crammed together like crowded teeth. That was when I saw her. Gloria had headphones on, bobbing and swaying to her music as she swept down the sidewalk. I couldn't get a good look at her new haircut, seeing as it was tucked under a robin's-egg-blue bandana, making her look like her mom. She looked up with a wave.

Was this a trap? I wasn't sure if I was allowed to wave back. "Audrey, what are you doing to me?"

"Relax, will you? She asked me to bring you here."

My body shook with each step. As we approached wherever it was we were going, Gloria brought her headphones down around her neck. "Hi."

I'd almost forgotten what she sounded like. Hearing that word, in her voice—it felt like an enormous weight lifted from me. I could breathe again. Gloria was talking to me.

Audrey watched Gloria and me staring at each other before flashing a peace sign. "Okay, this is weird. I'll let you two catch up."

Gloria opened a door for Audrey to step through. "My mom's almost finished with that skirt. Go on up. Take the stairs behind the counter."

Above the door was "Lucecita's" in big, bold red letters. A pair of scissors snipped the flowing tails of a ribbon, a ribbon that was tied to a tamale bundle.

"Whoa, what? What is this?" I stepped out into the street to get a better look.

"It's our restaurant slash tailor shop. Like, a for-real one. Mom thought it was time for a change, even though I begged her not to use my nickname."

"Lucecita's," I said, trying it out loud. There was a nice ring to it. "It fits. I'm so happy for you guys." And it was true: I was excited that the Buenrostros finally had a real storefront. I couldn't wait to hear more about how all of it had come to be. But Gloria and I had unfinished business. Our fallout over the Roosters. What the deal was with Conrad Pritchard. And, of course, our kiss.

I followed Gloria inside as she gave me the grand tour. The front of the house was tiny, barely enough room to walk in, only to turn around and walk out, but they'd made use of every square inch. I couldn't believe how much the Buenrostros had put into the store within a week's time. There was a full kitchen in the back to make their signature tamales. An old cash register sat at the counter, and next to that was a stairwell where I could hear the whir of a sewing machine. There wasn't any room for tables, so the leftover space was utilized by means of a clothing rack, displaying a few special custom-made items.

"How do you like the new digs, Rizzo?"

Rizzo the Mannequin posed by the front window, one hand on her hip and a bag of takeout in the other. She sported a pair of flip-flops and a ruffled lime-green skirt. Fully clothed this time.

"She's missed you."

"She hasn't aged a bit," I said.

Gloria circled behind the counter. "I missed you too. I needed time. It was . . . a lot."

"I'm so sorry for the whole Roosters thing," I said, forcing myself to look straight at her even though I wanted to crawl into a hole. "It was gross. Cruel. Selfish. Infantile." I paused. "You can stop me at any time."

"Keep going." Gloria leaned on the counter, chin in her hands. She wasn't wearing her whale charm bracelet anymore. "I think you missed a few adjectives."

I puffed out my cheeks and sighed. "I'm sorry, Gloria. For all of it." Now that Gloria knew all about the Roosters, I never wanted to talk or think about them ever again.

She stared back at me, her eyes unblinking, as if she were weighing her options on whether or not to forgive me. I wouldn't have blamed her for showing me the door.

"You messed up."

"I know."

"Shall I break it down for you?"

"I wish you wouldn't," I mumbled, my face buried in my hands.

Gloria counted on her fingers anyway. "You stole something extremely precious from me in hopes of getting into a super-secret slimy society where ghouls collect private items from teenage girls. And then you tell me that they had a whole scheme concocted that would get you inducted into their club if you kissed me. Did I get all of it?"

I wanted to melt into a pile of goo, sink into the tiled floor, and disappear forever. "I think that about covers it."

Her fingers strummed the countertop, her gaze never breaking. I half expected her to punch me in the teeth. The wait was agony.

"Come on," she said, lifting the door to the counter. "I want you to tell me if the tamales taste different now that they're being made in an industrial kitchen."

I exhaled. And just like that, my appetite was back.

Audrey came down the stairs with the skirt slung over her shoulder. Gloria set down two Mexicoke bottles and a bottle opener. "Audrey? You want in on this?"

"I'll take one to go." Audrey grabbed a tamale and something off the rack. "And this beanie. How much?"

"Discount for my fellow fair-worker. I'll send the bill home with your brother."

Audrey turned to me. "I guess that means you're sticking around?"

"Yeah, I'll figure out a ride back."

Audrey nodded and left.

Gloria rested her chin on her hand again. "It's a miracle you haven't gotten sick of these yet."

"Never." I peeled back the husks and tore in. One bite of the Buenrostros' signature steamed pork with red sauce and it was like all the awkwardness of the past week melted away. I was whisked back with Gloria on the tandem, making our rounds, before everything got so complicated.

"Looks like Audrey might be coming around. Giving you a ride? That seems promising."

"Yeah. I was kind of surprised by that myself. She probably only did that because *you* asked. You tend to have that effect on people."

Gloria shifted in her seat. I hadn't been away that long, but I had already forgotten how she hated to be complimented.

"So I take that to mean you're not any closer to finding out what happened while she was away at college?"

"No idea."

"You need to talk to her. Ask her what's wrong. You might be surprised. Look, if you could tell me about the Roosters, you can muster up the courage to talk with your sister."

"I'm not having the best of luck going the direct route. Preston's not talking to me, either."

"Oh no, what happened?"

"Wasn't too happy that I botched our chances of getting into the Roosters," I said, fiddling with the bottle opener.

"I see," she said, chewing on this new revelation. "I don't really know him that well, but I guess I'm not surprised by anything anymore."

I used the awkward silence to pop the tops off our Cokes and take another look around the shop. Paint cans sat in the corner below a half-complete orange wall. A shop vac lay on its side among a pile of broken drywall. On the wall next to the cash register was a series of framed pictures. One of Gloria and her mom in their backyard, making tamales. Another was a beautiful black-and-white photo of Gloria's mom hunched over her sewing machine. My favorite was one I remembered seeing displayed on a hanging shelf in the Buenrostros' kitchen—a photo of Gloria on her bike laughing on her first day of deliveries, trying to cover her face right as her picture was taken.

A sadness washed over me. I should have been there to help out with all this prep. How could I have missed everything?

"I think maybe we've grown apart," I said, remembering that she'd asked about Preston. "I dunno. We're not the same people we were when we were kids." I rolled the bottle back and forth in my palms. "I don't want to bring down the mood by talking about him. Tell me about the store. When? How? Tell me everything."

"It was the fair! Can you believe it?" She beamed, slamming her hands on the table. I almost fell back in my chair. "When my aunts saw how much money we raked in, they offered to be partners in a real business. My mom had already been eyeing this place for months. You'll never guess who helped us with all that confusing paperwork."

I shrugged.

"Victor!" Another slam on the table I wasn't prepared for. "The job offer he got? It was for a property management company! He got us in practically overnight. It all happened so quickly. And that's pretty much it. We got ourselves an actual store. I mean, we're only renting, but still! No more sharing a bathroom with half-dressed mannequins! And I have room to eat at the breakfast table without worrying about dripping strawberry jelly on someone's altered pants."

"That's great, Gloria. You deserve it." She did, too. I meant that.

Gloria blushed and hid behind a bite of her tamale. "My mom wants to throw some kind of party when we officially open. As if we have time for that."

"You have to celebrate, Gloria. This is huge."

"Can you believe we open next Friday? Look around! The paint's still drying."

This was the opening I had been waiting for. A chance to casually bring up the subject of Conrad without coming on too strong. "Hey, if you need help making deliveries, you know I'm not going anywhere."

She lit up. "Oh! I almost forgot to tell you. We don't have to waste the rest of our summer riding tandem anymore!"

The smile plastered on my face was frozen, even though I knew what was coming next wasn't going to be good.

"Conrad has been driving me to make deliveries all week in his car. It's saved us so much time. Oh! And the air-conditioning! My God, Gary. No longer will we be swampy, soggy messes at the end of the day!"

There it was. The confirmation I was dreading.

How could Gloria not understand that her hanging out with someone like Conrad Pritchard would devastate me? Could she be that clueless?

My poker face betrayed me once again. Or maybe I was smiling too long. Either way, Gloria reached across the table, shaking my elbow. "What? I thought you'd be happy about this. We have our summers back!"

"Guess it was time we finally put the ol' tandem out to pasture." I grinned through my lie. Getting on that bike with Gloria was what I'd looked forward to every morning. Maybe she and I weren't on the same page after all.

Gloria's wide smile morphed into a subtle grin. "I think you'll like him, Gary. He's not like those other guys. Seriously. He should be here any minute. He can give you a ride back."

It took every ounce of energy I could muster to force another smile. "Nah. I could use a walk." I pulled out my phone and pretended to actually care about the time. "I should leave now if I'm going to make it back in time for dinner." I didn't give Gloria a chance to stop me. Instead I cupped my hands around my mouth and called up to the stairway. "Bye, Ms. Buenrostro. And congrats!"

"Wait. Wait. Wait." Ms. Buenrostro appeared at the top of the stairs. "Gary! You're leaving already?"

"Mom's frying a whole fish tonight and you know you can't reheat that stuff."

"Not bad, huh? Be back here on Friday! It's gonna be huge!" She pointed a finger at me. "Promise me."

I looked at Gloria for support. She shrugged. There was no getting out of it.

"I promise."

I waited for Ms. Buenrostro to leave before rubbing my nose. "Didn't you say your mom wanted to go all out? A formal gala sounds out of my orbit. I don't really have anything to wear . . ."

Gloria laid a hand on my forearm. "Well, then it's a good thing you know a couple tailors. And it's not a gala; it's a grand opening for a store." She must have noticed the unfiltered look of disbelief in my eye. "It'll be classy, but not over-the-top. Don't worry. I'm already thinking of a great idea for you. Come on. Please. We couldn't have done this without you. You have to come."

In what universe could I refuse an invite from Gloria? My fate was sealed. "I'll be there." I started to plug the bus route into my phone when Gloria grabbed my arm.

"Hey, just because we're not doing deliveries anymore doesn't mean anything's going to change. You know that, right?"

It would be the first lie Gloria ever told me.

TWENTY-SEVEN

THE WEEK LEADING UP TO LUCECITA'S GRAND opening was a confusing mix of ups and downs. Because I was off the hook to do deliveries, there was no reason to keep the bike out, so I returned it to the hooks in the garage. Who knew if I'd ever ride it again. I considered asking Mom if I could sell it. Maybe there was someone else out there who needed a cheap mode of transportation for their summer crush.

I'd wake up to a text from Gloria, asking me what I was up to. My stomach would twist itself in knots before I'd ask her what her plans were rather than admit that I had nothing on my agenda. Then she'd propose going to the Club, assuring me that Conrad would be more than happy to get both of us in with his family's platinum membership standing.

Of course I'd decline and make up some excuse that I was sure Gloria saw right through. But I wasn't about to be the third wheel in whatever it was that was going on between the two of them. Which threw me into a tailspin, wondering what exactly was going on. Could Gloria really have feelings for someone like Conrad Pritchard? Anytime I felt those thoughts starting to creep up, I stomped them back down. Sure, the guy was loaded and good-looking, but I kept convincing myself that Gloria couldn't be wooed that easily. Not to mention that I still had the unaddressed kiss in my back pocket. That had to mean something. I needed to find out what that something actually was.

I had hoped to take things slow, to wait for the perfect moment to bring it up. But the whole Conrad situation was forcing me to make this happen quicker than I had intended. I couldn't sit on it any longer. If it was true that she was developing feelings for Conrad, I had to say something before she was too far gone. I needed to tell Gloria how I felt about her, but more important... I needed to know how she felt about me.

The only problem was, I was agonizing about how I was going to pull that off. There were nights I'd stare at the dreaded blinking cursor of my computer screen, hoping the words would magically come to me. I'd stay awake, fingers poised on my phone, only to delete the entire wall of text. It took me about a hundred attempts before I realized that what I needed to tell her had to be said in person.

Wednesday night, two nights before the Lucecita's grand opening, Gloria came over, armed with a tape measure, to do some last-minute measurements for the outfit she'd promised me. She'd only been over once before and refused to divulge anything about whatever it was she was making me.

"You're not going to show or tell me anything?" I asked, holding my arm out for her to assess.

Gloria spoke around the two pins jutting from her clenched teeth. "That's the whole point of a surprise, isn't it?"

I kept staring at those glass-head pins, delicately balanced on

Gloria's lower lip. God, I was jealous of those pins. I shook my head, recalibrating my focus. "Hardly seems fair. I'm going to be the one wearing this. You're making it from scratch?"

Gloria reeled back, eyebrow cocked. "No way. Have you learned nothing from this summer? I'd need more than a week to pull that off. And that's with my mom helping."

As I stood there, watching Gloria work, I would have stood there all afternoon if I had to. She always measured twice. Pinned here. Pulled a fold taut there. Always methodical, like I was fragile, as if I would crumble under her touch at any moment—it was like I was one of her tamales. When she draped the tape measure around my neck, her face inches from mine, I almost brought up the kiss and spilled my guts with all the reasons why we should be together. I searched her face to see if I could find any indication that she was thinking about the kiss, too. Her brow scrunched in deep focus, her eyes flickered with intensity—she wasn't thinking about anything but the task at hand. She was lucky. Our kiss must not have been completely consuming her every waking thought like it was doing to me.

I chickened out and said nothing.

"Finished!" That snapped me out of my trance.

"That was quick," I said, clearing my throat.

Gloria scribbled down her final measurement and tossed her supplies into her backpack. "Come by the shop at seven. That should give us plenty of time to get you ready for the ball, Cinderella." She looked over her shoulder. "Everything all right?"

"I'm fine. Little nervous about dressing up for a party, I guess."

"I wouldn't let you go out there looking anything less than

spectacular. Don't you trust me?" Her dimple deepened, practically melting me where I stood.

Did I trust her? At this point, Gloria could drape me in a garbage sack, call me Prince Charming, and I'd strut through the Met Gala with my head held high.

"Yeah, I do."

"Good." Her manicured fingernails strummed the doorframe as she gave me one last once-over, and then she was gone.

If there was any truth to my suspicions that Conrad was homing in on Gloria, I couldn't hold back. I knew that the moment I expressed how I really felt about her had to be perfect.

I had to tell her everything.

It had to be the night of the grand opening.

BY FRIDAY, I WAS A TREMBLING MESS. MY head was like a colander—any thought I tried to hang on to slipped right through. Video games weren't a strong enough distraction. I even pulled out my old paint set to work on some unfinished models, hoping that would keep my mind off Gloria and the gargantuan task ahead of me. It was no use. There was no going back. The longer I agonized over it, the more I was convinced keeping all my thoughts and feelings inside was slowly poisoning me.

As promised, I arrived at the brand-new Lucecita's before the actual party—thirty minutes earlier than expected, in fact. Not wanting to get in the Buenrostros' way, I looked at my phone and paced out front until Gloria came outside.

"What are you doing?" She poked her head out. Gloria was still in a tank top and pajama shorts.

"I got here a little early. It's no big deal. I'll look at my phone until you're ready."

"Get inside, you weirdo."

Part of me was wary that the Buenrostros could pull off a party of this magnitude in such a short amount of time. The other part of me knew better than to underestimate the Buenrostro women. Bright orange and yellow streamers dangled from the ceiling. The glass display case even seemed to shimmer. There wasn't a speck of grit or chunk of drywall on the tiled floor. Some industrial fans were pointed at the walls and set on full blast for last-minute paint drying. The Buenrostros had spared no expense. Out back was a patio big enough to accommodate a decent-sized crowd. There was a long table displaying heaping platters of tamales and a make-your-own raspado station—shaved ice with five different kinds of colorful syrup ranging from hibiscus to vanilla. And, of course, it wouldn't be a Buenrostro party if my man Elvis Crespo wasn't blaring from the strategically placed speakers.

I followed Gloria upstairs to where all of the alterations were done. It was a small attic—I nearly bumped my head on the low ceiling. Boxes filled with restaurant supplies were crammed in every corner. Reams of fabric were stacked in piles that reached the rafters. Clothes in various forms of completion hung from anything that could support a hanger. A full-length antique mirror stood next to Ms. Buenrostro's sewing machine, which had two dresses draped over it.

"Oh man, this is really going to help us get organized for drop-offs," I said, crossing to the only window. Beneath it was a dresser made of cubbyholes, and each slot had the name of a customer written in block letters. Some were already stuffed with folded alterations wrapped in brown paper, tied with twine.

"You like that? I had that idea years ago, but we never had any room for it."

"I still can't believe how quickly you guys put this whole restaurant slash tailoring shop together," I said, taking the whole room in. "It's like a total transformation."

Gloria sat at the sewing machine, elbows on her knees. "Tell me about it. I still have grime under my nails from the last-minute cleaning. You know my mom. When she sets her mind to something, it's going to happen no matter what. Fresh nail polish be damned." Gloria gave a forlorn look at her hands, then clapped. "Let's get to it. Tell me. Are you ready for your final fitting, Mr. Võ?"

"Ready when you are."

There was a giddiness to her step as Gloria disappeared behind a stack of boxes and returned carrying something on a hook. I didn't have a clue what she might come back with. My intestines twisted in knots. What if she thought I could pull something off that I absolutely had no business wearing? That would be just like Gloria—to convince herself I was better than what I was. Already I was planning a hundred different ways to get out of attending the party.

But then she came around the corner, laughing. "Here it is!" She held up a suit jacket—a midnight blue so dark, it could have easily been mistaken for black. Slung around her arm was a pair of tailored slacks. In her other hand dangled a leather belt with matching freshly polished leather shoes.

My knees nearly gave way. I was sure my mouth was gaping. "No way. Are you kidding me?"

"I don't joke around about tailored suits." She thrust the jacket into my quivering hands. "Well, what are you waiting for? Try it. I'm dying to see if everything fits."

There was a heft in the jacket that felt foreign to me. Never in my life had I held a piece of clothing this nice before. A suit, no less. A suit that I wouldn't have to return. A suit that was made for me. I couldn't wait to put it on.

I could have cried right there. I wanted to say thank you, but I knew if I tried to say anything, it'd come out as a blubbery mess.

Gloria was already halfway down the stairs. "Feel free to move that stuff off the mirror. I'll be right back!"

I waited until I could no longer hear Gloria's footsteps before shedding my clothes and stuffing them into my backpack. The slacks slipped on with ease—no scratchiness like I'd usually endure with the dress pants I was forced to wear. The clean coral shirt was crisp and cool. But it wasn't until I put on the jacket that I truly felt transformed. Everything fit just as it was supposed to. When I turned to look at the mirror, I didn't recognize who was staring back at me. I ran my hands over my chest, my stomach. Nothing felt bunchy or loose. Before I met Gloria, I went about life always feeling a perpetual twinge of hunger. I never ate until I was completely full—I always stopped myself before I was satisfied. But now I could fill out a suit. I actually looked cool. It was the only time I felt like I deserved to be by Gloria's side.

As I slowly turned in front of the mirror, taking every detail in, I thought about what must have gone into this suit. I imagined Gloria coming home from another full day of deliveries, forcing herself to sit down at the sewing machine. I could see her hands covered in the day's grime, carefully pushing fabric through while the whir of the machine's needle hummed. How many hours had she put into this? All the planning, all the snipping, the measuring, the actual sewing.

And she'd done it for me.

"You decent?" Gloria called from the stairwell.

"That's an understatement." I couldn't break away from the image in the mirror, too stunned by my own reflection to notice she was standing right behind me. When I turned to face her, it felt like someone sucked all of the oxygen out of the room. I had forgotten how to breathe.

Gloria had snuck off to try on her own dress. It was strapless—the pale violet fabric flowed over her like it was an extension of herself. The skirt stopped right above her knees. It looked simple enough; there was nothing over-the-top or showy about it—it was perfectly Gloria. I didn't know how she managed to not only make my suit, but her own dress. She was radiant.

"I was worried it might be a little too dressy for an event like this." Gloria twisted and turned in the mirror, her head cocked to the side and her hands on her hips. She'd cleaned up the impromptu haircut she gave herself the night of Conrad's party. So, gone was the waterfall of black hair that stretched just below her shoulder blades. In its place was a sort of elegant bob, I guess. It didn't matter. Gloria Buenrostro could pull anything off. "What do you think?"

"It's perfect." I was about to ramble on about how stunning she looked, but remembered our exchange back at Poppy House. "You put a lot of work into it. That's obvious. It's really nice, Gloria."

"Thanks, Gary."

It was my moment to say something about the suit she'd made for me. But of course I couldn't find the words. Instead I looked at my leather shoes. "Care to explain how you got these beauties?"

"Remember the guy who works construction over on Baker Street in that pink apartment building? His son is about the same size as you. I traded him a batch of chicken-and-cheese tamales and two tailored shirts for them." She snapped her fingers. "Oh! I forgot about this!" Gloria opened a drawer next to the sewing machine and pulled out a small, thin box.

"What is it?" I asked.

"Open it. No, wait. Before you do that, let me help you with the suit." Gloria tucked the box into the inner pocket of my jacket.

I flushed. Was I wearing it wrong? I knew I couldn't get

through this without messing something up. "No one has actually taught me how to wear a suit properly."

"You're fine. It just needs to be smoothed out in some places."

Her fingers moved with precision. She pulled a wrinkle out here, tugged taut a loose section there. Then she brushed her hands over my shoulders, down my arms, around my waist. A flash of goose bumps spread over me. There was a gentleness and delicate touch to her movements. It was like she was wrapping the corn husks of her tamales. She stepped back. Looked at me with a satisfied smile. The smile that was burned into my retinas. The smile that was the last thing I thought about before I fell asleep.

"There," she said, smoothing my lapels.

I couldn't hold it in any longer. If I didn't say anything, I was going to combust.

"Gloria, be with me."

The words gushed out before I had a chance to censor myself. As if I didn't really have a choice in the matter, that destiny was punting me out of the driver's seat and slamming its foot on the gas. Then the words hung there. Suspended.

"I mean, I think we should be together. Like, for real. These last few weeks have been the best weeks of my life. I don't want that to end."

Gloria's hands dropped to her sides. "Gary, that's the nicest thing anyone has ever said to me, but—"

But? I didn't plan for a *but*. There wasn't supposed to be a *but*. Whatever was going to come next wasn't going to be good.

It felt like an icicle had shot straight through my rib cage and gone clean out the other side. The walls felt bigger now, the attic much smaller—cramped and suffocating. I couldn't breathe. And it wasn't because there was no air-conditioning in the building. I felt ill. A very specific kind of illness you only experienced when you knew that the ground was going to give way from under you.

"But what?" I asked, not really wanting to know the answer.

There was a glaze in her eyes. I wouldn't know until later that it was because she was on the brink of crying. "These last few weeks have meant so much to me. And yeah, I had some complicated feelings I needed to sort out and get to the bottom of, so I went for it. I had to find out.

"My worst fear is losing you, but I guess if I am going to be the friend I want to be, I need to be honest and say that I just want to be friends. Not more."

My stomach frothed with a sick bubbling acid. She was lying. She had to be.

"*You* kissed *me*, Gloria."

Gloria fiddled with the hem of her dress. "I know I did. And I know that we haven't really had a chance to talk about what happened that night. I've wanted to, but I couldn't figure out how to bring it up."

She collapsed at the sewing machine. As if all her energy had been sapped from her. "For the first time in my life, I just went by my instincts and wondered . . . what if. So I kissed you. I was trying not to let myself overthink it, and maybe in this instance, I should have. I'm sorry."

She looked so sad over there by herself. I started toward her, but stopped myself by planting my feet on the creaky floorboard. I needed answers. For me.

"Do you regret it?"

"No, of course not. Not in the way you mean." She looked at the rafters, as if the words she was searching for were carved into the beams. "I wish I could go back and think about things a bit more before acting on an impulse. Believe me, I never wanted to hurt you."

"Impulse. Right." I was barely listening. We'd spent over half the summer together. She'd shared her secrets with me. Secrets she'd never told anyone else. Did any of that matter to her?

"Gary." She reached for my arm.

I jerked my elbow away. The hurt was steadily creeping up my throat, choking me. I didn't want to fight it. I wanted that pain to completely take over—spill over so she could feel it, too. "So what? I'm just supposed to forget about it? 'Just kidding, let's go back to being friends and pretend nothing happened'?"

"I made a mistake."

"I didn't know Gloria Buenrostro made mistakes." I knew that would sting. I wanted it to.

"That's not fair. I know that it must have messed with your head. And I don't mean for that to come off as cold or dismissive, because I swear to God, I am sorry." Her arms crossed as she held her elbows, cradling herself. "But a kiss also isn't a promise of anything . . ."

"Then why'd you do it?" I wasn't sure if I really wanted to hear that answer, either.

My question hung in the air. For a moment I thought I'd

actually found a question that could stump Gloria. Then she raised her head to look at me. Straight at me. "At the fair, we had a moment. The way you looked at me. The way you talked about me. It made me feel seen. Like I've never been before. And I got caught up in that. I wondered if maybe there was something there between us, something more than friendship. I acted on something I felt in the moment without thinking about what it might do to you. And I'm sorry." Her eyes bore into me, unblinking. I didn't have it in me to look back at her.

"Next thing you're going to tell me is that you have feelings for Conrad Pritchard." I said it as a joke. What I hoped would be a joke.

Gloria sighed. She wasn't denying it. Why wasn't she denying it? Why weren't her knees buckling from laughing so hard, telling me that I was being preposterous?

"No. You're kidding me," I said, my stomach dropping. "Conrad Pritchard? What is this? Some kind of new costume you're trying on while you're stewing in your rebellion?"

"Conrad is actually a nice guy. He offered to let me use his car for the rest of the summer. Plus he even bought all the painting supplies I needed to repaint that community fridge. He came back later with enough food to fill it and a couple others around town. And remember that broken-down intercom box out in front of Ms. Espinosa's apartment building? Conrad hired some guys to finally haul it away! You might like him if you got to know him. He's even asked about you a few times." She rose from her chair. "Jealousy doesn't look good on you, Gary."

I shouldn't have been surprised that Gloria could strike back, but I wasn't prepared for it.

I couldn't stay in that attic. Not with her. I needed to get out of there, get my mind right. "You know what, I don't think I can talk about this right now. I need to get out of here."

"Okay, I get that you're pissed. You have every right to be. But I think we're better than this. Let's talk. We can still go to the party and have fun, right?" She took a step toward me. I took a step back.

"You think I'm going to stand around all night while you dangle off Conrad Pritchard's arm? No, thanks."

"Now hold on a second." There was a fire behind her glare. "Now you're just being mean. I didn't take any low blows when you told me about the Roosters."

"Is that why you had me around all summer? So you'd have a lackey to do your bidding?" I knew I was going for the throat, but I didn't care. I was hurt and I needed her to hurt.

"That's what you really think of me?" Gloria threw open a drawer and shoved a stack of cash at me. "Fine. Here, take it. Your cut. It's probably not enough, but I'll figure out how much I owe you and pay you the rest. Wouldn't want you to think I'm shortchanging you."

My cheeks puffed out as I struggled to come up with a decent retort to hurl right back. Instead I said, "I'm done," and headed for the stairs.

She stood there, still holding the money. She could keep it.

"So is that it? We're not friends anymore?"

I paused on the second step. "I told you I wanted to be more than friends, Gloria," I said, unable to bring myself to look at her. "How are we supposed to go back to how we used to be?"

I didn't wait for an answer. I continued downstairs, but before descending completely, I forced myself to peek through the slats between the railings. I took in one last look, knowing that it very well could be the last. Gloria stood next to the sewing machine, oddly still, her fists clenched around the wad of cash. Her eyes wet with tears, still trying to process it all. A pang of tenderness overwhelmed me. She suddenly looked different to me, like a child playing dress-up in a woman's cocktail dress. I shoved down an intense urge to rush over to her and tell her to forget everything I'd said, so that things could go back to the way they were. But another, stronger, more raw part of me knew that it was impossible. There was no going back.

And that was where I left her. Alone in the attic. Looking beautiful and lonely and hurt.

TWENTY-EIGHT

ON MY WAY OUT, I KEPT MY HEAD LOW TO avoid the long line of people waiting to get into Lucecita's. I would have draped my jacket over my head if I didn't think it'd draw more attention to me. Every person on our old route was there, dressed up in clothes that the Buenrostros had created or altered in some way. Victor was in the same suit I'd last seen him in, carrying a bouquet of flowers. Jorge had even combed his ring of hair for a change. Ms. Romano rocked her stroller back and forth in an effort to keep Petey asleep. Even the baseball coach who'd had patches sewn on the uniforms had brought his entire team. I ducked out before I was recognized—I didn't want to explain why I wasn't sticking around.

But I caught a glimpse of Conrad Pritchard. He wore a crisp beige suit perfectly tailored to his sculpted body. I tried not to wonder if Gloria had done his alterations as well. Ms. Buenrostro held his jacket while he balanced on a ladder, replacing some broken bulbs on the string lights.

It made it even worse that he seemed like a decent guy.

After a long bus ride, with a few transfers, I was back home. As I was reaching for the knob, Audrey yanked the front door open. She was wearing makeup, which was a first. All dressed up and ready for a grand opening.

"I thought you left hours ago. What are you doing here?"

"Nothing. I don't feel well."

I pushed past her and opened the fridge. Of course it was practically empty.

Audrey gave me a once-over, like a vet analyzing a sick puppy. "No, seriously. What happened?"

I was too exhausted to make up a convincing lie, so I decided to take a gamble and tell my sister the truth. "I told Gloria how I felt about her."

"And?"

"What do you think happened? I'm here and not there."

Audrey arched her eyebrows. She wasn't used to me snapping at her like that. But the fury I felt at the injustice of it all kept leaking out. I had to admit that it felt good to allow myself to get truly and unapologetically pissed off. And it didn't help that the first time Audrey showed any kind of interest in me all summer was after I'd just been utterly humiliated.

"She kissed me, Audrey. At the fair. But apparently it didn't matter."

Even Audrey didn't have a snappy comeback. "Oof. That's rough," she said. "What did she say? That she made a mistake?"

There was that word again. *Mistake*. Why was *mistake* the Get Out of Jail Free card everyone was playing? "As a matter of fact, she did," I said, slamming the fridge door. "And I hope that that mistake was worth it, because I'm never talking to her again."

"You can't mean that."

"How am I supposed to face her after this? I spilled my guts to her and she just . . . didn't care." My eyes started to burn. Tears were imminent if I kept talking.

"Don't do anything stupid," said Audrey. "She's your best friend. She cares a lot about you."

"God, you too?" I didn't want to hear it. Why couldn't Audrey feel the same anger I was feeling? Couldn't she see I was hurting here? That I'd been trampled? That my heart had been pulverized?

Why wasn't she on my side?

"It's called being human, Gare Bear." She lowered her voice. And not in a gentle way. More serious and grave. "Deep down, you know that Gloria wouldn't do something to purposefully hurt you. I know you're upset and I understand why, but think about that for a second. She kissed you, and then she changed her mind. That sucks and I'm sorry it didn't work out how you'd hoped, but she's allowed to make mistakes. That doesn't negate everything you two have—"

Mistake.

"Leave me alone." I pushed past Audrey. I was done hearing anything she had to say.

IT WAS A LITTLE PAST TWO O'CLOCK, AND MY eyes were still glued to the ceiling. I didn't bother changing. I simply flopped on my mattress and didn't move. I guessed it was shock. I couldn't believe what was happening to me, that Gloria was doing this to me. Before I came clean about the Roosters, everything had been perfect. I did everything right. I was there for her when she needed me. I was always the first one to come to her when she needed help. And now I was alone.

Every time I shut my eyes, all I could see was Conrad and Gloria hand in hand, making their rounds at Lucecita's. Saying hello to their friends, having a laugh with Eliza, Nicole, and Jess, and Gloria introducing her new boyfriend to the Buenrostros' loyal customers. And then Conrad would offer to make Gloria a raspado, drizzling tamarind syrup over her cup of shaved ice. A drip of dark orange sweet syrup might dribble on her chin, and Conrad would be there to wipe it off with his thumb. Then he'd take that opportunity to go in for the perfect kiss.

A kiss that I wished, more than anything, had been mine.

FOR THE FIRST FEW DAYS, I WAS DETERMINED to not let Gloria's rejection ruin what little was left of my summer vacation. Turned out, easier said than done. I was not prepared to admit how much Gloria Buenrostro had managed to permeate my life in the few short weeks I'd known her. She was everywhere. I took the bike out for a ride, in hopes of exhausting myself so I could sleep better at night. On my long rides I'd avoid the Jig and I didn't have any reason to be anywhere close to downtown, but we'd spent the summer together riding all over the town. Every street, every intersection, every shortcut reminded me of her. It eventually got so bad, I stopped taking the tandem out altogether—besides, I felt like a clown riding alone in the neighborhood on a bike specifically built for two.

It didn't take long to discover that my bedroom wouldn't provide the respite I was hoping for. Everywhere I turned, I'd get sniped by something that reminded me of Gloria. The Club's polo shirt hanging in the closet. My dark elf archer figurine. On the rare occasion I had an appetite, I'd drag myself to the kitchen and search the fridge to improvise something to put into my stomach. But I'd pull out an onion or a wilted carrot and I'd wonder what Gloria and I could whip up together, and I wouldn't be hungry anymore. There was no escaping her.

Once I found myself so bored, I decided to reorganize my entire room, and I stumbled across the sun-bleached copy of Shakespeare's plays. An empty gum wrapper from the night she'd stayed over doubled as a bookmark. I flipped to where I'd left off. It was the part of *Twelfth Night* where everyone laughed at Malvolio's humiliation. All because he'd loved.

Feste wasn't the only fool.

Time works differently during summer vacation. The days melt together, making it feel like one long, exhausting time loop. And when you were all alone with nothing but your thoughts, time trickled like thick black tar. I was trapped in some sort of punishing, cruel time loop. I wouldn't fall asleep until the early-morning hours, sleep in, scavenge what I could from the kitchen, only to retreat to my room. I'd replay the same games on my wheezing, sputtering desktop, goof around on my phone until I was convinced I'd reached the end of the internet, tried picking up painting figurines again, and napped more than I ever had before. At some point I dumped all of my paints and figures into the trash (yes, including Gloria the Ravenous). I couldn't find the flickering bit of joy I'd once gotten from them. I hit a point when just looking at the time bummed me out. There was nothing left to do but to unplug all of the clocks around the house and use sticky notes to cover up any clock setting I couldn't turn off. It was easier not knowing how much time had passed. If you didn't know the time, you didn't know how much of it was wasted. My room was practically a Las Vegas casino.

Despite how determined I was to cut Gloria from my life, every now and then I'd hit a weak moment when I checked my phone, hoping to see a text from her. But Gloria proved herself to be as stubborn as I was. Or maybe she was giving me the space that I demanded, calling my bluff. Either way, she gave me nothing.

Audrey and I weren't talking or even acknowledging each other's existence. We'd avoid each other, which wasn't that different from how the summer had been, seeing that she continued to stay cooped up in her room as well. At Sunday dinner I'd keep my eyes on my rice bowl, refusing to make eye contact. If Mom worked late, I ate in my room. That is, if I ate at all. I wasn't exactly eating full meals. I never felt hungry. I avoided mirrors, knowing that I was probably losing weight again now that I wasn't scarfing tamales whenever the mood hit me. I'd gotten so used to eating whatever new food Gloria wanted to venture out and explore during our afternoon breaks. My shirts were looser, my pants sagged off my hips on the few days I chose to wear them. I took a lot of showers—a lot of very long showers. I'd stand there, letting the scalding hot water flow, and replay our last conversation over and over in my mind, wishing that I never said those words to her. I'd catch glimpses of my face in the steamy bathroom mirror. My cheeks were sunken. Pathetic patches of facial stubble sprouted. My scowl might as well have been permanent. I didn't like what was looking back at me, but I didn't care to do anything about it.

Meanwhile, as the back-to-school letters began piling up and my summer reading list lay barren, my brain kept replaying what had happened in the attic. The embers of my anger cooled, turning into a kind of deep sadness—a lamenting of what could have, should have been. Every stretched-out minute of those excruciating long days, all I could think about was Gloria. I wondered how the restaurant was doing or if Gloria was rehearsing her lines or what musical soundtrack she'd be singing that week. Then I'd think about her doing those things with Conrad Pritchard and make myself sick all over again. I meant nothing to her.

I don't remember exactly what finally got me out of the house, but I hit a point when I couldn't stand being cooped up in it any longer. My body felt brittle. I needed to get out. I needed to move. I had no choice but to dust off the tandem. It didn't take long for me to get her back to riding condition—a little oil here, replacing the rear tube. By the time I'd finished tuning it up, I almost whipped out my phone to take a picture for Gloria, only to remember we weren't speaking to each other. But there was something inside me that wanted to connect with someone. Gloria and Audrey were out of the picture. Then I remembered Preston.

Maybe I could explain to him what had happened. That everything had played out exactly like he'd predicted. There was a chance that after the Roosters had cooled off, they'd actually initiated him. Maybe then he could put in a good word for me, ask them to give me another shot.

Riding by his house, I didn't see his car, so I took a chance and biked to the Club. Sneaking back in again wasn't an option, but fortunately Gloria had told me of a secret get-around where I could get a good look at the pool from the outside.

Not surprisingly, the pool was packed. It was another scorcher. I'd definitely made the wrong decision by wearing a button-down, even if it was cuffed. It was like I had been inside for so long, I'd forgotten what weather was like.

I scanned the pool, the high dive, the cabana before finally catching sight of Preston. He strolled out of the main building alongside Jordan and the rest of the Roosters. He must have splurged on a new set of swim trunks and flip-flops. I had to hand it to Preston: I knew that he would find a way back in with those guys. Although I was sure he'd sacrificed a piece of his soul to do it. But hey, at least he had friends. Good for him.

I had my phone out, ready to shoot him a text when I caught something out of the corner of my eye.

It was her. I could always pick her out of a crowd within seconds—before, I might have considered it a gift. Now it was a curse.

She was sunbathing. Sporting one of her custom swimsuits, no doubt. Her big sunglasses were back again. Nicole was next to her, scrolling through her phone. She leaned over, showing her screen to Gloria. They both shared a good laugh.

I didn't even know who she was anymore. How much time passed before someone you thought you knew so well completely changed?

Then an employee dropped off a plate of fries to the table next to her. Gloria waved to someone in the pool. He glided out of the water. A perfectly muscled back. And somehow not a hair out of place. Dark magic, I was sure. Gloria tossed him a towel and he bent down to kiss her cheek.

Preston had the Roosters. Gloria had Conrad. Here I was, crouched in the bushes like some ugly little troll.

That was enough for me. I wasn't going to subject myself to any more of it. I hopped back on the tandem and headed home.

Preston was right. I guessed I was more like my dad than I thought I was—I had gambled everything I had, and I'd lost. Now I was left looking like a complete buffoon. Everything Preston had said about Gloria was right. Each of his words pierced my brain like a barrage of arrows. There was no deep hidden mystery behind her—she was so much simpler than that. She kept to herself because she thought she was better than all of us. No one was allowed in because she only cared about herself. That day I met her, she'd spotted an easy mark. Someone she could dupe into helping her with her chores. Now she didn't need me anymore.

I was used, discarded, forgotten.

Like I didn't matter at all.

TWENTY-NINE

IN A FEW WEEKS, I'D OFFICIALLY BE A JUNIOR in high school. I'd moved on from my anger, my sadness stage, and slipped into a kind of inexplicable numbness. Accepted my fate. I was an island. Pretty much how I was before Gloria came into my life, but now I had the misfortune of having something to compare it to. If I allowed myself to think about Gloria too much, I'd start to feel that gut-churning feeling creep over me. If I could allow myself to stay angry, there wouldn't be any room for sadness or humiliation, which would keep me hardened. It was easier that way.

One night, after not being able to sleep, I decided to start foraging for my back-to-school kit earlier than usual. Audrey and I did it every year. We treated it like a big scavenger hunt—we wandered the house looking for anything we could scrape together for school supplies—notebooks that still had blank pages in them, pens, pencils, hidden change to use for vending machines. It saved us from having to buy all new materials.

I was rummaging through my closet when I came across the suit Gloria had given to me. I pulled it out when I felt something bulky in the pocket. Inside was the thin box, the gift Gloria had given me right before our big fight. I'd never opened it.

I set the box on my bed, then sat back in my computer chair, staring at the gift as if I'd uncovered some ticking time bomb. A standoff. I wasn't sure what to do next. All this time, I had put so much energy into trying to forget about Gloria. Opening her gift would be like ripping off a scab that had never healed. Did I really want to know what was inside? Was I prepared for it?

I sucked in a breath and pulled off the twine. Inside lay a necktie. I picked it up, twisting the silky fabric between my fingers. A creamy salmon pink. A closer look revealed a pattern. Tiny green bicycles. Tandem bicycles, to be exact. This wasn't something Gloria had found on the internet. This was another Gloria Buenrostro original.

I brushed my thumb across the tandem patterns, taking the time to feel each individual thread. Serious care and consideration had gone into every stitch of this. I couldn't believe that she had gone to the trouble of sewing me a tie, on top of gifting me a pair of shoes and altering a suit to my exact measurements.

No. That wasn't true. I could believe it. Making me a custom tie based on one of our inside jokes was exactly something Gloria would do.

I wasn't alone. I had never been alone.

As my tears fell on the tie, blotting the hand-stitched tandem bikes, I felt a longing that I had forgotten about, one that I stubbornly refused to admit to myself—I missed my friend. All of my anger and embarrassment and confusion—everything building steam inside me was suddenly released. Gone. Evaporated. What was the point in holding on to all of it? What was the point of fighting it . . . whatever *it* was.

Gloria wasn't selfish or conceited or soulless. She was the type of girl who would surprise me with my favorite blend of Slurpee (three quarters piña colada with exactly two pumps of wild cherry, obviously) or save a gum wrapper to tell me an egregiously corny joke, or when it was her turn to steer the tandem, lead us on the long way home just to squeeze in a few extra minutes of laughs with me. How lucky was I to find someone who was always thinking about me? How lucky is it for any of us to find someone who wants the best for us? And as much pain and embarrassment as I'd felt those last few weeks, Gloria didn't make my life worse. She made it better, and it was a lie to pretend otherwise. This was the girl who was my partner in crime. She listened to me—really listened to me. She fed me. She clothed me. And she opened up my world and showed me that I could give something back. She didn't owe me. She didn't owe me her time, her patience, herself. If anything, I was indebted to her. She was my friend.

When I decided to open that box and hold that tie in my hands, it was like touching a live wire jolting me out of whatever dark, putrid funk I'd allowed myself to fester in for so long. I didn't want to feel this way anymore. I didn't want this to be who I was. The poutiness. The petulance. I'd always thought I was a little better than all that—that was how the Jordans or the Prestons might react when things didn't go as they'd hoped. But turned out I had allowed part of that poison to seep into me. If

Gloria were around, she'd call me out, and she'd be right to do it. But she wasn't, because I'd shoved her away.

Audrey was right. Maybe Gloria had messed up by kissing me that night, but it didn't mean that she should be punished for it forever. I'd accused Gloria of acting on her emotions without thinking of me, but now that the dust had settled, I found myself guilty of that exact crime—I'd let the bitterness of my own humiliation consume me without thinking of Gloria. She hadn't led me on. She'd changed her mind. She was human just like any of us, a notion she struggled to remind anyone who would listen.

Gloria had forgiven me for making an awful mistake. It was time for me to forgive her.

I hoped she'd accept my apology. But would I be too late?

THIRTY

AS MUCH AS I WANTED TO HEAD STRAIGHT to Lucecita's to find Gloria before my nerves gave out, I knew I couldn't see her in my condition, let alone be seen in public. I showered, shaved, and threw on a fresh T-shirt for a change. It was the first time I'd felt clean in weeks. Taking the tandem out again, I made it to Lucecita's a little after two o'clock. Perfect timing, since I wanted to avoid a massive lunch rush.

Despite my carefully planned timing, I still had to wait in line. Someone I didn't recognize was working the cash register. It looked like the Buenrostros were able to afford some extra help.

The cashier was so busy taking orders that he didn't look up at me when I approached the counter. I recognized him as Matty Silverman—he was an anchor for the morning news at school. He looked a little stressed out. No surprise, considering the line outside and he was the only one manning the front.

"What can I get for you, man?" There was a blip of panic in his eyes as he gawked at the sizable crowd out front, no close to thinning out.

"Is Gloria around?"

Matty punched buttons on the old cash register before giving it a good smack. "God, why don't they upgrade?" he muttered to himself.

"Uh, Gloria?" I tried again. "Is she working today?"

"Nah, man. I think she's on vacation or something."

"Do you know for sure?"

Matty puffed out his cheeks in frustration. He called over to the kitchen. "Hey, Estrada! Where's Gloria again?"

A squat man popped his head out of the door. So they could afford *two* extra sets of hands. The Buenrostros were on fire. "She's at home, packing for her trip."

Trip? What trip?

Matty turned back to me. "She's packing for her trip."

"Yeah, I got that. Thanks." I stuffed a crumpled dollar bill into the tip jar.

I didn't know how much time I had. With only so much time left in the summer, if she was going on a trip, I wouldn't see her until school started. I felt the tick of the bomb in my chest—I had to speak with her, to get the words out, even if I wasn't exactly sure what I was going to say when I saw her.

I'd never biked so fast in my life. So much for my shower. My legs had gone wobbly and numb, but the adrenaline coursing through my body was enough to push me through. A giddy excitement throbbed in my chest. I couldn't wait to see her again. To salvage what was left of our summer. My heart thundered. But then it stopped.

Sitting next to the dumpster was a dark cherry sports car in the driveway. The trunk was open. I slammed on my brakes, pulling to the side of the road. Out of the back entrance came Gloria with an armful of snacks, followed by Conrad carrying a suitcase and a duffel. He tossed both into the trunk. Gloria climbed into the passenger seat. The car pulled out and sped away.

I threw the bike to the sidewalk and sprinted to the door. Gloria's mom answered.

"Gloria, you have everything you need, I promise—Oh, hi, Gary."

"Hi, Ms. Buenrostro. How are you? It's been a while."

"It has. We missed you at our opening."

"Yeah, I'm sorry about that. I wasn't feeling well. Haven't been feeling that great for a while now."

Her hand went to her mouth. "Gloria didn't mention that. All better now?"

"Yeah," I said. "I'm fine now. Or at least I will be."

"Oh good. I'm happy to hear that," she said. "If you're looking for Gloria, you just missed her."

"Any idea when she'll be back?"

Ms. Buenrostro sighed. "A couple weeks. She's going to some camp. She said it was a youth group retreat with her . . . her . . ."

"Boyfriend. It's all right." I was surprised by my own words. I meant it. It *was* all right.

She nodded. I guessed we both weren't quite sure what to say next, so I decided to cut the discomfort. "Well, I'll try calling her or shooting her a text—"

"You can't." Ms. Buenrostro reached into the little car key dish kept by the front door and pulled out Gloria's phone. "No phones. The camp doesn't allow them."

That took the wind out of me. I thought for a moment that

my knees would give out from under me and I'd crumple right there on the stoop. She really was gone. I wouldn't see her until school and even then, would she even care? Would she hear me out, or would too much time have passed?

"Well, if you talk to her, will you tell her I stopped by?"

"Of course."

I got back on the tandem and went home the long way. I had time to kill. Where else was I going to go? What else was I going to do?

I pedaled around the city, along our old delivery routes, until my legs felt like overcooked noodles. I hated myself for missing her by only a few minutes. No, it was worse than that—I hated myself for allowing this bitterness to fester in me for so long. I thought about Preston and Audrey. I wondered what my relationships with each of them would have been like if I'd had the courage to say how I really felt, instead of sitting on the sidelines. It was too late for Preston, but maybe there was a way I could salvage things with Audrey.

It was only when I was all out of thoughts and all out of steam that I decided to head home. I'd lost track of time, but I was shocked to see the garage door open. My mom's car inside. I brushed my hand on the hood—still warm. She must have gotten off of work early. A rare surprise.

I slipped into the kitchen. She was at the stove, hunched over a pot billowing with steam.

"Hey, Mom."

The bun in her hair was loose like it typically was after a full day's work at the restaurant. The wispy black and gray strands tumbled around her face. She looked even more tired than usual.

"Hi, con. You eat yet?" She didn't even wait for my answer—she was already ladling some canh chua into a second bowl.

I sat at the table, suddenly realizing how exhausted I was. I could have laid my head down and fallen asleep right there.

Mom slid a bowl of steaming soup to me. Only the sounds of our slurping could be heard. I picked out the pineapple chunks like I always did. Mom plucked chunks of fish from her bowl and placed them into mine like always.

"This is nice," she said, finally breaking the silence. "I never get to eat with my boy anymore."

I nodded, swallowing a mouthful of tangy broth and rice.

"This morning I saw Audrey pulling your little model paints and statue things out of the garbage. Why did you throw them away?"

Audrey? Doing something nice for me? It didn't compute. "I have no idea." I shrugged. "We're not exactly talking."

Mom shot me one of those classic mom-disapproval frowns. "She's your sister. You shouldn't be fighting."

"Audrey hates me."

Mom clicked her teeth disapprovingly. "Why would you say that? She doesn't hate you."

"It's not like she's been the easiest person to deal with this summer."

She chewed on a bit of boiled tomato. She couldn't argue with that. "Give her a break. It's her first year back from college. You should try talking to her."

I gave my best noncommittal grunt. My mom was right: I needed to make amends with Audrey. But like all of my relationships, I didn't even know where to begin. I didn't even know if Audrey would hear me out.

"What happened to that cute girl from the fair? She seemed nice." Her mom-radar had picked up on something.

That was when I started to tremble. Like a dam had burst open. I was too tired to stop it. Hot tears streamed down my cheeks. I wasn't sure what had come over me. It wasn't like she'd said anything profound. Maybe it was all the exhaustion from the last two weeks finally taking its toll. Or maybe it was one of those mom-moments where they somehow drew it out of you without even trying.

My mom leapt from the table and rushed over to my side, cradling my head. I don't think she'd done anything like that since I was a little kid. And like a little kid, I held on to her arms as I sobbed into her sleeve. There was nothing quite like a mom-hug to catch you at the right moment and crumble every barrier you'd ever put up. The smell of her perfume, oil from deep-fried fish, and nước chấm was a welcome comfort. She did the best she could to smooth my hair down.

"Shh. Okay, okay. What's wrong, con? What happened?"

"I messed up, Mom," I blubbered. "I messed up big-time and I don't know if I can fix it."

I wanted to tell her everything. But it was too complicated, too long to explain. Not to mention that I didn't know if I could bring myself to admit to her how much of a jerk I had been. Besides, she needed to sleep. Not listen to me go on about teenage drama.

"I know my son, and I know that when he makes a mistake, he doesn't stop until he fixes it." She kissed the top of my head. "You're stubborn that way. You get that from me. It's the Vietnamese in you."

"What if I apologize and she never talks to me again?"

"Well," she said, "if that happens, then you have to let her go. You can't force someone to forgive you. She either will or she won't. There are some things you can't control. Things you shouldn't control."

It wasn't the answer I was hoping for, but maybe I needed to sit with it. "Thanks, Mom."

"Are you still hungry?"

"No." I walked our bowls to the sink. Two days' worth of dishes were piled high. "I'm going to wash these."

"Don't stay up too late."

Mom gave me another kiss and shuffled off to her bedroom. A warm breeze caused the curtains above the sink to billow. I found an Elvis Crespo channel, set my phone on the windowsill, and scrubbed until my hands were raw.

THIRTY-ONE

THE DAYS OOZED ON. TOO HOT WITH TOO much time to be left alone with my thoughts. The kind of stifling, choking heat that made you feel like you're on another planet. On the days I could muster up the energy, I'd paint the tabletop figurines Audrey had saved for me. Despite how much I tried not to let my mind wander, I kept imagining what Gloria was doing at camp—paddleboating around a sparkling lake, staying up late goofing off with a fresh batch of friends, snuggling with Conrad under a blanket next to a roaring bonfire. It was all I could do to force those thoughts from my head.

But the worst part was that there was still no word from Gloria. I'd refresh my email, hoping to see her name. I even checked our mailbox—multiple times a day. I thought about writing her a letter, but then I remembered I forgot to ask where the retreat was located. I could have asked Ms. Buenrostro, but I'd bothered her enough. I was out of options.

But life has a way of delivering when you've given up searching.

It was nine o'clock—9:17, to be exact. It was supposed to be the final day of a four-day heat wave, but it didn't feel like it was letting up anytime soon. Not a single window was closed in our house—there wasn't even a spontaneous bit of breeze to provide relief. I was already regretting promising my mom that I'd organize the garage. It was a monumental task, given her hoarding problem. The air was thick. My shirt clung to my back. And I could hardly move more than a few boxes before I had to give myself a break.

I was sorting through a box of winter jackets dating back from when I was in elementary school when I heard my phone rattling. It startled me and I almost dropped the box. No one ever called me.

When I somehow managed to find my phone in the maze of towering waterlogged cardboard boxes, I was worried whoever was calling would hang up. It was from a number I didn't recognize. I answered it anyway.

"Hello?"

"Hey, Gary."

My body went cold, then hot. I sat right where I was standing, right on a papier-mâché Trojan horse from one of Audrey's old history projects. A crackle swept through my body—a jolt of excitement and relief. I'd almost forgotten her voice. I tried to steady my own.

"Gloria. Hey."

"I'm so relieved you picked up. I was worried you wouldn't answer."

"Yeah, sorry. I'm actually in the garage right now. My mom's making me clean it out."

"No way. I've seen your garage. We'll be picking up our diplomas before you come close to finishing!"

"You're telling me." It was like we hadn't skipped a beat.

"I don't know how much time I have. I'm using a pay phone." I detected a slight tremble in her voice. My body chilled.

"Are you okay?"

There was a long pause and then a sigh. "No. I'm not. I mean, physically I'm fine. It's not like I've been bitten by a rattlesnake or anything." The line went quiet again. "It's so embarrassing... I couldn't even call my mom. I don't know how much I can tell you before I'm cut off."

Her voice warbled. Gloria was scared. Gloria was scared and alone and she'd called me for help. My friend was in trouble. I had to go to her. It was the only option.

"Where are you?"

"It's called Camp Woodchip. I don't even know the address..."

"I'll look it up. It's fine. I'm on my way."

"How?"

"I don't know. I'll figure it out. Don't go anywhere."

There was a click, then silence. A sick panic trickled down my spine. A quick Google search pulled up the location of Camp Woodchip. It wasn't close—about a three-hour drive. The image of Gloria waiting that long, sitting alone by a pay phone, burned in me.

The question was, how was I going to get there? Tandem was clearly out of the question. It wasn't like I could take a bus to a remote location. There was only one option. I guessed I wasn't going to have to find the perfect time to talk to Audrey. The perfect time had found me.

I stood outside Audrey's bedroom. My hands jiggled at my

sides. I didn't have time to build up my nerves. I had to go in there and force her to listen to me. I knocked once, and then again. When she didn't answer, I pushed open the door.

The lights were off, except for the soft glow coming from the laptop splayed in front of her. Audrey was bent over low, typing furiously, hyper-focused on whatever she was doing.

"Audrey?" I whispered. The last thing I wanted to do was wake my mom up. "I need help."

"Jesus, Gary, you scared the shit out of me." Audrey took out her earbuds. "What is it?"

"I . . . I don't . . . I can't," I stumbled over my words. Asking Audrey to do me a favor was completely foreign to me. It wasn't how we operated.

"Whatever it is, we can talk about it tomorrow." Audrey got up and ushered me out of the room.

But I had to break us out of this routine. She was going to listen to me whether she wanted to or not. I just needed to find the words. I shoved my foot in the door before she could shut it completely.

"No. I'm not leaving." I made a point to stare back at her, unblinking. She needed to see I was serious. How much pain I was in. "I'm calling in a solid sibling favor."

Audrey slowly opened the door back up. From the look in her eyes, she knew I wasn't kidding around. This was different.

"What's going on?"

"I need you to drive me somewhere. Please. I'll pay you back somehow." I exhaled, steadying my breath. "Please."

Audrey looked at me like I was about to pull a knife on her or something. "Gary, it's like ten at night—"

"It's Gloria." My voice warbled, but I didn't care to mask it.

I didn't know what Audrey saw in my eyes, but she stared at me before she closed her laptop. "Grab my keys. Let's go. Quietly."

THIRTY-TWO

NOW

I KEEP CHECKING MY PHONE, WONDERING IF Gloria will try to call back. The freeway lights zip by—it's rhythmic, almost hypnotic. My mind goes blank as I watch the shadows flit over my knees. Shadows, light. Shadows, light.

Audrey and I have time to kill. If there ever was a time to make things right with her, this is it. There's no bedroom for her to escape to.

"Hey, Aud?"

"Yeah?"

"Mom told me you were the one who pulled my paints from the trash. Thanks for that."

"Don't know why you threw them out. I know you love those things." Her eyes are focused on the road. The speedometer's needle is a few notches above the legal limit. She knows we don't have much time—Gloria is waiting for us.

"And thanks for doing this."

She gives me a little nod. Neither of us is used to this mushy brother-sister stuff.

I let a few seconds pass before asking my next question. Old Gary would have clammed up and let things be, but I'm on a different path tonight. I can't let her off the hook on this one; I have to keep the pressure on. I have to get through to her. "What's going on with you? Not just now, but since you came back from school. You haven't exactly been yourself lately. Should I be worried?"

Audrey sighs. Adjusts her grip on the steering wheel. "I know. And I'm sorry about that."

"I want to know what's going on. You don't have to share details if you don't want to. I just want to know if you're okay."

"I got put on academic probation. And up until yesterday, I thought I was going to lose my scholarship, too."

Now it is my turn to be speechless. Academic probation? That isn't like Audrey at all.

Sensing my complete shock, she continues. "You don't need to have a heart attack. It's cool now. I'm not getting kicked out of school. The scholarship is safe. I'm fine. Well, finer."

"That's why I haven't been around much this summer. And why I haven't been in the best mood. It's not something I even wanted to acknowledge was happening, let alone chat about with my little brother."

"Come on, Audrey."

"I'm teasing, I'm teasing," she says, shaking my shoulder. "I needed to deal with it on my own. I didn't want to bring anyone else into it. It wasn't exactly my brightest moment."

"Does Mom know?"

"God, no. Are you kidding? As if Mom needs something else

to stress about." Audrey cracks her neck. "But I'll tell her at some point. I'm just . . . working my way up to it."

"So . . . what happened?"

Audrey looks at me, then back at the road. "I keep forgetting you're going to be a junior next year. I guess you're ready for this kind of stuff. I was in a pretty dark place."

I nod, even though I'm not sure why. It feels like the right thing to do.

"I'm still working through it. I don't really share this kind of thing with you." She checks on me and must notice I look a little stung by that, because she follows up with, "I don't share it with anyone. And that's kind of the problem."

Audrey sucks in a breath, steadying her voice. I've never seen her like this—she's usually so calm and collected. "The first few months of school were fine, but then, well . . . it's kind of hard to explain what happened. A dark sadness closed in all around me. I wasn't talking to my roommate. I didn't really put in an effort to make friends. The classes were harder—so much harder than anything I'd ever taken in high school. My grades were slipping. I knew my scholarship was at risk. Everything was building up, closing in, suffocating me. I was sleeping all day long. I started skipping class. I missed a bunch of exams. I couldn't figure out what was wrong with me. I was scared, like, really scared. I mean, I know that depression is a thing, but I didn't even consider that it could happen to me. I was numb. Lost in a fog. I'm still figuring it out with my therapist."

I catch Audrey quickly wiping her tears with the back of her hand. I know Audrey hates it when she cries and hates it even more when people see her crying. I make it a point to keep my eyes on the road.

"That sucks, Aud."

"Yeah, it's not fun." Her voice cracks, but she recovers by clearing her throat. "So, one day someone on the scholarship committee came to check on me. When the lady came into my room, I hadn't even tried to hide the pile of unopened letters from them warning me that I was about to lose everything. She put me in touch with a counselor, who recommended a therapist."

"Are you okay?"

"I am now. Or at least, I'm getting there. But to be honest, I was freaking out. That's part of why I haven't been a great big sister lately. What do you think I've been doing since I got back home? Not only have I been doing remote therapy sessions, I've been trying to sort out this whole mess. It's been nonstop emails and phone calls back and forth with the school trying to explain everything. My therapist finally got them to agree to lift the probation, and I get to keep the scholarship. It was only yesterday that all this got sorted out."

I feel a wave of relief wash over me. I don't know what would have happened if Audrey had lost her scholarship. Mom can't afford to send Audrey back. It would have been a total nightmare.

"I know we don't really talk about this in our family," says Audrey. "But talking helps. It really does. And I'm still working on it. Sharing all of this with you is a step." Her fingers strum the steering wheel. "If you let all that poison bottle up inside of you, it'll kill you. It's nice to have someone who can listen. I can't tell you how good it felt just to talk to someone who wasn't directly connected to my shit-web, you know what I mean?"

I don't exactly, but I nod anyway.

"And speaking of things we don't say in our family, I want to say sorry for not being there for you this summer. I know you were going through a lot with this Gloria thing and I should have checked in with you. I'm going to try to be better about that, okay? It's hard for us to apologize, I know, and I'm trying to be better about it. If you ever need to talk to someone, I'm here for you. And if there are things you don't feel like getting into with your big sister, and you feel like you might be interested in talking with someone professional about school or family or girlfriends or just to talk . . . I can help you with that, too."

"Someone outside of my shit-web?" I smile.

"Now you're getting it."

I've never once considered therapy. But seeing Audrey smile, I think talking to someone doesn't sound like a bad idea.

Audrey changes lanes and uses the opportunity to look at me. "And I know Gloria hurt you. It sucks that she doesn't like you the way you like her, or maybe she did and changed her mind . . . I don't know. But people like Gloria, *true* friends, don't come around very often. Once in a lifetime, if ever."

"I know that now."

"And sorry again for not being around this summer, Gare Bear."

"You had a lot going on. I get it. I'm glad you told me."

"I'm glad you forced it out of me. I know getting this deep

isn't usually our thing. Next summer I'll make it up to you," she says.

As I roll down the window, a rush of cool wind whips my hair. "You're taking me on a last-minute six-hour round trip in the middle of the night. I think we're even."

THIRTY-THREE

IT'S A LITTLE PAST MIDNIGHT BY THE TIME WE reach Camp Woodchip. Audrey could push the speedometer on the freeway, but when we pulled off and started on the roads leading into the woods, she had to slow it down or else risk wrapping the car around a pine tree. Road signs to the camp are few and far between. Our cell phones can barely find a signal to keep our navigation open. I squirm in my seat and I rub my nose so hard that I wouldn't be surprised if it fell into my lap. I wonder if we're ever going to find the camp.

Finally I see the entrance to the campground. "There, Audrey! Right there!" I shout, tapping her arm.

"I see it. Relax."

Audrey downshifts, causing her wheels to slowly crunch over the gravel. I fling off my seat belt and lean out the window, craning my neck, searching for any sign of Gloria. There's a flagpole planted in a grand roundabout displaying the camp flag. A massive elaborate log cabin, which has to be the main house. There are a few lights in the windows, but the place looks quiet.

Then I see her. By a mini pay phone bolted to the side of the building. Some moths flit around the dim lamp hanging above it.

Gloria is bundled up in an oversized hoodie, fast asleep next to her suitcase and duffel bag. Her hood is up. Her arms are crossed for warmth. She looks small and fragile.

Audrey keeps the engine running. I jump out and run to Gloria. She doesn't hear me approach, so I gently shake her and she blinks, slowly waking herself up. She beams when she recognizes me. It's a smile I didn't know I needed—one that I'll keep forever.

"You came."

"Of course I did. Come on, let's get out of here." I toss her suitcase into the trunk.

I buckle in the passenger seat while Gloria hops in the back. "Thanks for coming to get me, Audrey."

"Don't sweat it. Should I go? Do you need to, like, check out or anything?"

Gloria pulls down her hood. "No, they know. Let's go."

Audrey gets us back on the freeway in no time, now that she knows where she's going.

For a while it's only the hum of the motor and the rhythmic thump of tires speeding along pavement that fills the silence. I know that it's killing Audrey that Gloria isn't giving up the reason why she asked us to extract her from a magnificent campground one week before she was supposed to leave. And it's not only Audrey who is desperate for answers. But neither of us has the guts to ask and Gloria doesn't act like she's in any kind of hurry to fill us in on the details. I sneak some glances in the rearview mirror. Gloria stares out the window, alone in her thoughts.

"I'm fading, guys," Audrey says, cutting through the silence. "I need some wake-up juice." Audrey pulls into the first gas station she sees. "Gloria, you coming with?"

Gloria doesn't look back, her focus still outside the window. "I'm good, thanks."

Audrey goes straight to the coffee station. I miraculously find a few bucks in my wallet to splurge on some convenience store snacks. I make my selection and meet Audrey at the front counter.

"Is she all right?" Audrey asks, waving at me to place my items on the counter along with hers. I shake my head, but she rolls her eyes before grabbing the snacks from my hands and pays for me anyway.

"I don't know. I don't think so. Something serious must have happened back there," I say, taking the paper bag from the cashier.

"Then I'm glad we got her when we did."

Back in the car, Gloria is asleep. Audrey sips her coffee, I crack open my Mountain Dew, and we're on the road again. Audrey is still on a pop-punk tear, but keeps the volume low. Every so often I'll look back to check on Gloria. She looks peaceful. Angelic. I feel an overwhelming sense of comfort blanket me. I have my friend back.

It's about an hour into the drive when Audrey pulls off an exit. "I'm dying here. I can't hold off any longer. You have to take over for me."

"You serious?"

"You can handle the last stretch, right?" The groaning creak of Audrey's car door opening causes Gloria to stir from her sleep. "Sorry, didn't mean to wake you."

"It's fine," Gloria mumbles through a yawn.

"My eyes won't stay open. Gare Bear is taking the wheel." We do a little car seat do-si-do—Audrey crawls into the back, I circle around to the driver's side, and Gloria buckles in next to me. Audrey flips her hoodie up and is out before I even hit the on-ramp.

I only stall the car twice before I manage to lurch us onto the on-ramp. Gloria tries her best not to laugh. I'm embarrassed each time I grind the gears, but I shift poorly on purpose, sending her into another fit of giggles. Once we're moving fast and I don't have to worry about shifting, it's a smooth ride.

I wait for Gloria to take the lead, trying to make peace with the fact that she may never tell me what happened. But the silence is killing me.

"Oh, I almost forgot. I picked you up a little something back at the gas station. It's in the glove box."

Gloria grins when she pops the compartment. Gum! Grape flavored, of course. She peels off the packaging, throws her head back, and tosses a piece into her mouth. "You know the way to my heart!"

"It's not a totally selfless act," I say. "My way of softening you up. I'm sorry about how I acted. I was being a baby. I know I hurt you and I guess that was the whole point. I think that, in a messed-up way, I wanted you to suffer like I was suffering. I'm so sorry."

"I hate knowing that I hurt you," says Gloria, her eyes glistening. "And thanks for saying all that, Gary. It means a lot. More than you know. And I'm sorry about kissing you and then taking it back. I never wanted to lead you on."

"You don't have to apologize again. I get it."

"I know, but I want you to know it wasn't something that I just forgot about. Or that I took lightly."

"Thanks. I appreciate that." And I mean it.

"Do you want to hear what happened back at the camp?"

"Only if you want to tell me."

Gloria squirms in her seat, chews on her pinkie. There's hardly any nail left. "So . . . remember Conrad Pritchard?"

"I'm vaguely familiar with the guy."

"If it wasn't obvious, we're no longer together. What he did—no, wait. Let me back up a bit. I should probably tell you about how I even ended up at the camp.

"It was his idea. He's been going there every summer since he was seven. They have campers there all the way up until you graduate high school. It didn't take much to sell me on it. It's basically the Club with a ton more activities on a massive plot of forested land, a huge lake, and no parents. All the same perks."

"Sounds expensive."

"I'm sure it was, but Conrad offered to cover it. I felt weird letting him pay for me, but he kept insisting that it was no big deal. My mom wasn't thrilled, but I finally convinced her to let me go.

"Anyway, when we get there, the place looks awesome. You saw it. It's, like, the Disneyland of campgrounds. I should have snuck you inside the kitchen—we could have had one last feast before hitting the road!"

"Why has breaking into luxurious, exclusive sites become our thing?" I say, shaking my head.

"I met a bunch of new girls in my cabin. Once they heard I

was dating Conrad, I guess they felt like I was in their 'circle' or whatever. They were my friends. At least I thought they were. I thought they genuinely liked me."

Gloria fidgets with her seat belt before continuing. "The first week was amazing. Everything I imagined it would be. Cookouts and fish fries every night. And they had open classes for anything you could want. If you ever wanted to learn how to fire an arrow, there were archery fields. If you had the urge to take up watercolor painting, there was an instructor who would lead hikes to the top of the mountain with easels already set up for you. I even learned how to catch a fish." Gloria zings me in the arm. "A fish, Gary. A fish! Can you believe it?"

"I can." I smile, rubbing my shoulder. I try to squash the pang of jealousy I feel hearing about Gloria's adventures. I want to have been there to experience everything along with her.

"Of course, I should have known it was too good to be true. The night it happened, Conrad had this big scheme for all of us to sneak out past curfew to go night swimming. By then there was a little group of us from the girls' cabin, and some of the boys from Conrad's cabin. It was fun at first—we were taking turns doing flips off the blob—"

"The blob?"

"It's like one of those giant inflatable balloons that sits on the water. You sit on one end of it while someone else jumps on the other end and it sends you flying. It's terrifying. You might like it.

"So this one girl Jules has the idea that we should all skinny-dip. Everyone seems into it, except for me. There's no way I'm taking off my bathing suit in front of these people. They kept trying to get me to do it. I kept saying no, trying to laugh it off. But they start to get like . . . I don't know, aggressive or something. Maybe it's because I'm the only one not doing it. They won't let it go. It gets real awkward real fast."

Now it's my turn to shift in my seat.

Gloria has moved on to chewing her other nails. "I keep hoping that Conrad is going to jump in, change the subject, anything, you know? And sure, he's not one of the people pressuring me to do it, but he's also not telling them to back off.

"Then one of the girls says something to Jules—kind of muttering under her breath, but definitely loud enough for me to hear it. Maybe she meant for me to hear it. Maybe she didn't. But I did. She said, 'I knew she thought she was better than us.'"

I suck in air. Ouch. Gloria's specific brand of kryptonite.

"I grabbed my towel before they could see me cry, and went back to the cabin. Do you know what my first thought was? I felt bad that I was ruining the night Conrad had planned. Can you believe that? Like, what's wrong with my brain? I kept telling myself that if I went to sleep, everything would be back to normal in the morning. I crawl in bed, trying everything I can to stop sobbing, when I hear someone open the cabin door. I figure it's one of the girls, but it's Conrad. And he's being so sweet and nice and apologizing for not sticking up for me. Just when I start to feel a little better, he starts . . . making moves."

My stomach drops. All I can manage is a nod. I wish Gloria would skip ahead so my imagination isn't filling in the blanks for me.

"So I push him away. He even tries a second time before I have to really shove him. Hard. That's when I realize that he didn't really feel bad for me back at the lake. And when I call him on it, he throws off the covers and heads for the door. I'm begging him to stay, but he won't even look at me. I know it hasn't been that long, but the entire time we were together he never once got angry with me. Not like that."

I feel a thick bubble of fury boil inside of me, tearing my stomach apart. "Gloria, did he—"

Gloria looks at me, confused. "Did he what?" Her face softens when she realizes my interpretation. "Oh! Oh, no, no. He didn't hurt me."

"Okay. Whew. Thank God," I say. My body relaxes. "Keep going."

"Then he goes off about how much money he spent. Then I remind him it's his parents' money, and that really frosts his apricots. And that's not even the best part."

"There's more?"

"I asked him to tell me what he meant by spending so much money?" Gloria lets a smirk slip. "Like, I wanted him to have to explain himself. Force him to finish that thought. Like, what does spending money have to do with dating me? That shut him up real quick."

"No way." A surge of pride fills my chest. "You said that? To his face?"

Gloria flashes a triumphant smile. "I'm sure no one has called him on it before. Then you know what he does next? Says I was a waste of time and storms out. He actually slams the door so hard, one of the cabin's old windowpanes cracks."

"Is that when you called me?"

"No. That's not even the worst part."

God. How can it get worse? I'm not sure if I want to hear the end of this.

"The next day, everything seemed . . . off. I knew something was wrong. People were staring at me. Whispering to each other as I walked by. You know—I've been picking up on these things for years. My radar is pretty honed.

"I finally confront the girls and find out that Conrad spread a pretty messed-up rumor about me. Told everyone that he dumped me after he barged in on me with one of the counselors. I laughed it off, told the girls what really happened the night before.

"None of them believed me. Not a single one. They all took his side. That's when it sunk in how many more days I was going to be trapped at this camp with Conrad. Trapped in a cabin with girls who were supposed to be my friends.

"I couldn't tell my mom. She didn't want me going in the first place and I can't tell her the truth about all the sick details. You were the first person I thought of."

Warmth fills me. To be the first person Gloria trusted with that phone call. The significance is not lost on me. After all this time, she still trusts me.

"That's it," she says. "I think you're all caught up."

"It sucks that Conrad is gonna get away with all that."

Gloria blows a bubble. "I wouldn't say he completely got away with it. If Conrad wants to find his ridiculously overpriced pomade, body wash, and facial cream, he's gonna have to check out a snorkel and some fins to do some deep-diving in Lake Woodchip."

I laugh. Apparently I'm not the only one who's gone through some bold changes this summer. "Whoa. I didn't even know you had a bad side, but now I'm terrified."

"You're safe as long as you don't get on it." She winks. Then Gloria shakes her head. "I dunno. I still feel like a chump. How did I let myself get duped so easily?"

"Don't be so hard on yourself," I say, remembering my own infatuation earlier this summer with the in-crowd. "It's like some messed-up utopia that digs its claws into you and doesn't let you go. I don't have to remind you about the Roosters."

"Ah right. Those losers." Gloria snaps her bubble. "What's wrong with us?"

I don't have an answer, so I keep driving.

"Okay, but can I say one last thing about the kiss?" she says, eyes twinkling. "I promise this will be the last time I bring it up."

"Sure." I chuckle.

"You're a good kisser, Gary!"

I hope she doesn't notice that I'm blushing.

THIRTY-FOUR

THE REST OF THE DRIVE IS UNEVENTFUL—at least on a surface level. A couple of friends catching up after being apart for too long. Lucecita's is a massive hit—in fact, it's so successful that Gloria thinks that they'll be well on their way to affording a small house. Nothing quite as fancy as her old place, but it'll be a house of their own. I'm not sure how to bring up the subject of her dad; I don't want to press my luck and ruin the drive. But since I've been on a roll of asking about whatever's on my mind, I ask her anyway. Now that Gloria's stay at Camp Woodchip got cut short, she's going to talk to her mom about staying with her dad until school starts—they're still figuring out visitation without getting the courts involved. At least her dad and her mom are talking. I hope for Gloria's sake it remains amicable, but I also know now that putting too much stock in things beyond your control will slowly poison you.

I somehow make it back to our neighborhood without crashing the car. Not only is it a miracle I didn't get us killed, I've also managed to stay awake the entire time. It reminds me of the nights in elementary school when Preston and I would stay up way past midnight goofing around, too hyped up on the fun we were having to let anything like sleep stop us. I start to wonder what Preston is up to, but shake my head to rid my thoughts of him. He's taken up too much of my time. I want to stay in this moment with Gloria.

When I pull up to the Jig, my smile evaporates. I fight the urge to downshift, to give us a few more minutes together. Gloria and I manage to slip out without waking up Audrey.

"Are you two good?" Gloria asks, nodding to Audrey snoring away.

"We are. Had a nice long talk."

"Sometimes that's all it takes, huh?"

I grab Gloria's suitcase and follow her to the door. She doesn't go in right away. There's so much more I want to say, but I can't quite figure out how to untangle all my thoughts. Gloria is silent, too. I wonder if she's struggling with the same thing.

"What are you going to do?" I ask.

Gloria takes the suitcase from me. "Sleep for a thousand years."

"And after that?"

"I don't know. I don't really have any plans. Do you?"

"Not really." I exhale and steady my breath. This is my moment to act. I know that I can climb back in the car and know that Gloria and I will be all right. But I don't want to just be all right—I want to tell her what I should have told her a long time ago. All the things that were rattling in my head when I was sulking in my bedroom for those long agonizing weeks. And I know that if I don't say it now, I might not ever say it. "Hey, so, I want to say thank you. For this summer. It was the best time of my life.

And that's all because of you—you're the best thing that's ever happened to me. I know how sappy all this sounds, but if you can forgive me a few more clichés, I'd really appreciate it."

Gloria doesn't say anything. Her mouth a thin line. She swallows and nods.

My mouth feels sticky, my throat tightens. How am I going to get through this without crying in front of her?

"Before I met you, I didn't know who I was. I mean, I thought I did, but I would have been fine just *being*, you know? Existing. Floating there. I didn't realize there was another way to live. There were days when I wondered, *why me*? I still wonder that. I'm nobody. I haven't done anything cool in my entire life. I'm nothing. But you made me feel like I was something. What did I do to deserve your friendship? No, that's not even it . . . It's that I *know* I don't deserve to be your friend after the way I acted. You stuck around. Always. After I pushed you away, I found myself in that floating place again—drifting without an anchor, and it sucked. A lot.

"That's all I wanted to say, I guess. And I'm so sorry for shutting you out. For acting like a child and pouting the way I did. You didn't deserve that. So, thank you. Thank you for being my friend. My best friend.

"Oh. I almost forgot." Before I give her a chance to react, I reach into my shirt pocket and hand her something I know she's been eying since the start of summer.

"Gloria the Ravenous! You finished painting her! Oh wow, you even gave her a dimple!" The duffel bag hits the ground and before I know what's happening, Gloria's arms are around my neck, pulling me in. "You're not a nobody, Gary. You're stronger and better than you think." She hugs me even tighter, which I didn't think was possible. "You were with me when I needed you most. I can always count on you. Thank *you* for being *my* friend. It's me who doesn't deserve you."

"*You* don't deserve *me*? I don't see how that's possible."

Gloria pushes me back, but keeps her hands on my elbows. She's not smiling anymore. "I know your default is to crack jokes, but no jokes this time." There's darkness in her eyes—she's dead serious. I fight back another joke, which is harder than I thought it would be. Her eyes burrow right into mine, as if she's searching for something. "You don't see it, do you? You really don't see it. You're a great friend. You know how to really listen. Do you know how rare that is? I'm going to make you see how great you really are. Mark my words."

Maybe she's right. Gloria Buenrostro rarely gets it wrong, after all.

But I still can't fully accept everything she's throwing at me. I do one of those half shrugs and turn away.

She tugs my chin so that we're both looking at each other. "Maybe that's the secret to all the best friendships—both people not thinking they deserve each other."

I think back to the start of summer. When I first saw Gloria walk through the front door of the Jig. By all accounts, it should have gone horribly wrong. I can't think of a worse start. There are a lot of things I can hate on the Roosters about, but, in some twisted way, they're the ones who led me to Gloria. I think about how scared I was to lose Preston and how, in the end, it didn't matter. Friendships change and evolve. The strong ones last, the weak links erode. Like everyone who knows her or has heard of her, I put Gloria Buenrostro up on a pedestal—someone who is unapproachable, someone who doesn't need anyone else because she has it all figured out. And I guess I still do that, but not in the way I did before. I'd only known her for a few short weeks, but in that time, I felt like more of myself around her than all the years growing up with Preston. She's true blue. The genuine article.

Gloria hates that people called her "beautiful"—well, I doubt she will be able to ever really escape that. She was. She is. But I think what Gloria wants is for people to stick around, to see that she is so much more than her thick curls or her eyes or her dimple. She is kind, and thoughtful, and funny, and messy, and human.

There's part of me that still has boyfriend feelings for her. I can be honest with myself about that. But those will fade in time. I almost threw it all away. Now I'm just happy to have found my best friend again.

There is a bigger part of me that's scared about what could have been, what I almost let happen. When Gloria told me she just wanted to be friends, I was angry and I wanted that fury to boil over. It was so easy to let it fester and blind me from everything but the pain I felt. I shudder to think about what would have happened if I'd let myself get swallowed up by all that bitterness. About what I would have missed out on if I'd held on to that fury. Gloria sees me for who I am. And I see who she is. And we didn't end up running away from each other. We leaned into each other. Like Audrey said, a friend like Gloria comes around once in a lifetime, if you're lucky. And I almost let that go.

There's still so much I don't know about her. There is so much I have to share with her. Now, as friends, we have a chance.

Gloria picks up her bag and suitcase and unlocks the front door.

"One more thing. I forgot to thank you for something." I straighten up, standing tall to give her a good look as I pull the zipper to my hoodie down. Underneath, I'm wearing a slightly wrinkled dress shirt with the tandem bike tie.

She snaps her fingers and points right at me. "I *knew* that tie would look good on you."

"Hey!" I say, one foot in the car. "See you on Monday."

Gloria smiles.

ACKNOWLEDGMENTS

The first book only gets made if people take a chance on you. This is for everyone who did.

    Friends and family who kept me laughing when I needed to laugh the most. My gals, Trixie and Margot—I do this for you. Mom and Jess, for all of the bedtime stories, never saying "no" to a book request, and for always keeping the family printer stocked with paper.

    My agent, Alyssa Jennette. It was your idea to start this journey together, and I'm so glad I said "yes." Your unflinching encouragement filled me when my well was dry. Thanks for the hustle. I'm glad you're in my corner!

    My editor, Trisha de Guzman. They say it only takes one "yes," and I'm so grateful that my first came from you. You gave me a shot and for that, I'll forever be in your debt. Your steadfast patience and your unique insight with story and character are unparalleled. Oh, and thanks for not hanging up on me when I nervously babbled this crumb of an idea to you while trying to pitch over the bird squawking at the Los Angeles Zoo. Thank you for watching out for Gary and Gloria.

    Eleonore Fisher and Naira Mirza. Your thoughtful questions

and suggestions were invaluable and pushed this story to a place I never could have imagined. You cared for these kids as much as I did.

Kaitlin Severini, for your thorough copy edits and laser-focused scrutiny. All writers need a Kaitlin in their corner! And Amy Cooper, Susan Bishansky, and Kelly Markus, for your sharp-eyed proofreading.

Diana Nguyễn. I pinch myself every time I look at your cover art. How lucky did I get?

Ms. Stone. In fifth grade, you thrust a copy of a book featuring a Vietnamese protagonist into my hands, knowing it would change my life, and predicted that you'd see my name in lights someday. Well, they're not lights, but lots of paper bound together. I hope that's enough.

Jesse Klausmeier. For talking me off many cliffs and graciously reading every document I threw at you. You've been my literary oasis from the beginning.

Kim Buenrostro Giron and Martha Buenrostro. For showing me how to fold a proper tamale and letting me borrow your beautiful family name.

Nick Edwards: my Shakespeare savior since high school. Hat Night Squad: Wylie Overstreet and Chris Rogers. Shannon Kirk, Elissa Sussman, Margot Wood, Samantha Berger, Casey Gilly, Kim Hutt Mayhew, and Isabel Galupo. The author's journey to getting their first book published can be a lonely one, but I'm grateful to my writer friends for lending me your shoulders to lean on.

Powell's Books (shout-out to the Rose Room) and Fort Vancouver Regional Library. Growing up, you were like a second set of parents to me. Thank you for always stocking your shelves with the good stuff.

Many hands make light work. Well, I don't know how *light* the work was, but a lot of talented hands touched this project. Much love to all of the folks at FSG who worked on this:

Mallory Grigg, art director and designer

Eleonore Fisher, assistant editor

Naira Mirza, intern extraordinaire

Joy Peskin, executive editorial director

Allison Verost, publisher

Lelia Mander, production editor

John Nora, production manager

Maria Williams, designer

Jen Keenan, designer and hand letterer

Sara Elroubi, publicist

For all the readers who pick up this book. I'm honored to share these words with you.

Lastly, my biggest thanks and gratitude go to Beth. You demanded I pick up a pen when I didn't have the courage to. Thank you for reading the first draft in one sitting. My favorite beta reader. And for all those late-night note sessions, you really only have your brilliant mind to blame. Love you.

PLAYLIST

1. Bob Seger: "We've Got Tonight"
2. Jack's Mannequin: "The Mixed Tape"
3. Jackson Browne: "Late for the Sky"
4. Jim Croce: "Alabama Rain"
5. Billy Joel: "Rosalinda's Eyes"
6. Elvis Crespo: "Suavemente"
7. Carly Rae Jepsen: "Gimmie Love"
8. Brett Dennen: "Little Cosmic Girl"
9. Local Natives: "Mt. Washington"
10. Vampire Weekend: "This Life"
11. Angels & Airwaves: "The Adventure"
12. Khruangbin: "Maria También"
13. Kacey Musgraves: "Golden Hour"
14. Joe Pug: "The Flood in Color"
15. The Avett Brothers: "The Weight of Lies"
16. Paul Simon: "Me and Julio Down by the Schoolyard"
17. The Beach Boys: "God Only Knows"
18. Yeah Yeah Yeahs: "Maps"
19. Phil Collins: "Take Me Home"
20. Radiohead: "Karma Police"
21. The Joy Formidable: "This Ladder Is Ours"
22. The Killers: "Smile Like You Mean It"

DISCUSSION QUESTIONS

1. What information does the cover provide? Gloria is front and center, taking up much more space than Gary. We see her face clearly. Gary's face is more obscured—he is shown from the side, looking up at her. Why did the author and illustrator agree this was the direction to go?

2. A tandem bike is an unusual device to appear in a contemporary young adult book. How is the tandem bike used? Talk about the tandem bike as a symbol.

3. In addition to the tandem bicycle, various modes of transportation are sprinkled throughout. What does each one tell you about each character?

4. Food, both Vietnamese and Mexican cuisines, is also prominently featured. How is food used to show relationships between the characters?

5. Preston refers to Gary as a "white knight." What does he mean by that? Do you agree or disagree with that assessment?

6. Different characters have various degrees of "control" at different points of the book. When does Gary have control? When does Gloria? When do Preston, Jordan and the Roosters, or Conrad? When does Audrey?

7. The charm on Gloria's bracelet is a whale. Is that significant? Why or why not?

8. Gloria offers to help Gary understand Shakespeare by reading the play *Twelfth Night*. Why does Gary get defensive over the character Malvolio?

9. Gloria asks Gary if he believes in second chances. How often do characters get second chances in this story?

10. The story opens in the present but quickly flashes back to the start of the summer until it catches back up to the present at the very end. Why do you think the story was structured in this way?

11. "Before I met you, I didn't know who I was. I mean, I thought I did, but I would have been fine just *being*, you know?" What does Gary mean by this? How does Gloria change Gary's life? How does Gary change Gloria's?

12. Gary acknowledges that Gloria hates being called beautiful, but at the same time he says she might not ever be able to escape that. What do you think he means by that?

13. The original title of the book was *This Is Not a Love Story*. Do you think this would have been an appropriate title? Why or why not?